Runaway

MARIE-LOUISE JENSEN

OXFORD
UNIVERSITY PRESS

OXFORD
UNIVERSITY PRESS

Great Clarendon Street, Oxford, OX2 6DP,
United Kingdom

Oxford University Press is a department of the University of Oxford.
It furthers the University's objective of excellence in research, scholarship,
and education by publishing worldwide. Oxford is a registered trade mark of
Oxford University Press in the UK and in certain other countries

British Library Cataloguing in Publication Data
Data available

ISBN: 978-0-19-273535-5

1 3 5 7 9 10 8 6 4 2

Printed in Great Britain

Paper used in the production of this book is a natural,
recyclable product made from wood grown in sustainable forests.
The manufacturing process conforms to the environmental
regulations of the country of origin.

ALSO BY MARIE-LOUISE JENSEN

✳

Between Two Seas
The Lady in the Tower
Daughter of Fire and Ice
Sigrun's Secret
The Girl in the Mask
Smuggler's Kiss

For Helle, Gregory, and Paul;
the centre of my world.

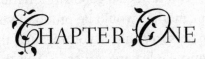CHAPTER ONE

'We'll be safe here, Charlie,' my father said as he shut the thin door of the new lodgings behind us. He put down our heavy trunk on the worn, creaking boards and rubbed his hands together to get the circulation going again.

I looked around the room with a sick rush of disappointment. We'd moved so many times in the last few weeks, giving a different name to each new landlord. Each time we moved, it was worse. Each room was shabbier and more run-down than the last. This one had been whitewashed once, but the grubby walls bore the traces of many previous occupants and there was a pile of refuse in one corner. The meagre furnishings were battered and dirty. The stairwell stank of cabbage, latrines, and poverty. Many desperate families were crowded into similar cramped rooms in the building. I could smell hopelessness mingling with the other odours. I could never have believed we'd end up somewhere like this.

I was increasingly concerned for my father's wellbeing. First my mother had died of that dreadful sickness. Then we'd left the Americas to return to England, where I knew not a soul. My brother, to my great distress, had chosen to stay the other side of the ocean. And now my father worsened day by day . . . But it wouldn't do to say so. 'That's good, father,' I said instead. 'I hope this move will give you some peace of mind.'

He embraced me and kissed me on each cheek by way of reply. 'You're such a good girl, Charlotte,' he said warmly. 'Your mother would be proud of you, God rest her soul. I'm so sorry to put you through this. Perhaps we made a mistake leaving America. You think we did, don't you?'

I sighed. 'I miss our friends,' I agreed. 'And I know we didn't live in luxury there, but this . . . ' I looked around the sordid lodging with distaste.

'I know, I know.' My father passed one hand over his face, rubbing his greying stubble. His once upright figure had become a little stooped of late and his former military neatness was sadly compromised.

'But this is temporary. I felt certain I was bettering us by returning to England. I had good reason for believing that, Charlotte. I still do! One day soon, you will see.'

My father began exploring the room, hunting for a loose floorboard. He found one beside the battered closet and concealed his papers there. Once he'd had valuables to hide too, but if there was anything left, I didn't know about it.

A sparkle came into father's eyes as he straightened up; a faint reminder of his former, cheerful self. I felt a surge of affection for him. Such a dear, loving father he'd always been to my brother and me.

'Here you are, my dear,' he said, delving two fingers into his coat and pressing a coin into my hand. 'Take this and go and find us a hot pie while I unpack. We must celebrate our new abode in style!'

I smiled back. Our pleasures were few nowadays and my father's joys were rare. I was more than willing to celebrate, however modestly. Standing on tiptoe, I kissed his thin cheek. 'Why don't you lie down and rest instead of unpacking?' I suggested.

'I *am* a little tired,' he admitted with a small sigh.

I hunted in my luggage for a brush and ran it through my long brown hair, which had been tangled by the wind earlier. My gown was patched and shabby, but I shook out my petticoats so they fell more neatly. I picked up the coin again and blew father a kiss. Closing the door carefully behind me, I ran down the creaking stairs.

The street was dusty and full of refuse. The stench was appalling. There could be no greater contrast between the poor quarters of London, teeming with ragged humanity and filth, and the places I had grown up, the open spaces of Newfoundland and Nova Scotia, where my father had served in a private company of the English Army. The land there was sparsely settled and the air crisp and clean. Here the air was rank with foul vapours.

My search for a pie shop led me to busier streets where horses, wagons, street sellers, and pedestrians thronged the thoroughfares. The rumble of wheels on cobbles, the clatter of hooves, the tramp of boots, and loud voices created a bewildering hubbub. I was anxious about becoming lost; London was a vast maze to me.

The sharp crack of a whip cut through the general noise. Startled, I turned. An elderly, rather gaunt bay horse was straining between the shafts of a cart. The muscles were standing out on his neck as he threw his weight into the collar. A searing memory tore

3

through me as I saw the horse. I'd been grieved to leave my own beloved bay mare behind in America. This horse was quite different, but the colouring reminded me of her nonetheless. The lash fell viciously again, this time drawing blood from the horse's shoulder. He snorted in pain and fright and redoubled his efforts, straining obediently until his eyes bulged, but the cart didn't move an inch.

'Get up, you lazy creature!' shouted the driver, raising his arm once more.

'Stop! Stop!' I cried, rushing forward. 'Try looking, before you lash your horse! Your wheel is jammed!' I ran out into the road and placed myself in front of the maltreated beast, putting a hand on his bridle. The man could not drive his horse forward over me, so lowered his whip arm and began shouting at me.

'The wheel of your cart is jammed between two stones,' I shouted over his obscenities. 'You need to back up, not try to force your poor beast forward!'

Several other passers-by had also stopped. A buxom woman with a basket had spotted the jammed wheel too and was crying shame on the driver. 'Don't beat the poor, defenceless beast for somethin' that's none o' his fault!' she shouted.

By the time three or four people had joined the fray, the driver finally stopped swearing long enough to take a look. As he climbed down to examine the wheel, I soothed his horse by stroking his dark, whiskery nose and speaking calmly to him. The horse rolled his eyes at first, quivering with fear and pain. Gradually, however, responding to my voice and gentle touch, he quietened.

I helped back the horse, while two men pushed at the cart to free it from the rut between the cobbles. 'Make sure you check your wheels next time, before you strike your horse!' scolded the woman with the basket once the cart was free again. I gave the horse a final pat, bid him a reluctant farewell and stood aside. I felt an ache in my heart as he trotted away. I'd spent my life with horses. The worst thing about being suddenly so poor was being deprived of their companionable, comforting presence.

Realizing I'd been gone much longer than planned and my father would be fretting about my safety, I asked the woman with the basket if she could direct me to a pie shop. There I bought a steak and kidney pie wrapped in paper and hurried back towards the lodging before it could cool.

CHAPTER TWO

I knew there was something wrong as soon as I saw the door was ajar. I'd closed it behind me, leaving my father resting; I knew that for certain. I climbed the last stairs silently, approaching the doorway with caution. I could hear a rustling and things falling to the floor. The hairs on the back of my neck rose. My father would never throw things around in that way. Was someone robbing us?

Softly, I laid the wrapped pie down on the dusty wooden floorboards and put my hand on the doorframe, trying to peer in. Perhaps I hadn't noticed a floorboard creak beneath my feet. Perhaps I cast a shadow through the doorway. Whatever it was, I gave myself away.

The door was yanked open; I was seized roughly and dragged into the room. I yelled once but before I could do more I was slammed against the wall, face first, and held there. My head spun sickeningly from the impact. A smooth voice spoke in my ear: 'There's a knife against your throat. No noise!'

Cold metal pressed against my warm skin. Terror flooded me, turning my limbs to water. In the mere second I'd had to glimpse the room, I'd taken in a scene of chaos; I'd seen blood.

'Where's my father?' I asked in a shaking voice. 'What do you want?'

'I want to know where your father's papers are,' the man's voice whispered, his breath hot on my cheek. I flinched away, but stopped short when the sharp tip of the knife pricked my throat. My breathing was coming in short gasps and there were black spots dancing before my eyes.

'I . . . don't . . . know,' I stammered.

'Tell me!' The man pulled me back and slammed me against the wall again. Stars exploded behind my eyes and nausea rushed over me. 'He doesn't . . . tell me. Why don't . . . you ask him?'

The man grasped my hair and twisted me brutally around, staying behind me, so that I could see the room.

The table and both chairs were overturned. The closet, the only other furnishing in the small room, was on its side, the door torn off. Our trunk had been emptied and smashed; its contents strewn across the room. The mattresses had been slashed open, their straw filling scattered. I saw all this in a few horrified seconds. And then I saw my father and there was no longer room for anything else in my mind.

Father lay sprawled across the piles of clothing in the far corner of the room. My first thought was that he looked broken; his body lay at a strange angle. Then I saw the deep cuts on his face and throat. Blood had soaked into his clothing and run onto the floor, staining it bright red.

I was used to the sight of injury and death. I was a soldier's daughter, after all. But this wasn't battle, nor was it the body of a stranger. This was my father.

I fought to get to him, but I was held impossibly tight. My head burned from the blows it had received and from the tight grip on my hair.

'Please,' I begged. 'Please let me go to him. He's hurt.'

My captor shook me. 'Nothing's hurting him any more,' he whispered. 'And if you don't want to end in the same state, tell me where his papers . . .'

There was a sharp rap at the door and we both froze. I considered crying out, but the knife was pressed harder against my throat. The man released my hair only to clamp his hand over my mouth, pulling me back against him.

'I've come for the rent,' said a high-pitched voice outside the room. It was the landlady.

'Don't think you can escape me,' the man hissed in my ear. 'I know who you are, Charlotte, and I'll find you like I found your father. No matter where you go or how well you try to hide. I'll get what I want sooner or later. Tell me now! It's the only way you'll ever be free of me.'

He lifted his hand slightly from my mouth, keeping it hovering there, ready to clamp back down if I tried to call out. At the same time he pushed the knife deeper. I felt it sting as it drew blood.

I kept stubbornly silent, my breathing ragged with pain and fear. The landlady was on the other side of the door, listening hard no doubt. All she had to do was open it, and I had a chance. She was nosy enough to do so, I knew. *Please*, I begged her silently. *Just push the door open!*

The handle turned and the door creaked open. My captor exploded into action. I was flung aside and crashed heavily into the overturned closet, striking my hip and shoulder so hard that I almost fainted from the pain. The man pulled the landlady into the room. No doubt he would have threatened her as he'd threatened me, but he was foiled. Outside the door stood her son and the two children from the room across the hall, all watching curiously. He couldn't kill all of us.

With a furious oath, he shouldered his way violently past them and thundered away down the stairs. I'd caught only a brief glimpse of his face, but I noted he looked like a gentleman, not the sort of ruffian you'd expect to find robbing paupers.

I picked myself up off the floor and staggered over to my father. The attacker was right. He was beyond my aid. His eyes stared, glassy and unseeing, at the cracked ceiling. His still-warm hand, when I clasped it, was limp. There was blood everywhere.

Behind me, the landlady approached, took in the sight of all the blood and my father lying lifeless, and let out a piercing scream. I jumped and looked up. Hands clasped to her mouth she stared at the spectacle.

'Dead?' she whispered at last.

I nodded. 'His throat's been cut,' I said. I couldn't recognize my own voice.

Shaking with shock, I bent over him, closed his eyes and pressed a kiss on his forehead. My vision blurred and a tear splashed down onto his face. I wiped it away with one trembling hand.

'This is a respectable house!' said the landlady, her voice high-pitched. 'We don't have murders and violent goings-on here! I must call a magistrate!'

I heard her leave the room behind me, shooing the

9

watching children away and pulling the door shut. My tears continued to flow, running unheeded down my cheeks. 'Oh, father!' I whispered brokenly. 'What have they done to you? And why?' I stroked his poor face and sobbed.

I recalled my father's terror, his certainty that he was being watched and followed over the last couple of weeks. I was ashamed now to think I'd dismissed his fears, believing them delusions. 'I'm so sorry,' I whispered, my tears still falling. 'I should have believed you.'

But even if I had, what could I have done? Could I have protected him in any way? The memory of the man's words echoed in my mind. *I know who you are and I'll find you.*

Who was I? No one of importance. What could we possibly have that anyone would want? Nothing. I wiped the tears from my face with my sleeve and attempted to marshal my wits. I had to escape. I sat back and took a deep breath. If I stayed here, that man would be back and my life might end the same way my father's had. If the magistrate came and began to speak of inquests, I would be trapped. I must flee now, during all the fuss.

I began to rummage through the clothes that had been tipped onto the floor, but couldn't think what I would need. I dropped them again and sat helplessly back on my heels. I couldn't think at all.

By the time the landlady returned with the magistrate, I was lying motionless on the floor, curled up in a ball beside my father. I sat up, numb with shock and grief. The magistrate was a spare, wizened man, with thinning grey hair and sharp eyes. He was puffing from climbing so many stairs. He stood in the doorway, taking in the scene in our room. 'Well, here's a to-do!' he said, once he had caught his breath. He looked around at the smashed-up room and then darted a glance at my father, lying in a blood-soaked heap. His face showed no emotion at all. He picked up an overturned chair, perched upon it, rubbed his hands together and drew a notebook from his pocket. 'Right, then,' he said, his voice business-like. 'Can you tell me the name of the deceased, young lady?'

The landlady stood beside him, her fierce, frowning gaze trained upon me as though I had conspired to arrange all this especially to cause her trouble. Her mouth worked angrily as I spoke.

'He was Andrew Smith,' I said shakily. 'My father. Formerly a soldier of the English Army.'

'That's not the name he gave me,' interjected the landlady shrilly. 'That's not the name he hired this room under. Brown, he said!'

'I know,' I confessed. 'He's been afraid for some time that he was in danger. He gave another name. He's been trying to hide, but I don't know why. I still don't know. Except that now . . . ' I gestured helplessly at the tumbled room.

'This is a respectable house,' repeated the landlady angrily. 'You've lied and brought trouble on me!'

'Thank you! That will do for now, Mrs Wickett,' said the magistrate, dismissing her. 'I'll call you if I need you.'

She backed out of the room reluctantly. The magistrate watched her leave and then turned back to me. 'I'm sorry for your loss, my dear,' he said. His words were kind but his voice cold. I sensed impatience beneath the surface. 'I'm going to have to ask you some questions. Can you manage to reply, do you think?' I nodded.

'Good. Your father was discharged from the army, you said?'

'Last autumn.'

The man took some notes. 'And your name?'

'Charlotte Smith.'

'And can you tell me what occurred here, Miss Smith?'

I told him briefly about the man I'd found here. 'I'd never seen him, to my knowledge,' I said at last. 'He was a stranger to me and I know of no reason why he should have hurt my father.'

'Has anything of value been taken? It is likely the motive was robbery.'

I shrugged helplessly. 'I have no idea.'

To my horror, the magistrate stood, bent over my father's body and searched his pockets. I had to bite my lip hard to prevent myself ordering him to show some respect. He drew out a purse, shook it and held it out to me. 'Empty,' he said. 'Was there money here before . . . ?' He gestured at the body.

I shook my head, wondering whether the coins for the pie had been his last. It was possible. 'I don't believe there was much to steal,' I told the magistrate, who made a note.

'Did you see the intruder's face? Would you know him again?'

'Only briefly, but yes, I'd know him anywhere. He was young, perhaps a few years older than me, brown-haired, and clean-shaven. His eyes were a very pale blue and he had a small mole just below his right eye. He sounded educated, not rough.'

The magistrate looked taken aback. 'I see. My goodness me. Yes, that is very . . . um . . . detailed. Now, you said your father had been afraid for some time. Did he have enemies?'

'Are you not going to write down my description? It could be important!'

'Oh yes, of course.' The man scribbled for a minute then looked up. 'Now where was I? Yes, enemies?'

'No. We know nobody in London. We've only been here a couple of months.'

'Debts or quarrels of any kind?'

'Not that I know of,' I said. I looked forlornly around the mess, at my father's body, lifeless on the floor. He had certainly sold the few items of value we'd once had.

The magistrate closed his notebook, rose and stood looking down at me where I sat upon the dirty floor. 'I shall have to send a message to the coroner. There will be an inquest,' he said. 'You'll need to stay here until after that. Do you have any relatives nearby? Your mother...?'

I shook my head. 'My mother died a year ago. I have no one in England,' I said.

A strange expression crossed his face. I wasn't sure why but it made me uneasy. Was it satisfaction?

'Very well. Stay here for now. It sounds to me as though it was merely a robbery that went wrong. You shouldn't be in any further danger. But perhaps, to be on the safe side, you should give those papers to me for safekeeping for now.'

As I stared up at him, my blood ran cold. He continued to look down at me with a condescending air. He held his hand out. 'The papers?' he asked again.

'I didn't . . . mention any papers,' I said slowly.

'Of course you did. You're confused, my dear.' He opened his notebook again. 'You told me the man demanded your father's papers from you. Now, what I suggest is that you hand them over to me for safekeeping and to look into. Meanwhile I'll call an inquest into this death.'

'Murder,' I said unsteadily. 'It was a murder.' My mind was reeling with shock and confusion. Had I really mentioned the papers? I was almost certain I had not.

'The inquest will decide whether it was murder or not,' he said. 'The papers?'

He held out his hand again. Was it my imagination or were his eyes glistening? If I was right, I was in far more danger than I had thought. 'My father had no papers,' I said. 'You are mistaken.'

The magistrate hesitated, then bowed briefly. 'If you're sure. If you remember where they are, do let me know, won't you? Mrs Wickett can always get a message to me. They could be important in tracing whoever did this dreadful deed.'

'I will,' I said, forcing myself to sound calm. 'Thank you . . . for all your help.'

The man nodded and left. I heard him descending the stairs.

My hands were icy in my lap. I was shaking. With difficulty, I rose to my feet, steadying myself by grasping the chair back. My head swam sickeningly. The weakness passed after a moment and I left the room, stepping out into the now deserted hallway and creeping down the creaking, filthy stairs after the magistrate.

When I reached the window on the landing below our room, I stopped and peered out through the grime-encrusted panes. I could just see down to the narrow street from here. I watched until the magistrate emerged from the building below me. He paused on the pavement below and wiped his thin face and hands on his pocket-handkerchief. Then he took a pinch of snuff from a box, sniffed it, and tucked the box back into his coat. Casting a glance around him, he crossed the narrow street and paused by a doorway, apparently exchanging a few words with someone, before walking on. I stayed where I was, watching, my heart thumping uncomfortably in my chest.

After a few moments, a man stepped out of the shadow of the doorway where he'd been concealed and looked up at the house. I caught my breath and drew back swiftly from the window. In that brief moment, despite the distance, I'd recognized my father's killer. The magistrate had been speaking with the murderer. Clearly he had no intention of arresting him. He knew him.

I retreated back to my room, closed the door and stood leaning against it, shaking. What had I told him? Dear heaven, I'd told him I would know the murderer anywhere. I'd given him a description that proved it. I'd surely signed my own death warrant with those words. My life was in danger and I had no one to turn to for help.

CHAPTER THREE

I needed to flee. To get far away from a killer who was so powerful he was in league with a magistrate. I tried to imagine what my father could possibly have that they wanted so badly, but I had no idea. We were poor. We had no connections of note, no influential friends. My father had been a mere major in the army, living on his pay.

I rummaged through my scattered effects. My head was clearer now, my senses sharpened by fear. What would I need? Some clean linen. I looked hopelessly at my few gowns. They had once been good quality, but now every one was patched and shabby. They made me pause and think: a gown was no good anyway. How was I going to escape from the house unrecognized? Where was I going to go? What would I do?

An idea came to me that gave me hope. I rummaged deeper to find garments I'd not worn for a while: my brother Robert's outgrown breeches, shirt, and jerkin. I was going to be destitute on the streets of a strange city where I knew no one. It would be safer to be dressed as a boy. I was used to it, after all. My parents had sometimes dressed me like my brother when we were travelling in America, to keep me safe. The murderer was looking for

Charlotte Smith, but he would not find her now, no matter where he searched.

I discarded the gown I was wearing, horribly stained with my father's blood, and dragged the breeches on with shaking hands, fumbling with the buttons. I wrapped a scarf tightly around my chest to conceal my breasts, put a shirt over it and pulled on a leather waistcoat. I knotted a shabby silk neckerchief around my neck to hide the knife cut that was still bleeding a little. I twisted my long, brown hair into a thick rope and pulled my father's cap over it.

I picked up a clean shift, the least worn of my gowns and an extra shirt, wrapped them hastily into a bundle and stuffed them into a leather satchel. As my only shoes were unmistakably girls' shoes, I pulled riding boots over my stockings. My disguise was complete.

To one side of the closet was the floorboard where father had hidden his papers. With difficulty, I prised it open with my fingernails, ignoring the splinter that stabbed under one nail and sent a sharp pain through my finger.

A bundle of assorted papers wrapped in oilskin and a leather pouch lay beneath the loose board. I stuffed them all hastily inside my shirt. As an afterthought, I picked up my father's cloak from the floor. Before I left, I knelt beside my father and kissed his brow one last time. 'I'm so sorry, dear father,' I whispered, fighting the tears that trembled behind my eyelids. 'If I could help you by staying, I would do so. But I cannot. Farewell.'

The light was fading outside the window as I slipped out of the door. I half expected the children to be there, gawping, waiting for something more to happen. But they had long gone and so, I noticed now, had my pie. It wasn't difficult to make the connection. I would go without food tonight, but it would be worth it if I succeeded in leaving unobserved.

I descended the stairs swiftly. From behind each door came the sound of voices, the bawling of children and the smell of cheap food.

Instead of leaving through the front door, the way I'd entered with the pie, I went out the back into the court-yard. Here was the stinking latrine that was shared by several houses, with a queue of people waiting to use it. Children played tag in the yard and mangy dogs sniffed at the rubbish that lay strewn about. No one so much as glanced at me as I walked by. They had no interest in a scruffy, unknown lad.

I paused, pulled my cap down low over my eyes, and joined a gaggle of other lads, all of them ragged and dirty, so that I wouldn't be leaving the yard alone. We passed right by the murderer. His eyes ran over all of us, but rested no longer on me than on the others. It took all my courage to saunter by casually when my legs shook for fear of my life, but somehow I managed it. The man stood slouched in a dark doorway, his pale eyes watching the coming and going from both the front door and the back yard. There was no other way out, and he was probably confident I couldn't leave the house unobserved. But he was looking for a girl.

As soon as I was well past him, I left the lads, disappeared into a back street and wove my way through a maze of narrow alleys. After ten minutes or so, I paused in a doorway and watched for a while. There didn't seem to be anyone following me. I leaned my forehead on a dilapidated wall, weak with relief.

I forced myself to move on along the unfamiliar streets with no clear idea of where I was heading. It was the strangest feeling in the world, to have nowhere to go. On the busy main roads, I was jostled and bumped from all sides by pedestrians and street sellers as I walked, and found myself drifting with the crowd. It was easier to follow everyone else than to fight my way through the throng. I glanced back often but saw no sign of the murderer.

I was soon hopelessly lost and the light was fading fast. Cold and hungry, with no money to buy food, I searched instead for a safe corner to spend the night. The bridges and doorways were full of ragged, destitute waifs, all of them keen to defend their sheltered spot. Eventually, the best I could find was a small space behind a wagon in a carrier's yard. It was open to the elements as well as being dirty and uncomfortable, but I crouched down to conceal myself, wrapped in my father's cloak, determined to stay awake all night.

I was chased out of my spot before dawn as the yard came to life around me and goods were loaded into the carts. The streets were already bustling and crowded, with stallholders calling their wares, servants fetching water and dogs nosing among the refuse for scraps. I had only two thoughts in my head. The first was how desperately hungry I felt, the second was that I had to get out of the city.

I dared speak to no one in case they remembered me. Fatigued, famished and frightened, I imagined everyone around me was my enemy. Fear drove me onwards through the city with no knowledge of where I was going. Some streets were wide and fine with grand carriages rolling along them; others were mean and narrow, peopled by ragged beggars and children, their faces pinched with want. Everywhere was equally unfamiliar to me.

A train of packhorses came towards me, carrying panniers full of winter vegetables. Somewhere in my dazed and shocked mind, it occurred to me they must have come in from the country. I headed in the direction they had come from.

Eventually, I found myself at a city gate. I had no idea which one it was; London was so unfamiliar to me. I followed the crowd out of the city and kept going along the road. I suspected I was heading west, as the sun was on my left, and that was confirmed when I saw a milestone beside the road bearing the information: *Bristol, 90 miles*. I kept walking. My father had never spoken of his childhood home, but I remembered my mother once saying that she'd grown up in the countryside between Bath and Bristol. I may as well head there as anywhere.

I hoped sleeping rough might be easier and safer in the countryside. Perhaps I could find a haystack or barn rather than risk another night beneath a bridge or in a doorway, where I might be robbed or attacked by one of the many ragged and desperate souls who eked out a miserable existence in the huge, grimy metropolis.

I found myself considering these things quite dispassionately, as though they were happening to someone else, not to me. For how could *I*, Charlotte Smith, respectable soldier's daughter, be in such a position? Meanwhile, I kept plodding westwards along the rough road.

As the light faded, the crowds thinned. Fewer people were riding or walking along the road. I kept going with dogged determination, putting off the moment when I would have to think about where I could sleep. My boots, never intended for walking long distances, pinched my feet and the satchel strap cut into my shoulder. My belly was aching with emptiness. I hadn't eaten since the early morning of the day before, and little enough then.

It was growing cold again and I needed to find somewhere to sleep. I turned off the road and crossed a field towards a barn. A dog frightened me away by barking fiercely. I could find no other shelter and ended up stumbling around in the darkness. Eventually I crawled under some bushes and lay down on a bed of dry leaves. I slept fitfully, curled around my satchel, my father's cloak wrapped tightly around me.

I awoke at dawn with the sickening knowledge of all that I'd lost. It was as though I'd scarcely understood until this moment. I'd acted by instinct, fleeing from danger. But now I truly realized that my father was gone. Murdered. Yet another member of my family torn from me. 'Oh father,' I whispered to myself. 'What shall I do now?' The grief that I'd been able to hold at bay up to now swept over me. I wept like a baby.

I caught my breath abruptly on a sob when something touched my ankle. I started in fear and jerked away from the touch, convinced I'd been found and would next feel a knife on me. A giant man in ragged homespun crouched beside me.

'You a'right, lad?' he asked, his rough voice gentle with concern. His face was dirty, his teeth bad, and there was a vacant look in his eyes that suggested to me he might be simple minded.

'I'm . . . fine,' I said, sniffing and dragging my sleeve across my tear-stained face. 'Th . . . thank you!' I pulled my cloak and satchel closer to me, edging away from the man.

'Don't be afeared,' he said. 'I wussn't goin' to hurt yer.'

Nonetheless, I scrambled to my feet and fled. Disorientated and weak, I stumbled through some trees, unsure of my way. Eventually I followed the sound of a creaking wagon back down to the road. I watched as it approached from the east, the sun low in the sky behind it and then turned and followed the wagon westwards, picking my way around the worst of the churned-up mud and deep ruts.

I overtook the laden wagon after a while as it lumbered ponderously along, jolting through potholes, pulled by six horses at length with a chain linking them. A gentleman's carriage came the other way, rattling towards the big city, drawn by four fine carriage horses, sleek and glossy. Some stable hand had worked hard to make them look so fine.

I passed another milestone: *Bristol, 80 miles*. I'd come a good distance already, but felt conspicuous walking along the road alone. I was convinced people were staring at me and might remember me if questioned. A

22

greater problem still was hunger. I'd eaten nothing for two and a half days now.

At noon, I left the road and concealed myself behind a hedgerow. Sitting on damp grass, I glanced carefully around me, to be certain I was hidden from prying eyes, before I pulled my father's papers and pouch from my shirt. First, I leafed through the papers, looking for bills. No such luck. If my father had had any large sums of money remaining, he would not have taken us into such poor lodgings.

I put the papers carefully aside and emptied the pouch into my lap. My father's precious gold signet ring rolled out. I gasped in shock. I'd mourned that ring as lost, certain it had been sold as everything else of value had been. I clutched the ring in my hand, shaking with unexpected gladness. Then I uncurled my fingers and studied it, so wonderfully familiar to me when all else was lost. The unusual design on the front, the stag in the ornate *R*, and the curiously wrong initials on the inside, curled around one another, *ASL*.

I'd asked my father once, years ago, with a child's curiosity, why he wore a ring with initials that were not his. A cloud had passed over his face and then he had smiled mischievously, grasped my hand and told me he had inherited the ring from his godfather. 'They're his initials, you see, Charlotte,' he'd said. And he'd winked at my mother. I'd never thought to ask him his godfather's name. I was far more curious now. In the light of everything that had happened, I was beginning to suspect my father had kept secrets from me. I slid the ring onto my finger, but it was too loose. I shook the bag, still hoping for a coin or two, but there was nothing. It appeared I was alone in the world with no more than a ring.

Next, I turned my attention to the papers, hoping they would tell me more. I sat for a moment, just holding them in my hands. I remembered my father as he'd been when my mother was alive: tall, dark-haired, strong, with bright, laughing eyes and smile creases.

I broke open the oilskin package and found a sheaf of letters and sundry other items. I took a deep breath and spread out the first letter. It was clearly old, the paper discoloured and the ink faded. It was dated July 1704, and addressed from *The Home Farm, Deerhurst Park, Gloucestershire*.

My dearest Andrew, it began. *I miss you more than I can say*.

I'd never heard of the place, but recognized my mother's flowing hand. This was from before my brother and I were born. A love letter, it seemed from the next few lines. I felt deeply uncomfortable; as though I were spying on something private and secret. Besides, this could not be what the killer had been hunting for. I folded it up and laid it aside.

I unfolded the next. A quick glance showed me it was another similar letter, but this time from my father, also dated 1704 but addressed from an army barrack in Plymouth. The tenderness of the opening lines brought tears to my eyes. I'd lost both parents, and so recently. I could not bear to read their private correspondence. I laid this letter aside with the first.

More than half the papers were personal letters between my parents, filled with endearments. They must have been deeply precious to them personally, but they had no value to anyone else that I could see. I folded them all carefully together and put them back inside the oilskin package before turning my attention to the remainder of the papers.

There were several documents connected with my father's time in the army: his joining papers dated some years before my birth, some commendations, a letter praising his bravery and confirming his promotion to the rank of major, and his discharge letter. I'd seen them all before. There was nothing either valuable or dangerous about them.

I'd come to the very last paper without discovering anything of importance. This one had been sealed, but the seal had been broken. I spread it out on my lap and saw it was dated just a few months previously and addressed to me. There was no message of any kind, however. Simply a name and address: *Henry Palmer, Seaview Cottage, nr Studland, Dorset.*

Henry was my father's friend and companion from America; it was a comfort to me to find his direction. The address was printed in my father's neat, elegant handwriting. But at the very bottom of the paper two words were scrawled: *Sorry, Charlotte.*

Remembering how his hands had trembled constantly in his final weeks, I could guess that these final two words had been added later during that dreadful time. My poor father.

Now at last I knew where I should go. I had someone in England who knew me and cared what became of me. As long as I could find him; for I had not the least idea where Dorset might be. England was almost completely unknown to me.

I put everything into the satchel with my few possessions. Wearily, I got to my feet and slung the satchel onto my back. I was shocked to find how weak I'd grown. My legs were reluctant to bear my weight and I staggered as I made my way back to the road.

Before I reached it, the faint sound of running water caught my ear. Following the sound, I found a beck that looked clean enough to drink from. The surface of the water reflected my image as I looked down into it; a pale, pinched face with an ugly bruise on my forehead, another on my cheekbone, and smears of dirt everywhere else. When I pulled my scarf aside, there was a dark scab where the knife had pricked my neck. I looked a vagabond already.

I drank deeply and seeing there was still blood on my fingers where I'd touched my father's body, I washed it away. My dear father would have a pauper's grave with none to mourn him, like any beggar or vagrant. And yet he'd been much loved. He'd been a good man, with an affectionate family and many friends in the army. It was frightening how quickly fortunes could alter.

I rejoined the road and walked on. At an inn, I enquired the way to Dorset and was told I should follow the Bath Road and, when I reached the city, head south.

'Is it far?' I enquired.

'Ah, it'd take you a good week afoot, I daresay,' replied the innkeeper.

I kept on, putting one sore foot in front of the other. I spent the night in a haystack beside the road. My belly ached so with hunger it was hard to sleep, despite my exhaustion.

Towards the village of Colnbrook the following day, a train of packhorses overtook me, led by a lad not much older than me. Despite the large bundles they carried, they were moving quickly westwards. A stout, grey-haired woman brought up the rear of the train, a staff in her hand. 'Hup!' she called out to the last pony as he showed a disposition to pause and nibble grass at the wayside. He tossed up his head and walked on.

'Good day!' The woman cast a curious glance at me as she passed by. I plodded wearily on. Only a few moments later, however, I rounded another corner, to be greeted with a scene of chaos. A wagon had overturned on the road, spilling both wares and passengers. Its horses, five of them pulling at length, were frightened and fighting their harness. The chestnut horse that led the line was down, its leg caught in the chain, screaming with fright and pain. The packhorses were trapped in the sunken road, unable to go on, milling about, made restless and edgy by the distress of the horses harnessed to the wagon. Casting cloak and satchel aside, I ran forward to the lead horse that was down. Its eyes were rolling wildly, its neck lathered in sweat as it fought to get up. The tangled chain pinned it to the road.

'Hush, there,' I murmured to it, putting a hand on its nose. 'Hush, I'll help you.'

I looked around, wondering why no one else was helping. I spotted the wagon master stretched out on the road. Two men were tending him and other road users were helping his passengers climb out from the wreckage of the wagon. That explained why no one had a thought to spare yet for the poor horses.

I turned back to the frightened chestnut horse, speaking soothingly to him, and gradually he stopped struggling against the chain and harness that bound him. I gently unbuckled his traces and untangled them, but on my own I could do nothing about the chain that had trapped him and was bruising his legs every time he tried to move.

After some time, the boy who'd led the train of pack-horses joined me. 'You done well to calm that one,' he said with a friendly grin. 'Now let's see if we can get 'im on his feet.'

He took hold of the chain and lifted it clear. I spoke to the chestnut horse again, encouraging him. He struggled to stand, scrabbling for grip in the mud and stones of the road. Then, with a great heave, he surged upright. The other horses, still unnerved by the accident, tossed their heads and tried to pull away. I took a firm hold of the injured horse's bridle and kept speaking to him. He trembled and snorted, but didn't fight me. The wagoner was back on his feet and staggered over to me, still looking dazed.

'I'll take him now,' he muttered.

'I'll be fine while you see to the others,' I tried to protest, but he was insistent. Reluctantly, I relinquished my hold on the horse and stepped back. It was sheer bad luck that at that very moment a chaise rattled around the corner from the London direction far too fast for the narrow road. Seeing the chaos ahead, the chaise driver pulled his lead horses up so hard that they sat back on their haunches, but it was too late. This latest incident was enough to make the injured horse, already terrified and in pain, rear wildly. He pulled out of the wagoner's hands and stepped back onto the leg of the lad from the packhorse train. The boy screamed.

Chapter Four

The boy's cry brought the woman from the packhorse train running towards us. She pulled the boy out of reach of the frightened horse, and was much distressed for him. The wagoner recaptured his horse, but the harm was done.

'You good for nuthin' reckless, rich idiots!' the woman bawled at the chaise driver. 'What kind of speed is that on these roads? Tell me that! Tell me how I can manage now for two months with no boy to help me in my work!'

She was so fierce the coachman practically cowered on the box of the chaise, holding his horses well in hand now. In no time at all, she'd made him promise to take up the injured boy and convey him to the inn at Maidenhead. The servants carried the poor lad into the chaise, trying not to jar his injured leg, and the gentleman joined him, having promised to get a doctor to the lad as soon as they arrived.

I was free to go on, but I didn't. So weak I feared I might faint, I sat on the damp grassy bank beside the road. I watched as the wagon was dragged clear by straining horses so that the chaise could go on past. I saw the packhorse driver pick up her boy's stick as well as her own and go to her lead horse who was grazing at the side of the road.

'Do you need help?' I called to her. 'I'm looking for work.'

She glanced sharply at me, her eyes taking in my bruised face. 'I could have done wi'out gettin' my boy injured,' she snapped.

My heart sank. 'I'm sorry I couldn't prevent it,' I said and turned my face away, wishing I hadn't asked. Who would want to employ me, after all? I realized she was still looking at me and flushed a little.

'You know horses,' she said. 'I could see that much. Driven packhorses before?'

I shook my head. 'Never, but I could learn.'

'Where are you headed to?'

'Dorset. But I cannot go so far without work.'

'You sound like a young gen'leman,' she said critically. 'Ever worked in yer life?'

She was looking at me quizzically and, despite my weariness, my hunger and my unhappiness, I felt hope. 'Not as such,' I admitted.

'Ah. A young gentleman fallen on hard times, is it? Well, there's no slacking on a packhorse train. Yer keeps up with the lead horse and keeps her outta mischief. As long as she keeps going, the others'll foller her. She knows the way. Think you can do that?'

I nodded. The woman rolled her eyes. 'I must be goin' soft in me old age,' she remarked to the road. 'I'm Martha Winters.'

'Charlie Weaver,' I said, standing to shake her hand. The world swam around me. I swayed and sat quickly back down. I mustn't faint. I tried to breathe through the dizziness that was sweeping over me, but stars danced before my eyes.

'If you will feed me,' I said in a faint voice. 'I'll willingly walk all day for you.'

'When did you last eat, Charlie Weaver?' Martha asked me.

'I don't remember. Three, four days ago?' I hated to confess to such poverty. It felt shameful. Martha sighed. 'I'm taking on more trouble here than is worth my while,' she complained to herself.

She called the horses off the road, some onto the verge and others into a gateway, and pulled a skin of ale from a saddlebag and handed it to me. I drank gratefully while she took bread and cheese out too and sat down beside me.

'I don't eat in the day as a rule,' she said. 'But if we're stopping . . . '

I fell on the bread, barely chewing in my rush to fill the yawning void inside me. 'Slow down!' Martha ordered me, snatching the bread back. 'Chew or you'll make yerself sick.'

Under Martha's watchful eye, I forced myself to eat slowly and politely. By the time I'd finished, I was still weak, but lights were no longer dancing before my eyes. Martha strapped my satchel to one of the horses.

'Right then, we'll walk together while I teach you the commands. Here's yer staff,' She handed me the boy's stick. 'Hup!' she called out to the lead horse. The horse jumped to attention and walked out into the road, heading westward. We both fell into step beside her and the other ten horses took their places in the train behind.

'They wants to reach the King's Head at Maidenhead,' she told me. 'Sooner they can get there, sooner they gets unloaded, fed and watered. It's not them you has to look out for. It's trouble from other road users, like that wagon and chaise. From robbers and no-goods. That's why I need help. With that and all the unloading and loading at the start and end of each day. I'm not so young no more.'

As we walked, Martha taught me the packhorse language, the 'hup' to encourage them on, the 'whoa' that was universal to stopping horses, and how to direct them to the right and the left. Apart from that, the main task was keeping up with the blistering pace the beasts set. I was half running some of the time.

At the Colnbrook tollgate, after Martha had paid the fee and all the ponies had passed through, she glanced at me. 'Holdin' up?' she asked.

'I'll do,' I said and then strode ahead with the lead horse. I was elated to have eaten and found myself work.

My relief was soon tempered by the weather, which rolled black and threatening from the west. We walked into a rainstorm that drove straight into us, drenching me through, despite my father's cloak. The rain soaked right through my cap, plastering my hair to my head. Water trickled steadily down the back of my neck into my shirt. My boots leaked mud and water so that my stockings and eventually even my breeches became mired from the muddy road.

I kept doggedly walking the weary miles, while the road became a bog. The horses at my side put their heads down in misery, but barely slackened their pace, their hooves squelching and sliding in the mud as they struggled onwards. My feet chafed raw inside my wet boots. The strength I'd gained from the meal leached slowly out of me. My only comfort was that I wouldn't be forced to sleep out of doors in this storm tonight.

The rain lessened at last. Towards evening the sun came out. My clothes steamed and so did the horses and their packs. Just as I thought I couldn't walk another step, we entered Maidenhead, crossed the bridge and the horses swung off the road of their own accord, through the archway into the inn yard at the King's Head.

Once we'd unloaded the packhorses, stalled them, groomed them, and Martha had checked they were receiving the full measure of provender she was paying for, she led me up to a plain room on the top floor and told me I'd be sharing a bed with her that night. Promising to come back and fetch me for supper, she disappeared to enquire after her injured lad.

Surprised but relieved that I wasn't expected to share with her boy or to sleep in the stables, I pulled off my wet clothing and hung it over a chair to dry, slipping on my one spare shirt to sleep in. I thought I'd just lie down on the bed for a few moments to rest while I waited for Martha. The next thing I knew, the early dawn light was peeping through the window, and Martha was shaking me awake.

'What?' I uttered, confused. 'Where. . . ?'

'Time to get up for breakfast!' Martha ordered, her voice loud in my fuddled head. 'We'll be off in an hour.'

Pulling my still-damp breeches and stockings on as quickly as I could, I collected my things together and stumbled down the creaking stairs after her. Eggs, bread, preserves and ale awaited us on a table in the taproom. Having missed supper last night, I made a hearty meal. Martha ate steadily in silence. On the way out to the yard, she remarked: 'You'll suit me if yer up to the work. Sleep instead of supper and a shared bed makes a cheap night. And no chatter. I like that.'

Together we loaded up the horses with no more talk than it took to instruct me on the correct way to tie on the packs and teach me some new words like 'wantyes' and 'sursingles': the straps that held the packs in place. 'A badly-tied pack ruins a horse faster than a bad road,' Martha told me as she checked each horse, adjusting the loads one final time.

'The Bear Inn in Hungerford, by nightfall,' she said. 'Off you go.'

And I went.

The second day was longer but less gruelling than the first. My feet hurt more, but I'd slept well and eaten breakfast. And it didn't rain. I was rubbing down the last of my six horses at the Bear when I noticed Martha leaning against a post, watching me.

'Ah. You really do know horses,' she said in her decided way. 'Time to eat.'

We washed at the pump and then entered the crowded taproom and found a place at a greasy table. Martha ordered the house supper for us; a generous portion of lamb stew with potatoes. I tucked in hungrily. After a while, I noticed Martha's steady gaze on me again. She was sharp-eyed, but so far my disguise seemed to have fooled her.

'How's your lad?' I asked. 'Will his leg heal?'

'It'll heal right enough. But not for weeks. It'll cost me an arm and a leg to put him up. He can't be moved yet.'

Her harshness wasn't convincing. I'd seen enough to guess that she cared for him. 'Is he your son?'

Martha gave a scornful grunt. 'Jason? Do I look young enough to have a nipper like him?' she demanded. I thought it tactful not to answer.

'Fifty year old and still trekking to Lunnon and back every week,' she sighed. 'That's the price of runnin' yer own business.'

'You don't have a husband?' I asked cautiously.

'Had one once. The packhorse train was his business, but I bin a widow these fifteen years. I kept the business goin' all this time. Three days up to Lunnon, three days back, and Sundays at home to rest.'

I nodded as I chewed. 'Are there many women in your line of work?' I asked curiously.

Martha's eyes on me were sharp once more as she replied. 'A few. You got to be tough to survive a life on the roads. Twice as tough if you're a woman.'

I hoped I was going to be tough enough to last the six or seven weeks it would take Jason to heal; if Martha would employ me so long.

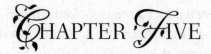CHAPTER FIVE

The road the next day took us through Savernake Forest. It was a wild place, a mixture of dense, ancient woodland, heath and grazing land.

The morning traffic on the road was busy. By noon, I'd overtaken several lumbering wagons with between five and seven horses drawing at length and any number of travellers on foot. I felt stronger after a day of good, nourishing food. The clean air and exercise out of the London smoke suited me too. I kept pace with the lead horse with ease, every now and then commanding her to 'hup!' if she slackened her pace.

On a deserted stretch of road in denser woodland, a bang echoed ahead of us. The lead horse, Magpie, threw up her head, but kept going. Another shot echoed and she shied violently. 'Whoa!' I called. I caught her halter, put my hand on her nose and spoke to her quietly.

'It's just someone out shooting rabbits or a deer,' I said soothingly. 'It's a way off. No need to fuss.' The mare dropped her head and looked trustingly at me. I gave her the word to go on, hoping whoever was shooting had bagged his prey.

A short time after, a chaise approached. It was a light, open, two-horse chaise, built for travelling fast. The horses were magnificent; elegant, high-bred carriage horses, groomed until they gleamed.

The chaise slowed as it approached and came to a smooth halt just in front of me. 'Whoa!' I called to Magpie, who obediently halted. I looked curiously up at the people riding in the chaise. A young gentleman was driving with an elderly groom sitting beside him. 'A word of warning,' said the young man. He had a pleasant voice, deep and relaxed. My eyes were drawn to him. He was finely dressed, in a brown velvet coat over a plain beige waistcoat. His cravat was a simple stock without lace, tied neatly with its ends thrust through his buttonhole. He wore a neat brown travelling wig, but looked fair and, I thought impulsively, very likeable. He was the kind of handsome young man a young lady like Charlotte might once have dreamed of: tall, slim, and graceful, with soft hazel eyes. But I was no longer that young lady, so I swallowed hard and met his eyes frankly. Seeing amusement there, I blushed, realizing I must have been staring.

'There are highwaymen in this part of the forest,' the young man warned me. 'We've just had a run-in with one. You might have heard the shots that were exchanged?'

'I did,' I said.

'I think Bridges here frightened him off, but we can't be sure. If you'll take my advice, you won't travel on without company this next stretch.'

'Thank you,' I said.

The gentleman nodded to me in a friendly way and gave his horses the office to drive on. I nodded back, but then remembered I was a lowly packhorse boy and should be more respectful, so I hurriedly touched my cap to him. There was once again a hint of amusement in the charming smile he cast me as he passed.

The crest on the carriage caught my eye as it drove by: a magnificent stag. It looked oddly familiar, but I couldn't place it. I shook my head, frowning to myself. Why would I recognize an English nobleman's crest?

I stood uncertainly in the road, wondering what I should do. Martha took her timekeeping very seriously and we needed to reach Hungerford by nightfall. On the other hand, I was unarmed and couldn't protect her horses or the goods they carried. Martha could be a long way behind me, for all I knew. She had parcels on the last two horses, to be dropped off at various inns along the road.

A rumble of wheels decided me. I would wait a few more minutes for the wagon approaching behind me. Once it reached me, I sent Magpie on and we proceeded on our way through the bright green of the spring foliage.

'You were slow today,' remarked Martha, when she walked into the yard of the Bear Inn in Hungerford as I was unloading the third horse. I explained what had happened and she nodded approval. 'I heard the tale,' she said. 'Mr Lawrence was the man driving the chaise. I works for the family from time to time. You judged rightly. That's a tricky stretch of road and company is always a good thing.'

'You didn't warn me,' I pointed out.

'You can think for yerself, can't yer?' asked Martha as she began to unload packs.

'Have you ever been robbed?' I asked her.

'Not yet,' she said and paused briefly beside me, opening her jerkin a short way to reveal the butt of a heavy pistol tucked in there. I was impressed.

'So what do your horses carry?' I asked Martha over plates of pulled chicken, mash and green peas that night. Martha popped a piece of chicken in her mouth, sucked her fingers and took her time replying.

'Goin' up to Lunnon, I mainly takes wool,' she said at last. 'That's our main trade down west. We can get it there a deal faster than any trundling wagon can.'

'And on the way back down from London?'

'Parcels for folks as want stuff carried, manufactured goods for the shopkeepers in Bradford and whatever else is ordered.'

'I've seen lots of other trains of horses. Do they all carry such things?'

'Similar. Lunnon's a hungry city. It needs food and raw goods to keep it goin'. Money, too, from the estates. There's a lot of fruit from down our way gets sold up in Lunnon. There's a packhorse train from the north, I've heard, that travels day and night to bring fresh fish into the city. That wouldn't suit me. I'm too old for that.' She sighed and stretched her legs out, taking a pull at her ale. 'That's enough gabbin' now. Get you to bed if you've eaten.'

The nights felt very short compared to the long weary days. I'd barely laid my head down each night when Martha was shaking me awake to begin the next day's work. But I was fed far better than before I met her, in fact better than I had been since my father was discharged from the army. The long months of poverty through the winter had been hard, with my father deteriorating day by day.

I snuggled down on the lumpy mattress in the attic room we shared and pulled the coarse sheets up around me with a sigh. The loss of my mother, followed quickly by giving up his profession, had broken my poor father. He'd told me several times that he'd returned to England for my sake and my brother's. I still didn't know the reason. A wave of sadness swept over me as I lay waiting for sleep. My life with my father already felt immeasurably distant. When I counted the days, I was astonished to find they numbered only five since the killer had crept into our room, altering the course of my life utterly. It felt more like five weeks.

After a final night at Chippenham, we moved on together, passing through Corsham and heading towards the Bath to drop off more goods. Before we reached the city of Bath itself, we branched off the Great West Road and headed down to a market town called Bradford-on-Avon.

This was a town built of yellow sandstone cottages on the side of a steep hill. A river ran through the bottom of the valley. We crossed the bridge at dusk and climbed the steep track up the hill between tall houses. Despite the long days they'd worked and despite the steepness of the hill, the horses walked briskly, their ears pricked forward eagerly. I panted and hurried, unable to keep up. I was walking beside the ninth horse, Sparrow, when he trotted into a yard at the top of Silver Street and joined his fellows at a water trough, drinking noisily and swishing his tail with contentment. The horses were home.

As I helped unload the packs, groom and feed the horses, I reflected that I had succeeded in fleeing my father's killer. I'd put many more miles between us than I'd thought possible. I had been incredibly lucky meeting Martha.

We turned the horses out into a paddock adjacent to Martha's cottage where they rolled and fell to contentedly cropping the winter grass.

'Well, Charlie,' Martha said after a supper of mutton and dumplings. She looked directly at me with her sharp blue eyes. 'How was driving a packhorse train?'

'I won't say it wasn't hard, but I enjoyed it,' I assured her. 'I love working with horses.'

'You did just under half a full run,' she told me. 'So by my reckoning, taking into account your food and lodgings, I owes you sixpence.' She put the silver coin on the table and pushed it towards me. I picked it up gratefully. A sixpence was little enough between me and the wide world, but it felt like riches compared to my previous condition.

'Now,' said Martha. 'I can pay a shilling for a full run. With Jason laid up, I'm going to need help the next weeks. Do you want the work?'

Gratitude and relief flooded me. 'Yes!' I said at once. 'Oh yes, please.'

Martha grinned: 'Tomorrow is Sunday so it's a rest day. We go to church together and then you have the rest of the afternoon off. But you're grooming and stalling the horses tomorrow night ready for Monday morning. So if you do go out drinking with the lads in the town, don't spend that whole sixpence at once, and come back sober enough to look after my horses! And if you get into fisti-cuffs as a regular habit, don't do it on my time.'

I grinned at the thought of going out on a spree with the local lads and rolling home drunk. 'I'll tend the horses,' I promised. 'Thank you.'

'It's only until Jason is back, mind you,' Martha warned. 'He's apprenticed to me and I can't afford to take on anyone else.'

'I understand,' I told her, hastily calculating that I might have earned six shillings or more before I was obliged to fend for myself again. A small fortune. I could then set out alone to find Henry in Dorset without fear-ing starvation.

As I settled onto Jason's straw mattress above the stable and pulled a blanket over myself, I felt more re-lieved than I'd been able to express to Mistress Martha. I pushed my remaining anxiety for the future away, and thought only of the security of the next weeks. Only one thing troubled me: I had to return to London each week. I would have to hope that my disguise and my new oc-cupation were protection enough for the hours I would have to spend there.

CHAPTER SIX

I quickly settled into the routine of the packhorse train. Being on the road with few possessions in all weathers was familiar to me from the years we'd spent following the army. My blisters healed and I toughened up. My skin grew brown from the early spring sun and my clothes were almost constantly dirty. I felt increasingly confident that even if the murderer were to see me in London, he wouldn't know me for the pale-skinned city girl he had threatened.

It was just as well that I looked so different, for the Castle and Falcon in Aldgate Street where Martha put up in London was uncomfortably close to those last lodgings where my father had met his end so horribly. I recognized the pie shop and the spot where the bay horse had got stuck. The thought struck me that the killer must have been watching us before he attacked. He knew we'd just moved in to that house and he even knew I'd gone out, leaving father alone. I shivered and cast a glance around me.

A shock awaited me, too, in the inn yard. A printed notice was tacked to the wall, offering a reward to anyone who had information on the whereabouts of one Charlotte Smith, wanted in connection with an unlawful killing. There was even a sketch of me that was a reasonable likeness, my long hair tumbling down around my face. I stared at the notice in horror. It was as though someone had dropped ice down my neck.

'A right scandal, that were, weren't it?' said a friendly stable boy, nodding at the notice as he passed by me. 'Did you hear? A young servant upped and murdered her master and robbed him too.'

'Really?' I croaked, horrified. 'It doesn't say so.'

'No, but it were in the papers,' said the lad. 'Mr Jones read it to us a couple of days ago. They even preached about the wickedness of the crime at church on Sunday.'

I gulped. 'But how do they know that's what happened?' I asked. 'If there's been no trial?'

'Oh, it's clear as day, ain't it?' said an ostler, joining us. 'T'was in the paper as how the landlady swore she was outside the door and there was no one else what could have done it.' He lowered his voice. 'She stabbed him seventeen times and ran off with all his valuables, the hussy!'

'I heard as how she cut him into pieces,' contradicted the stable boy. 'Sawed his head clean off!'

Fearing I might be sick, I withdrew to the stables and leaned my clammy forehead against Magpie's neck. The stall was in semi-darkness as the daylight failed and I could stand and shiver without being observed.

'They must have bribed the landlady, Magpie,' I whispered, trembling. 'Now I'm a wanted felon.'

It struck me that the two stable boys had discussed the crime with me right in front of the poster without so much as a curious glance at me. I hoped that meant my boy's clothing was protection enough for now. This thought gave me courage and I pulled my cap down low and went into the inn. But I avoided the taproom and my dinner, going straight to bed.

Early the following morning, I tore the notice down when no one was looking, ripped it up and stuffed it in the midden heap. But there were others; I saw them here and there in the streets and on buildings. I couldn't possibly remove them all.

I breathed more freely as we passed out of the city gates into the open countryside again. Each trip into London was fraught with danger and I dreaded it.

I cared for Martha's horses conscientiously. She was quick to spot an unbalanced pack or a badly tightened girth, but I knew when horses were sickening and what remedies to use. I'd always spent as much time as possible in the stables with my father's comrade and groom, Henry. He'd taught me how to spot the first signs of lameness, how to brew and apply poultices, and how to groom and turn out a horse so it looked its very best. And I'd learned the trick of calming a horse when he was angry or frightened.

I wondered what Henry was doing in Dorset. We'd parted company at Plymouth, after just a few days back in England and I missed him a good deal. His presence might have helped father in his troubles. But he was obliged to find a way to make a living just as we were. I hoped he'd succeeded.

I sighed as I trudged along beside Magpie. She turned her head towards me at the sound and whickered softly.

I laughed and patted her neck as we walked. 'Don't mind me, Magpie,' I said. 'I'm thinking. This has been an interlude, working with you. I have to face the future again very soon.'

Should I write to Henry to be sure he was where I thought? It might save me a long, arduous journey in vain. But I dismissed the idea for the same reason I'd not written to my brother: what if those men were watching the post? What if it led them to me, or to Henry, or to my brother, Robert? They had put up notices and paid bribes. Who knew how far their powers extended? I dared not risk it.

'Martha, where is Gloucestershire?' I asked her that evening as we rubbed down the horses and settled them for the night. She straightened up from inspecting Sparrow's hooves with a grunt.

'Gloucestershire? It's north of Somersetshire, of course.'

I looked blankly at her. 'And do you know Deerhurst Park?'

'Ah, I do that. It's the seat of the Rutherfords. I carries goods for 'em, now and then, like I told you before.'

'How far is it?' I felt a little spurt of excitement at the thought that my mother had once stayed or lived so close to where I now spent my Sundays.

'A day's walk, give or take,' said Martha. 'Why?'

'Oh, just that I'm so ignorant about England,' I said quickly. A day's walk. Unfortunately that put a visit there out of the question. I had only part of a day a week free. But I stored the information in my mind for the future. If I could go there, perhaps I might find someone who remembered my mother. I pondered what my parents had told me of my family, but could come up with very little.

That was strange, now I thought of it. I frowned. A distant memory returned to me of asking my mother whether she had an elder brother like I had. She'd said no, I dimly remembered. Then I'd asked her more and she'd fallen silent.

At Maidenhead, we found Jason much improved but heartily bored. He was a skinny, freckled lad with a cheerful smile and it was easy to see why Martha was fond of him.

'Can't I come home, Mistress?' he begged when we'd stabled the horses and gone up to visit him. 'Look, I can move my leg a bit now. You could put me on a wagon and I'd be home next day!'

'It'd be cheaper than keeping you in luxury here, eating your head off at my expense!' said Martha caustically, but Jason only grinned. 'It would!' he agreed. 'You see to it, Mistress. I don't want to cost you no fortune!'

The following morning, Jason was packed off in the back of a wagon, and we took the packhorse train ahead of him. My time with the packhorses was drawing to a close.

Chapter Seven

The following Monday saw me setting out from Bradford-on-Avon to London for the last time. I'd packed all my belongings and taken them with me. Jason was up and about, hobbling around the stable and lending a hand. He was far more experienced at loading the horses than I. By next week he would be strong enough to make the trip instead of me.

I picked up my staff, took my place beside Magpie and cried 'Hup!' The horses, full of energy after a day of rest and freedom in the paddock, threw up their heads and surged out of the yard onto Silver Street, their shod hooves clopping on the cobbles. We turned right and headed out to the Bath Road without passing through the town. I didn't look back. That part of my life was over.

The nearer we drew to the great city, the more the sight of it reminded me of what I'd experienced there and that soon I would be leaving Martha with only a few shillings in my pocket. I'd tried to hoard every penny I'd earned, but I'd needed to take my boots to the cobblers twice and to purchase new stockings. What remained was inadequate.

Once we'd reached the Castle and Falcon and supper was done, and whilst Martha took a drop or two of liquor in the taproom 'to warm her bones', I went out to the stables to check on the horses. It was my job to ensure they received the full measure of provender Martha was charged for and to check they were comfortable. I ran my hands over each horse's legs, checking for heat or swelling, but they all seemed fit and well.

Feeling restless and too anxious about the future to fall asleep readily, I decided to risk a walk along the street adjacent to the inn. I didn't normally venture out in London, but I needed some air.

The streets were quieter at this time of day. There was less horse-drawn traffic and fewer traders, though the city was still bustling with people on foot. Men and women were walking home from work, couples were out strolling arm in arm, looking in shop windows or talking together. Children played in every yard and side street or hung about hoping to earn a penny taking a message or holding a horse.

I paused to look at hats in the window of a milliner's shop on Aldgate Street, wondering if I would ever wear such garments again. Most were ugly things, but there was a modish bonnet that I thought would suit my brown hair. I sighed and shook my head. I was just about to walk on, when I glanced over my shoulder and saw a face I knew. My heart jumped into my throat. My father's killer was walking along the street behind me.

Heart pounding with fear, I slipped into a doorway beyond the milliner's and shrank back against the door, pulling my cap down low over my face. In just a few moments, the man walked swiftly past me. He looked neither right nor left, and didn't glance in my direction.

It was him, beyond any doubt. Those pale eyes and that small mole were unmistakable.

I stood trembling, trying to master my fear. I had been guilty of gross stupidity, walking around unnecessarily in London. Even worse, I'd been gazing at girls' adornments in a window. No boy would do such a thing. I cursed myself.

I fled back to the safety of the Castle and Falcon and crept into bed beside Martha. I could tell she was awake by the absence of rumbling snores, but she said nothing. I curled into a tight ball beneath the blankets and shivered.

The day came too soon for my sleep-drenched mind. Martha had to haul me out of bed to pack and go down to breakfast. 'Late to bed ain't no excuse for rising late,' she grumbled at me as I staggered down the steep staircase, clutching my things.

Breakfast scarcely kept me awake, but checking that I wasn't being watched as I left London certainly did. Afraid I might have been followed last night, I glanced around constantly. I closely scrutinized every ostler, coachman, and groom, in fear they were covertly watching me. As I made my way out of town along the road, I looked fearfully behind me. It wasn't until we reached the inn at Maidenhead for the night that I began to relax and stopped startling at every unexpected noise.

Scarcely had I entered the yard and drawn a sigh of relief, than I saw another notice with my face on it plastered on the wall for all to see. I forced myself to stay awake until darkness and peace had fallen over the inn, then I crept down the creaking stairs with my heart hammering and tore down the notice.

At Hungerford, as we reached our room for the night, Martha startled me by telling me they were looking to hire a boy in the stables of the John of Gaunt inn. 'It's a fine coaching inn, the biggest in the town. You interested?' she asked. 'I've recommended you.'

I caught my breath. 'Really?' I asked. I hadn't planned to look for more work yet. I'd set my heart on finding Henry. But I couldn't afford to turn the job down when I had so little money left. 'Thank you,' I stammered. 'That's very kind of you.'

'You'll be a stable boy. It'll be hard, but you'll be fed and have a roof over your head. I wasn't easy in my mind turnin' you off,' she said, shedding her shawl and plumping up her pillow. 'I'd feel a deal more comfortable knowin' you have a place.'

'You've been good to me Martha,' I told her gratefully.

'Ah well, it's a dangerous world for a slip of a girl alone,' she said. I cast a shocked glance up at her.

'Oh, don't think I didn't see through that disguise o' yours,' she said impatiently. 'Dressed as a lad often enough myself as a child. You have to get up early in the morning to fool *me*!'

'Has everyone else guessed too?' I asked in a low, mortified voice. I thought of those posters in London and elsewhere and felt sick.

'Not as they've said to me,' said Martha, slowly. She was sitting on the bed staring at me. 'What's troubling me is whether you've run off from some school or yer father. If there be kin that are worried sick about you, I can't go on helping you.'

I shook my head. 'No, Mistress Martha,' I told her, the words wrung from me by necessity. 'My mother's dead, and father died of . . . an illness in London.' I felt bad lying to such a kind friend.

'An illness, was it?'Martha said solemnly.

Seeing suspicion and understanding dawning in her sharp eyes, I opened my mouth to speak, to deny the crime of which I was accused. But seeing me about to speak, Martha held up a gnarled finger for silence. 'No! Don't say nothin', for I don't need to know!'

I suspected she'd guessed my story, or a version of it; it had been in the papers and much talked of. But, to my great relief, it seemed she intended to let it pass for now, and after a moment, she said, 'You can't do better than earn an honest living. But before you go, I think we'd better cut your hair, hadn't we? If you want people to believe you are a lad, that is.'

'How long have *you* known?' I asked.

'From the first day. You didn't eat like a lad. More like a bird. And you slept in your cap. Once I'd suspected, it was clear enough.'

I felt rather low. If Martha had seen through me so quickly, how was I to maintain the pretence in the long run? I foresaw many difficulties ahead.

'Ah, don't fret,' said Martha, guessing my thoughts. 'I sees further than most. There's plenty of folk as never see past their noses.' She pulled a pair of scissors out of her bag and snipped the blades together invitingly. 'So. We goin' to cut it off or would you rather return to your life as a young lady?'

'I don't have a life to return to,' I told her sadly. I pulled my cap off and my brown hair cascaded down over my shoulders. I touched it sadly, remembering how I'd admired ladies' hats in a shop window only a day or so before. On the other hand, knowing I was being hunted as a girl, I should have cut it off long ago. 'It needs to go. If I'd had scissors to hand the night I fled London, I'd have done it then.'

Martha stood over me, lifted my long tresses, and looked at them for a moment. 'Ah, 'tis a pity. But you'll be safer this way.' She snipped my hair off short. I watched it fall to the floor and bit my lip. I was leaving the very last of my old life behind me, and with it at least half of who I was.

After Martha had finished, I put my hands up to touch my shorn head. It felt strange; not me at all. Martha bent and gathered up my long hair, wrapping it all in a scarf. 'This'll fetch a bit,' she said. 'I'll sell it quiet-like and drop off the money for you on my next journey through.'

I nodded sadly. I really was Charlie now. There was no turning back.

CHAPTER EIGHT

'Oi, new boy! You not got that stable mucked out yet?'

'I'm nearly done!' I called, heaving a heavy forkful of muck into a barrow.

'Get out here right now and help Tom hitch up this team!'

I threw the fork into the half-full barrow and hurried out of the gloom into the brightness of the yard. Tom was leading two horses towards a smart carriage that had come in late last night. The occupants had stayed overnight at the John of Gaunt, and were now ready to continue on their journey west.

The blow came out of nowhere, sending me reeling onto the cobbles, my head spinning. I hadn't seen Phillips standing by the door to the stables or I would have at least tried to dodge his meaty fist. He was a large, powerful man, with unusually long arms and eyebrows that jutted out and met above his eyes, giving him a permanent scowl.

'Get up, lad, and stop blubbing like a girl,' ordered Phillips harshly. 'This team needs to be harnessed and ready. The owners have been calling for it these five minutes. We don't keep no one waiting here! D'yer hear me?'

I scrambled to my feet, my breeches soiled with

that particular mix of mud and horse dung that is to be found in every stable yard. My hands were mired too. Wiping them on my breeches so as not to dirty the carefully cleaned harness, I hurried to Tom's aid. As he backed the first pair up to the carriage, either side of the shaft, I threaded the harness through their collars and strapped the reins to their bridles. The moment they were hitched, Tom hurried to fetch the next pair, leaving me fumbling with unfamiliar buckles. I'd ridden my whole life and knew as much as anyone about grooming and care of horses, but harnessing them to a carriage was new to me.

'I thought you knew horses, damn it,' snarled Phillips, watching my clumsy efforts with growing anger. 'I employed you on that understanding!'

'Not carriages,' I confessed timidly. 'I'll learn fast, I swear.' He was approaching me again and I had no way of escaping another blow, the buckle only half threaded as it was. The clout felled me again and I sat, winking away the spots in front of my eyes, under the horses' feet.

'Not fast enough,' he said, aiming a kick that I wasn't quick enough to dodge. 'Get inside and carry on mucking out. It's all you're fit for.'

I crawled away from him and staggered unsteadily to my feet. Ever since Martha had left me here yesterday, I'd wished I'd set out for Dorset instead, whether or not I had enough money for the journey.

I rubbed my aching head as I set to mucking out the empty stall again, lifting the trodden-down mixture of horse dung and straw one heavy forkful at a time into the barrow. When I'd tipped the last barrowful out on the midden, I hauled heavy buckets of water up from the well and sluiced the stable floor clean, sweeping the sludgy liquid into the guttering that ran the length of the floor.

No sooner was that stall finished and strewn with fresh straw, than there was another to do and then another. By the time I was sent in to breakfast, I ached from head to foot.

I walked into the room where the stable hands were served their meals. A huge cauldron of stew and dumplings stood on the straw-strewn floor, a ladle resting in it. The smell set my mouth watering. I grabbed a wooden bowl from its place on the shelf and helped myself. Then I sat down on a rickety bench. As I began to eat, Tom came and sat beside me. He stirred his stew, examining the lumps of carrot and stringy meat in the brown gravy.

'You mustn't look so afeared of ole Phillips,' he told me. 'The thing is, you got to show him you're useful. Then he won't bully you no more. Work alongside me and Sam the rest of the day,' Tom offered kindly. 'Learn the ropes. Come on. That's the bell ringing. That means there's a coach coming in that needs a change. Go fetch two fresh horses and I'll unharness theirs.'

Swallowing my last mouthful of food, I hurried to the stables. On the left were the horses that had already done a stint that day. I knew because I'd groomed them, washed the mud from their legs, and fed and watered them as they came in. To the right were the fresh horses. I picked out two and led them out into the yard. They followed me out, their hooves clattering on the cobbles, their ears pricked up. Tom had unhitched a sweating, steaming pair from the carriage. I led them away, handing Tom the fresh horses. Ben, a skinny, dark-haired youth, was helping him hitch them to the carriage. They worked so fast that the carriage was rolling out of the yard before I'd tethered the tired beasts in their stalls.

As the horses drank, Tom climbed up to the hayloft and tipped fresh hay through the slots into their racks. Meanwhile I sponged their mud-spattered legs, then rubbed one horse down while Tom saw to the other.

We had barely finished before the bell was ringing again. 'Those two!' Tom ordered, pointing at a bay and a skewbald horse in the stalls. He ran out into the yard to begin the next change as I untied the pair to lead out. Tom and Sam, an older boy with huge hands and feet, had unhitched two more sweating horses, but we'd barely led them from the shafts when another coach rattled into the yard and rang for the change, this time with four horses harnessed to it.

As I led away the tired pair, the coachman was already bawling complaints at us for slowness and Phillips was looking thunderous.

There was no time to feed or groom the horses now until we had the coaches done. I led out one pair and then another, while Tom and Sam tackled the harnesses and handed me the tired beasts to lead away.

It was a cool day, but I grew steadily warmer, required to work constantly at a run. When there was a brief respite from travellers, we rubbed down, fed and watered the tired horses. By late afternoon, most of them were going out for a second stint.

'Is it always this busy?' I asked Tom breathlessly, as we forked hay down from the loft into the horses' racks.

'This time o' year it is. Bath season just beginning and everyone a-travelling down from Lunnon,' he said briefly.

'Are you wasting time talking up there?' demanded Phillips' angry voice from the stalls.

'No, sir, just giving instructions,' Tom called down, and grimaced at me. We finished our task as quickly as possible and hurried back down the ladder, thankful that another peal of the bell had called Phillips back out into the yard.

I was about to run out to fetch the horses when I spotted a figure I recognized in the yard. I stopped so suddenly that Tom collided with me.

'What's up?' he demanded. 'We gotta hurry!'

'Stomach ache!' I improvised, bending over and clutching my belly. Tom sighed and pushed past me, running to take the horses and calling to another boy to help. I stayed out of sight, watching a thin, wizened man with stooped shoulders holding a roll of papers speaking to Phillips. It was the magistrate without a doubt. When Phillips nodded, he thanked him and went to nail a notice onto the wall. I knew what it was without going to look. I shivered and drew further back into the shadows. When Tom came running in leading the two steaming horses, I took them from him at the door and led them into the friendly gloom of the stalls.

So I was still being hunted. I rubbed down the horses with shaking hands and found excuses to stay inside the stable until the magistrate was long gone. Late that night, I crept out of the straw where I slept wrapped in a moth-eaten blanket, tore the notice down, ripped it into tiny shreds and buried it in the midden heap.

The bell that rang to wake us in the morning dragged me from the deepest sleep. For a few moments, I couldn't think where I was. The stable was still in darkness, and all I knew was that I ached all over. When I remembered, I groaned and dragged myself out from under my blanket, trying to force my heavy limbs into action. Around me, the other boys were emerging yawning and stretching from whichever corner they had crawled into to sleep. In theory, we slept in the stable to keep watch over the horses. In practice, I doubted a thunderstorm right overhead would have woken us until morning.

Instead of growing used to the long days, I was constantly tired. 'How are you getting on, Charlie?' Martha appeared beside me in the stables one evening as I was grooming. I gave her a weary smile without pausing in my work. Her familiar face was a welcome sight. 'I'm well enough, thank you,' I said.

'Getting enough to eat?'

'Plenty to eat, just not enough time to eat it.'

'Posting houses are busy places,' she acknowledged. 'I'm on my way back from Lunnon. Thought I'd see how you was settling in.' She leaned closer. 'No one suspects?'

'The latrine is tricky,' I told her, keeping my voice low. 'There's always a queue during the day, and no time to wait in it. The other lads piss in the midden and can't understand why I don't.'

Martha nodded. 'And?'

I grinned. 'I'm developing a strong bladder.'

'And the sleeping arrangements?'

'I'm in the stables with the horses.'

Martha nodded. She handed me a small package of coins wrapped in paper. I took it, looking questioningly up at her. 'Money for your hair,' she whispered and winked. 'Got a good price for you.'

Phillips came striding through the stables just then, so Martha gave me a nod and departed. I hurriedly stuffed the packet into my shirt and kept working. I was sorry to see Martha go. I missed my days on the open road with Magpie, Sparrow, and the other packhorses.

CHAPTER NINE

'This horse has a strained hock,' I told Phillips two weeks later. He was walking past me as I groomed a tired horse from a team that had been brought in sweating and straining from one of the overloaded stagecoaches.

He checked the bay gelding over, running his hand over his leg and shook his head. 'I can't see anything wrong.'

'It's heated,' I insisted. 'It'll be swollen by morning and needs to be cooled and poulticed now.'

Phillips stared down at me, his lower lip jutting out and his frown pronounced. 'Nonsense!' he said. 'Are you setting up your knowledge against mine?'

'No, of course not,' I faltered. 'I just think that . . . '

I reeled back as a blow caught me on the side of the head. I fell back against the horse's flank and sank to the floor. The gelding startled and pulled on his halter, snorting in shock, his hooves narrowly missing me where I lay in the straw.

'Get on with your work,' snapped Phillips. 'Or you'll be out of a job by tomorrow.'

As Phillips stalked off, I staggered groggily to my feet and leaned against the gelding, putting a soothing hand on his neck. 'There, boy,' I said softly. 'Don't fret.' He grew calm again, turning his weary head to nuzzle me. 'They work us all to death, old boy,' I said sadly to the horse, stroking his velvety nose. 'Horse and human alike.'

By morning, the bay gelding had a swollen hock and was dead lame. Tom tried to lead him out only to find he could barely walk. 'This one's lamed, Phillips,' he called out.

Phillips cursed colourfully. 'Put him across the other side,' he said, nodding at the stalls where the horses that had already done a stint rested. The bell rang in the yard once more. 'I'll look at him later,' he added, hurrying out to direct the next change.

Phillips tended to the horse himself. I didn't expect him to admit I'd been right, of course. But neither did I expect to be hauled in front of him at suppertime by Matthew, his senior groom, and told I was dismissed. 'I want you gone within fifteen minutes, no gossiping to anyone in the yard,' Phillips ordered me, leaning against the wall of the tack room. Matthew, an ill-favoured rogue with a sneer, lounged behind him, grinning. I felt the shock catch me like one of Phillips' blows.

'Dismissed?' I heard my voice say faintly. 'What about my three weeks' pay?'

'Your pay is forfeit for injuring that horse. We can't afford to have animals standing idle because they've been lamed by clumsy stable hands who don't know their work. Nor to employ lads who aren't strong enough to lift a shovel full of muck.'

I bit my lip and flushed with anger. 'You must know I didn't harm him.'

'Get out, Weaver,' spat Phillips.

'I won't miss the place, or you!' I retorted. 'You're a cheat and a liar!' I dodged out into the yard before he could think about belting me.

An open carriage had arrived with two fine-looking horses between the shafts. It was late and most of the boys were at dinner. They'd sent Jim, the youngest lad, out to deal with the carriage; none of the older boys would leave their meal unless they had to. Young Jim approached the high-bred horses nervously. 'Stay away from them,' called the driver from the box. 'They aren't used to strangers!'

I looked up at the driver of the vehicle. Both his appearance and his voice were familiar to me. His groom, an elderly man, was climbing down from the carriage to go to the horses' heads. The black horses were pulling and fretting on the reins restlessly, and I guessed from looking at them that they were a young pair only just broken to traffic and still unpredictable. One was a stoned stallion, huge, strong, and fiery. Such horses were always difficult to manage.

At that moment a chaise drawn by four horses, driven at a shocking pace, swept under the archway and into the yard. It took the driver a moment to react to the fact that there was a vehicle straight ahead of him and to pull his horses up. Before he could stop entirely, there was a glancing collision and frightened screams from the horses involved.

Complete chaos ensued. The black stallion reared wildly, and then dropped to all fours and kicked out with tremendous force. There was a splintering sound as the dashboard of the open chaise stove in, and then the horse was on his back legs again, screaming out a wild neigh, his fore hooves pawing the air. His fellow tried to make a break for it, and succeeded in dragging the shattered chaise sharply to the right. The elderly groom, still in the act of climbing out of the carriage, was thrown headlong onto the cobbles.

The horses of the chaise and four were hardly in any better case. One had been kicked by the young black stallion and was frantically trying to back away from him. Another horse had got his leg over the trace, whilst the driver, who appeared either drunk or incompetent, failed to get his team under control or away from the enraged young horse.

It was no longer any part of my duties to help. I was free to collect my belongings and walk away from the John of Gaunt for ever. But I could no more see horses in trouble and not help them than I could cease to draw breath. I plunged into the fray.

It was the young pair that most needed calming. The team with the chaise were blown and sweating and would calm of their own accord if the firebrand stallion could be removed from their midst.

I dodged flailing hooves and made for the young stallion's bridle. As I approached, he laid his ears flat back, bared his teeth, snaked his neck and bit the lead horse from the other team in the neck, causing him to scream and plunge forward afresh. I managed to reach his side. Ears still flat back against his head, he lunged at me, his handsome face twisted with fury, his lips drawn back over his white teeth. The strong teeth caught me a vicious bite on the arm, but I managed to catch his bridle.

'Stop it,' I told him firmly. 'Stop it now. Listen to me.'
I began to speak soothingly, with the mixture of words
and meaningless sounds I'd always used to communi-
cate with horses, which often seemed to calm them. The
stallion tried to bite me again, but this time it was a half-
hearted effort and, using all my strength, I managed to
hold him. I kept talking.

He was back down on all four hooves now, teeth no
longer bared, though his ears were still flat against his
head. He was trembling, snorting, and sweating, with
the whites of his eyes showing. But I had his attention.
His nostrils quivered as he sampled my scent. His head
dropped a little lower and, though he stamped his back leg
one more time, I could see the tension going out of him.

Behind me, I was aware that the chaise and team had
managed to back away. There was nothing further to
trouble the young stallion. But I didn't take my eyes off
him and kept talking softly. A little more time, and his
ears came forward. He dropped his nose into my hand
and I stroked him. Only when I was quite certain he was
calm did I risk a glance up at the driver. He was sitting
quite still on the splintered box of the light chaise, the
reins gathered in his hands. As I met his astonished gaze,
I recognized him as the handsome young man who had
warned me about the highwaymen in Savernake Forest. What had Martha called him? I'd forgotten. But I
remembered she'd said he was from Deerhurst Park.

I gave the stallion's nose a last stroke and then stepped
back. The elderly groom had staggered to his feet and
was now standing unsteadily at the other horse's head.
Tom had taken charge of the team and Phillips himself

was back in the yard now too, drawn by the rumpus. I noticed the stallion's driver beckoning me.

'Thank you, my lad,' he said as I approached. 'Did he bite you hard?'

'It's nothing, sir,' I lied politely.

'Here's a shilling for your trouble,' he said, holding out a gleaming coin.

I recoiled instinctively. 'Oh no,' I stammered. 'You don't need to . . .'

I didn't notice Phillips coming up behind me until he took me by the collar and shoved me away with a kick to the seat of my breeches.

'Sorry the little varmint is bothering you, Mr Lawrence,' he said obsequiously. 'We've just had to dismiss him for laziness and impertinence. He's not at all the sort of urchin you'd want to tip. Scram!' he said fiercely, rounding on me. I fled.

It didn't take me many minutes to pack up my belongings, tuck my few valuables into my shirt and leave. As I left the inn yard, I heard the young man giving orders to put up for the night and to have his carriage repaired.

It was late and as I walked along the high street, the heavens opened and the rain soaked me. Instead of setting out for Dorset at once, I was forced to find a shabby little alehouse that rented out a few tiny rooms to travellers far poorer than those who used the main posting houses. I broke into the money I'd got for my hair, ordered a jug of hot water, enjoyed a thorough wash, and sent my clothes for laundering overnight.

When I opened my eyes, the sun was shining brightly outside. I yawned, stretched, and took a moment to enjoy not having been up for several hours already, mucking out stalls. I sat up, wincing at the pain in my arm and pulled up my sleeve. The whole area was bruised purplish-blue and very sore.

I was halfway out of bed when I heard footsteps and a knock at the door. 'Who is it?' I asked nervously.

'Gen'leman to see you,' the innkeeper's voice announced through the door. 'Waiting downstairs.'

I sat frozen to the spot as his footsteps receded back down the rickety stairs. A 'gentleman'. The only gentlemen who might be looking for me wanted nothing good. I remembered the smooth, well-spoken voices of my father's killer and the equally presentable magistrate. A man was waiting for me downstairs and it could be either of them. It had been a close call in London. Perhaps the posters had worked and they'd been given information leading them to me.

With a shudder of fear, I silently fetched my laundered clothes from where they'd been left in the corridor and dragged them on. I couldn't risk using the stairs; they took me straight down into the grubby taproom below. Instead, I forced open my narrow casement window. It gave onto a small yard and a woodpile was stacked up below me. There was no one about, so I dropped my bag through the window, wriggled through the small opening, and jumped down after it. Swiftly leaving the yard, I fled up the road.

CHAPTER TEN

I hadn't gone far up the busy street before I heard footsteps behind me. There were plenty of people around, but fear gripped me and I broke into a run. I pushed past a farmer and slipped by a stout woman with a basket on her arm, desperately trying to lose myself in the throng. The footsteps behind me quickened, keeping pace easily.

My terror made me behave stupidly. Instead of staying in the busy thoroughfare, I dodged down an alleyway, my urge for swift flight winning over my wiser instinct to stay among people. The footsteps were drawing closer behind me. I dared not even take the time to glance back. I raced around a corner only to find myself trapped in a dead end.

I attempted to dodge my pursuer; as I ducked past him, his hand grasped my sleeve. I used the force of it to swing around and let fly a blow to his face. It was too late to stop by the time I realized that I did know the face, but it wasn't either of the ones I'd feared.

Even as my eyes widened in horror at the mistake I was making, my fist connected with his chin. I felt the pain of the blow through every bone in my hand and gasped. The young man released me and reeled back, clutching his jaw with an oath.

I staggered away from him but didn't flee. Instead, I nursed my bruised hand, watching him from a safe distance as I caught my breath, both wary and apologetic.

'What are you chasing me for?' I gasped.

'There's gratitude for you,' said the young man, shaking his head as if to clear it. He bent over, panting and rubbing his jaw ruefully, his eyes on me. They were hazel; striking in his rather pale face. As he straightened up, I realized he was quite a bit taller than me. His face looked stern.

'I sent you a message and the next thing I knew, the maid told me you were running off up the road. You *are* the lad they call Charlie, are you not?'

'I am.' I was still wary, watching him suspiciously, wondering what he wanted from me. Was I in some kind of trouble, more than I knew of?

'Do you recognize me?' he asked.

'Yes. It was your stallion last night.'

'That's right,' he nodded. 'We met once before, didn't we? On the road to London? You were with Mistress Martha.'

I gave a wary nod, still wondering what he wanted. 'Why were you chasing me?' I asked again.

'I'm clearly mad. I was impressed with your handling of my young horse. I was considering offering you work.'

'You were?' I could hear my voice was suddenly eager.

A slight smile crossed the young man's face. 'They let you go from the John of Gaunt. Why was that?'

I frowned. 'You heard what Mr Phillips said.'

'Yes, but I'd like to hear your version of it,' he replied.

'He didn't like that I noticed a horse was injured before

he did. And he didn't think I worked fast enough.'

'I see. Well, I know you worked for Mistress Martha while her boy was laid up. I know she was pleased with you, because I've seen her and spoken with her recently. I need a new personal groom. Mine is elderly and the work is too much for him; it's time he had someone to start training up. I've rarely seen a lad who can handle horses like you showed me you can yesterday. Nor do I often see lads with that kind of courage. My horses take some handling. If you are honest and hard-working, I'm interested in giving you a chance.'

I stared up at him. 'Really?' I managed to say at last.

His eyes twinkled, making his face look less severe. 'Really. How old are you?'

'Thirteen,' I said. It was safer to give him a younger age to explain why I wasn't as strong as other boys.

'Parents?'

I shook my head.

'Bailiffs or constables after you?'

'No!'

'Then why were you running off?'

'You frightened me.'

'Not in any trouble I should know about are you?'

I shook my head vehemently. He definitely shouldn't know anything about it. 'I've done nothing wrong,' I stated honestly.

'What experience do you have?' he asked me.

'I've spent my life around horses. I can ride them, groom them, care for them when they're sick, injured, or in foal.'

'Can you care for their tack, their harnesses?'

71

'I can.'

'What about driving?'

'No,' I said regretfully.

'That's something we can address. I think we might suit,' said the man. 'You would be paid a shilling a week, after board, lodgings, and clothing have been subtracted. Will you come and work for me?'

I grinned at him, struck by the absurdity of the situation. A few moments ago, I'd been fleeing from him, convinced he was someone trying to kill me. 'I know nothing about you,' I pointed out. 'Except Mistress Martha told me you worked for some lord or other.'

This drew an answering smile from him, and I thought once more how it suited him to smile. He was a quiet, serious man. I had the impression he was as reserved as I was, but his smile seemed to hint at another side of him.

'I'm sorry. My name is Lawrence. I'm steward and cousin once removed to Lord Rutherford of Deerhurst Park. You'd be working in the main stables at the park.'

I was actually being offered a job at Deerhurst Park! How could a more perfect opportunity possibly come my way? I instantly put my plans to find Henry on hold once more. I would be earning money *and* perhaps I could learn something about my parents.

Lawrence smiled again and I found myself smiling back. I liked what I saw. This was a young man I could imagine working for happily. He would not bully or browbeat. I was amazed he would look twice at a scruffy lad like me.

'Lord Rutherford was a keen horseman in his younger days and still keeps a large stable. He indulges my interest in gentling difficult horses. You'd have responsibility for some valuable beasts. I need someone with both courage and talent.'

'And do you often take on new staff by interview in the middle of the street?' I asked, amused.

'Rarely,' he said, ruefully rubbing the bruise I'd given him.

'I accept,' I told him.

'There will be a trial period of a month,' Lawrence told me. 'You'll be working under my groom and learning the ropes. Presumably you can start right away?'

'I can.'

'Come with me then, Charlie Weaver,' said Lawrence. He turned and strode off back down the alley. I trotted after him in wonder. I had no idea what a household such as his would be like. It sounded very grand. I knew nothing of the British nobility, having spent my childhood in the Americas. Would I manage to fit in better than at the John of Gaunt? Mansions were even further outside my range of experience than packhorse trains or posting inns. I simply needed to be thankful, I told myself, that such secure, respectable work had come my way. The relief of not being adrift in the world again, with only the vague possibility of finding Henry, was intense.

It was very strange to enter the yard of the John of Gaunt again. I attracted a few surprised glances from the other boys and a deeply disapproving one from Phillips. He drew Mr Lawrence aside and whispered in his ear, but I was relieved to see Lawrence shake him off in some irritation.

'Fetch me my carriage and let my groom know I'm ready for my horses, if you please,' he told him firmly but politely, 'You can leave me to make my own choice of staff.' He turned to me. 'You can put your bag in the chaise. Then Bridges will no doubt be grateful for some help bringing out the horses.'

I stowed my satchel and hurried into the stables. It took me only a second to spot the stallion and the gelding that had pulled the carriage the night before. Both had been groomed far more thoroughly than anyone employed at the John of Gaunt would have time for. I guessed that Bridges was responsible for this. It gave me a good opinion of him.

I soon realized this good opinion wasn't reciprocated. His expression, when his eyes fell on me, was disapproving. In fact, he looked as though he had smelled something distasteful.

'Mr Lawrence sent me to help you,' I said by way of explanation. 'I'm Charlie.'

'Hmm,' was all the response I got as he took hold of the stallion's lead rein and led him out of the stall. I hadn't been told what to do, but decided I should lead the gelding out after him. However, before I reached the horse, I was intercepted by Phillips and the eldest stable boy, Matthew. They didn't look as though they'd come to congratulate me on my new employment.

'Sneaking off to ingratiate yourself,' hissed Phillips. 'There's half a dozen lads here should've had this position ahead of you.'

'You're nothing. Dirt under our feet,' added Matthew.

I tried to slip past them, not wanting to get drawn

into an argument. But Matthew stuck out his foot and I tripped, falling full length onto the mucky floor of the stalls. I picked myself up, but Phillips caught my arm and Matthew punched me in the stomach. I doubled over, winded, gasping helplessly for air. The stalls and my assailants swam giddily before my eyes for a moment. I thought I was going to throw up. Something in me snapped suddenly. The fear I'd been living with, the bottled up grief, my anger at their resentment; all combined to make me feel red-hot rage. I threw myself at Matthew, clawing at his face and kicking him. I caught him off guard and bore him backwards into the straw. I bit him on the ear and punched him in the face before a hand grasped me roughly by the seat of my breeches and hauled me off. Still spitting with rage, I fought to get away, until I realized it was Bridges. I went limp in his grasp.

'Are you going to lead out your new master's horse, boy, or are you too busy brawling?' he asked icily. They were the first words he had spoken to me.

Hot with anger, my throat choked up, I couldn't speak a word in my own defence. Instead, I limped to the gelding, who was fretting at the noise and disturbance nearby. I soothed him with soft words, stroking him before I untied him. The necessity of being calm for the horse, and his familiar, comforting scent, helped me let go of my anger. When I led him out, both the horse and I were quite collected.

I walked past Matthew and Phillips without looking at them, my chin jutting defiantly. I hurt all over. My belly felt tender and bruised, as did my ribs, and I suspected from the soreness of my face, that I would soon have a black eye once more.

'You fight like a girl, Weaver!' Matthew taunted me as I passed. I flushed deeply.

Lawrence looked narrowly at me as I led his gelding to the carriage, but he said nothing. His gaze shifted to something behind me. I glanced over my shoulder to see Matthew had emerged from the stable, a dirty pocket-handkerchief held to a bleeding ear, his face scratched. He was glaring at me. Lawrence exchanged a glance with Bridges as I backed the horse up to the carriage beside his partner. Bridges helped me harness the horse in silence. I knew I was in disgrace. My heart sank to think I had made such a bad start to my new employment.

When both horses were harnessed, Bridges climbed with some difficulty into the seat beside his master. I looked up questioningly, wondering where I was to travel. 'You can stand up behind, Charlie,' Lawrence told me.

I'd often seen grooms and servants perching on the back of a chaise, but had never tried it myself. I scrambled up so my feet were on the narrow ledge that protruded from the back of the carriage. There I clung as Lawrence drove the horses out of the yard and onto the road. I felt precarious in the extreme, every bump of the road threatening to shake me free. My existence, I felt, was as precarious as my perch.

CHAPTER ELEVEN

I was used to long days in the saddle and all kinds of weather. And I'd become used to long days of walking with the packhorses. But the next two days tried me nonetheless. The clouds brought several heavy bursts of rain and the wind was sharp. We travelled slowly to spare the horses as they were accomplishing the whole journey without changes.

We broke the journey, of course but, when we stopped, my duty was to care for the horses, not to take a rest myself.

'Take the gelding, boy,' Bridges ordered me each evening as he led the beautiful stallion to the stables. I groomed Velvet, the gelding, to the best of my ability but Bridges always went over him as though I hadn't done a proper job. He rarely spoke to me.

Once or twice I cast an envious glance at Mr Lawrence as he escaped the cold and the rain, disappearing into an inn to warm through and rest while we fed, watered, and rubbed down his valuable horses. Only when they were comfortable could we take a bite to eat and a sup of ale ourselves.

I slept in the stables overnight. 'Stay away from that stallion! He's in my charge, not yours,' Bridges ordered me as he went off to sleep in the quarters for the senior servants. I made myself a nest in the corner of Velvet's stall. He seemed quite happy with the arrangement, especially as I'd managed to beg a carrot for him. Before I slept, I couldn't resist disobeying Bridges by trying to befriend the stallion, Pitch.

In the adjoining stall, the gleaming black horse greeted me with laid-back ears. I could see the whites of his eyes in the darkness as I approached. I stopped, standing quite still, out of the reach of those strong teeth, and simply talked to him. I kept my voice low and soothing.

It took the best part of an hour before I could approach closely enough to touch him. He was jittery and I was wary of being bitten again. But the longer I spent with him, the calmer he grew. When I finally lay down in the straw in Velvet's box, I hoped it had been time well spent.

I woke in the early morning to find Velvet standing over me nuzzling me, blowing in my hair. I laughed sleepily and pushed his head away. He snorted, turned back and lipped my ear playfully.

'That's enough, you,' I said, rubbing my sleeve over my face and yawning. I stroked the horse's nose affectionately. Then I realized there was someone watching me.

'Mr Lawrence,' I said, appalled, scrambling to my feet, trying to brush straw out of my hair. 'I didn't see . . . didn't realize . . . '

'Good morning, Charlie,' he responded, completely relaxed. 'Thank you for guarding my horse. I wanted a quiet word with you.' He paused as though uncertain how to continue then finally said: 'Bridges is bound to resent you at first, Charlie. At present, he neither wants to retire nor understands the need for it. He's been a loyal and trustworthy servant and I don't want his feelings hurt. I rely on you to win him over as skilfully as you have won over my horses.'

'I'm not sure I'm as good with people as I am with horses,' I admitted ruefully.

'I'm beginning to see that,' replied Lawrence. His eyes rested on my new bruises. I lifted a hand to touch my sore cheekbone and blushed at the appearance I must present.

'Do you want to explain this latest to me?' Lawrence asked sternly. I shook my head. I peeped up at him nervously and was relieved to see smile creases in the corners of his eyes. He wasn't really angry. The irony of acquiring a reputation for brawling wasn't lost on me. A small answering smile crept onto my own face. I winced as it hurt my bruised cheek.

Mr Lawrence gave me a nod, and left, presumably to be served his breakfast. I turned to Velvet and patted him. 'Let's get you groomed and presentable for the day then, shall we, boy?' I asked him. He twitched his ears and nudged me by way of response.

Our last stop was the bustling city of Bath with its sandstone buildings and bustling, narrow streets. How I'd longed to visit it when we first returned to England and how different was my actual arrival. Instead of entering the city as a young lady with expectations of pleasure, I clung to the back of a chaise, soaked through and grimy, my bitten arm and bruised face aching. My hair was hacked short and I was dressed in boy's working clothes.

Up to now, I'd been so grateful to have escaped death and to have found work to keep myself from destitution that I'd dwelled little on my losses. But the bustling city, thronged with sedan chairs and filled with elegant ladies in beautiful gowns, and gentlemen gorgeously attired in bright colours, brought my fallen fortunes home to me in the most brutal way possible.

My father wouldn't have been able to afford the best lodgings or the finest gowns for me, not even before things began to go wrong for him, but I would at least have been respectably, perhaps even prettily, clad. I would have come here for parties, not hard work.

I roamed the streets for the hour or so I had free while Mr Lawrence transacted some business. I watched the street sellers hawking their wares, saw a pickpocket at work and clutched my own meagre purse tightly to me. I watched stray dogs picking over piles of rubbish in the street.

There were sites where stylish new town houses, grand squares, and wide streets were under construction, extending the city to the north and west. Sedan chairs passed me, carrying elegant gentry to their places of amusement, and I cast them longing glances. But that life was no longer for me. I must be grateful for what I had.

The Lansdown Road out of the Bath was steep and rutted. Lawrence took it at a steady walk, allowing the horses to pace themselves without actually stopping on the sharp incline. When we reached the top, a magnificent landscape burst upon us; the rolling downs and far views drew a gasp of admiration from me. The country was verdant, with tall trees just bursting into leaf. Lawrence half turned to me as he drove.

'Nearly home now, Charlie,' he said. 'Just a few more miles.' He was smiling and I could tell the view pleased him too, though it must be a familiar sight. 'All this land belongs to Lord Rutherford's estate,' Lawrence added, with a casual wave of his hand.

We drove up and down the rolling downs for another half an hour or so before Lawrence turned the weary horses to the left and allowed them to slow to a walk. Before us were shining new lodge gates. At the sound of carriage wheels on the gravel, they were quickly thrown open to welcome us by a man with a beard and battered cap on his head. A woman with wispy grey hair escaping from a bun emerged from the neat new lodge cottage beside the gates. She was hastily removing a floury apron and bobbed a curtsey when she saw us.

'Good afternoon, Mrs Saunders, Mr Saunders,' said Lawrence with a friendly nod to the couple as he tightened his hold on the reins, drawing the horses to a halt beside the woman. 'I hope I find you both well?'

'Very well, thank you, sir,' the woman replied. 'I hope you had a good journey?'

She darted a curious glance at me as she spoke, and froze, the colour leaving her cheeks. I squirmed uncomfortably. The chaise started again with a jolt and rolled forward. I cast a quick glance back to see the woman still standing on the carriageway, watching us. Her mouth was agape and one hand was clutching her chest.

Did she think it strange that Lawrence had picked up a guttersnipe and brought him home? Is that what all the people here would think of my arrival? I must certainly look disreputable with my dirty clothes and bruised, cut face. I was nervous, now that we were so nearly there, about meeting so many new people.

The ground fell away before us revealing a vast, cultivated park. In the distance I could see a herd of deer grazing. Ahead of us, nestled in the landscape like a precious gem, was a magnificent honey-coloured house with a grand facade filled with huge windows over three floors and topped with balustrades. I thought I'd never seen anything so beautiful.

Mr Lawrence must have heard my sharp intake of breath, for he glanced briefly over his shoulder. He was smiling slightly.

'You approve of your new home then?' he asked.

'How could I not?' I responded, still awed by the sight. Bridges sat silent at his master's side. It occurred to me to wonder what his fate was to be, if Lawrence considered him too old to work much longer. Was he perhaps to be banished from this place that he had learned to love? If so, I had my first inkling of why he might feel resentment towards me.

'What about you, Pitch?' Mr Lawrence asked the stallion. The stallion's ears flickered as though he knew he was being addressed. 'This is where you'll be living from now on,' Lawrence continued. 'So I hope you'll settle in too and unlearn your less appealing tricks. I'm relying on you two, Bridges and Charlie, to teach him better.'

I smiled at the prospect of working with the magnificent stallion, but Bridges responded with a stiff half bow and a reproachful look at his master.

Mr Lawrence chuckled, not noticing his servant's resentment. 'He's too tired to make much trouble now,' he remarked. He steadied the horses, slowing their pace as we followed the sweep of the wide carriageway down the contours of the hill towards the house. The whole valley sloped towards the house which dominated the view. The sun was setting to the left behind the vast building and, as we dropped down closer to it, I could see it was all very new. The honey stone was newly cut and bright, the edges sharp and free from creepers or weathering. The house looked almost as new as the half-built houses at the Bath had looked. 'It's all been newly built in the latest style,' Lawrence explained. 'And the park fashionably landscaped. His Lordship felt in need of a large project.'

To our right, a stream flowed down towards the house, cascading from one pool to the next. The grounds had been arranged formally but with great elegance. Before the house lay a neatly-scythed lawn. A gardener worked to one side of it, tending rose bushes in the evening sunshine. I couldn't even begin to imagine the number of staff they must need to run a house and park on this scale.

The carriageway reached level ground in front of the house, swept to the left through wrought iron gates and then to the right again along the front of the stable block. Mr Lawrence slowed the horses again for a sharp left-hand turn through an archway to a courtyard. The surface here was cobbled and the horses' hooves clattered on the stones.

Before us was a large block of stalls ending in another

archway that led through into more gardens. I caught a glimpse of another lawn and shrubbery beyond the arch in the setting sun. To my left and behind me were loose boxes. Several horses looked curiously over their half-doors at us.

The yard was swept and clean, free of the clutter and dirt that clogged most inn yards. Two smart-looking grooms emerged from a doorway and came towards the carriage. I noted they looked well-dressed, well-fed, and alert, and my hopes for life at this place rose still higher.

I jumped down from my perch the moment the carriage drew to a stop, but the grooms in the yard were quicker. Pitch threw up his head in indignation as they approached him and, despite his tiredness, backed up, ears flat, preparing to fight.

'Wait!' Mr Lawrence called, tightening his hands on the reins. 'This new horse is unpredictable. Let Charlie see to him.'

The grooms fell back as I stepped forward, letting the stallion see me before I approached him. His head dropped when he realized it was me. The time I'd spent with him over the past couple of days was beginning to pay off.

'Take care of Charlie, won't you Bridges?' Lawrence said as he got down from the carriage. 'Show him the ropes!' He turned to me. 'You're in good hands, Charlie. See you soon!'

He left us to unharness his horses and strode off through the archway to the adjoining main house. I felt friendless and forlorn to see him go, but threw myself into the work of rubbing down the weary horses while the other grooms prepared the stable for the new acquisitions. When Pitch was ready, Bridges led him into a loose box and then returned for Velvet. I stood back, pleased with my work as Bridges untethered him. The horse was shining and magnificent; worthy of these fine stables.

I gathered up the brushes as Bridges led the horse away, then waited for him to return, but he did not. I couldn't see anyone at all now.

'Bridges?' I said tentatively, walking to the stables. I went right up to the loose-box door. Velvet stood with his rump towards me, munching hay contentedly. He was alone. I looked over the neighbouring loose-box door and Pitch flattened his ears, stirring restlessly in the strange surroundings. Bridges wasn't with him either. He'd left me alone.

CHAPTER TWELVE

I stood feeling foolish. I had no idea where to go. Where was I to sleep? Was there food? I'd eaten nothing but an apple since breakfast. Who would show me around and tell me my duties? The grooms who had appeared when we arrived had pulled the chaise into the coach house and vanished. My satchel lay just inside the door of the main stable block, but there was no other sign that I belonged here. I swallowed hard and picked it up. I walked over to what I guessed was the tack room, looking for someone to ask. The sound of cheerful whistling from within heartened me. Peeping around the door, I saw a red-haired lad with a freckled face and blue eyes polishing the harness from the carriage. He looked up as my shadow fell over him and grinned at me, revealing a broken front tooth and a dimple in each grubby cheek.

'Lookin' for work to do?' he asked with a cheeky smile.

I stepped into the room and picked up a rag. 'By all means,' I said. I was dead tired, but some friendly company was most welcome.

'I were only joking,' replied the boy looking a little startled as I sat down beside him. 'This is my work.'

'It's no problem. What's your name? I'm Charlie.'

'Heard that. You're to be trained as Mr Lawrence's new personal groom, huh? Plenty of us would have fancied *that* position.'

My hands, which had already picked up a bit to clean, fell limply into my lap. 'Will everyone resent me then?' I asked timidly. 'Bridges already does.'

'Ha! Won't accept he's past it. He'll get over it. He's not a bad sort, really. The lad grinned again. 'I'm Ben.'

'Hello Ben, pleased to meet you,' I said with a smile.

We worked side by side for a few moments in silence. Eventually I got up the courage to ask: 'So where do we get meals here?'

'The kitchen maids bring over pots and pans for us to the room next to this. We dish up there.'

'Not welcome in the house then?' I said, remembering life at the inn.

'Whiff of the stables an' all that,' said Ben with a comical grimace. 'They thinks theirselves a cut above us lot, the house servants. More *refined*,' he added in a mock genteel voice, holding up his nose.

I chuckled and felt the tension in me lessen. I rubbed at the leather harness for a few more minutes and then yawned.

'Dinner's served when the stable clock strikes six,' Ben told me. 'Then we got to feed and water all the horses and check 'em afore we get to turn in. And I got to finish this harness first an' all.'

By the time the clock struck, we'd cleaned the entire harness. I was so tired I stumbled wordlessly after Ben, and barely knew how to eat my stew and dumplings. The small, crowded room where the men and boys who worked in the stables enjoyed their dinner was noisy with chatter and laughter. Everyone was friendly and introduced themselves to me, though their names and faces blurred before my weary eyes. There was a Joe and a Peter around my own age as well as Ben, all loud and cheerful, and several men besides. The contrast with the John of Gaunt couldn't have been greater. Despite my weariness, I felt at home here at once.

I got through my evening duties somehow, but the moment I'd taken a blanket off the pile in the stables that evening and laid down in the straw, I was deeply asleep.

Ben shook me awake the next morning. It took me a moment to remember where I was. The stable yard was already bustling. I could see from the stable clock high on the tower that it was just after six. Two horses had already been led out of their stalls and were standing in the yard being groomed. Stable boys were mucking out the stalls or boxes, carting the soiled straw to a towering midden in the corner of the yard. I looked at Ben enquiringly. 'What am I to do?'

'Bridges has put you on mucking-out duty,' said Ben. 'Why don't you take Belle's box? Bring her out and tie her out here for grooming first.' He pointed the way.

I headed across the yard to the loose box he indicated. I wondered what kind of horse answered to the name of Belle. It sounded like a lady's horse. A showy, spoiled pet, perhaps. I imagined her grey, with some Arab blood. None of my idle imaginings prepared me for the sight that met my eyes when I peeped over the stable door.

In the gloom of the loose box stood the most beautiful

horse I'd ever laid eyes on. She was a dark, glossy bay, with a gleaming black mane and a shining tail that almost swept the ground. Her hide was a rich, burnished red-brown, darkening to black on her legs. Everything about her was elegant and beautiful. She was sheer perfection from the tip of her pricked ears to her neat hooves.

I caught my breath. For a mad instant, I'd thought it was my own Mahogany, whom I'd had to leave behind in America. The parting had almost broken my heart. But, I had to confess, this horse was far finer. My father could never have afforded such a magnificent creature. This horse had thoroughbred blood, I was sure. Arab too, by the look of that beautiful arched neck.

I stood staring, lost in admiration. The mare looked back at me from dark, liquid eyes. She arched her neck and blew out through her nostrils. Spellbound, I un-latched the half-door of the stable and stepped into the loosebox. I approached the mare cautiously, rev-erently, but she was perfectly relaxed and friendly, stepping forward and nosing me in search of some treat. Sorry I had nothing for her, I stroked the horse's glossy neck. She was in tip-top condition; gleaming with health and vitality.

'So you are Belle,' I said softly to her. She pricked her ears forward, looking at me endearingly from intelligent, kind eyes.

Belle was already wearing a halter. A leading rope hung on the wall near the door. I unhooked it, clipped it on to her halter and led her out into the yard. She stepped out beside me, so light on her hooves it seemed as though she were dancing.

I tethered her in the yard and continued to pet her, quite forgetting I had work to do, until Ben called me away, a spade in each hand.

'What a beauty!' I exclaimed.

He grinned. 'A costly piece of horseflesh,' he agreed. 'You wouldn't believe the long price his lordship paid for her.'

'Does he hunt her?' I asked. Her delicate good looks and her name still made me think her a lady's ride.

'Lord love you, no,' said Ben, shaking his head and accompanying me into Belle's loosebox, where he threw me one of the spades he carried. 'Clean straw this side, soiled the other,' he said. 'I'm to show you how we muck out here.'

I nodded, my mind still on Belle, as I raked out the soiled straw and piled it on one side. I looked questioningly at him.

'Belle belongs to Miss Judith,' he said. 'Or she will do when . . . '

'Less chit chat in here and more work,' interrupted a stern voice from the open doorway. A shadow fell across me and I jumped and flinched, afraid of a blow. When I dared looked up, I saw a smart-looking groom with neat whiskers looking down at me. He was tall and spare with something of a military air about him, which made me warm to him at once.

'You're the new boy,' he stated, looking distinctly unimpressed.

'I know,' I replied cheekily.

Instead of lashing out, he grinned at me. 'I'm Steele. I'm the head groom here. Lawrence might have employed you, but you will need to prove yourself to me. You look a skinny little excuse for a stable lad. Get this box done! No slacking! There are three more to do before you get your breakfast.'

Chapter Thirteen

The footman made sure I removed my muddy boots at the door before he turned and led the way into the house. As we left the servants' quarters and entered the main rooms, I caught my breath in wonder. I'd rarely seen such affluence. Furnishings, hangings, chandeliers, and carpets; all were new and looked costly. I stepped nervously, hoping no straw or manure was clinging to my clothing to soil such splendour.

I'd been at Deerhurst Park a week, but this was the first time I'd been into the house itself. I'd spent my days and my nights in the stables; most of my waking hours had been devoted to mucking out and cleaning tack.

The footman paused outside a heavy oak door and cast a disparaging eye over me. I probably had dirt on my face and looked disreputable. I'd been given no notice of this summons, but had been fetched directly from mucking out stalls. I removed my cap, smoothed my shorn hair nervously, then quickly replaced it, worried that it was a girlish habit and would give me away.

The footman was still looking down his nose at me. From his expression, I guessed I smelled bad. With a disapproving 'Ahem', he knocked and opened the door.

'The new lad from the stables, Mr Lawrence,' he announced in a voice of doom.

I stepped nervously into the room, but there was nothing within to terrify me. The room was an office. There was a small fire in the grate, casting a cheerful glow over the panelled room. A few bookcases stacked high with ledgers and papers drew my eye, as did a huge mahogany desk covered in more paperwork. My grubby, stockinged feet sank into a thick carpet that hushed the sounds of the fire and the door closing behind me.

Lawrence was writing at a desk, but looked up as I came to stand before him. His expression was friendly, so I had a glimmer of hope that I hadn't been brought here to answer for any misdeeds.

'Charlie,' he greeted me, laying down his pen. 'Are you settling in well?'

I grinned nervously in relief and, belatedly remembering my manners, whipped my cap off my head. 'Thank you, sir. Yes, I am.'

'Good. It's a fine place. I hope you'll be happy here. Any problems, you can always speak to Bridges or Steele. I've just spoken to Bridges and he tells me you're shaping up well.'

I cast Lawrence a look of disbelief. 'I don't get the impression Bridges trusts me with the horses, sir,' I said respectfully. 'He sets me to clean tack and muck out mostly.'

Lawrence frowned. 'Of course you'll have those duties too, but the priority is the new pair. I've ordered you a set of livery too. Those clothes will do about the stables, but if you're to accompany me out or if visitors are to come, I'll need you looking smarter.'

I nodded, aware that the process of being measured and fitted for livery might present a new danger to me.

'In fact a good wash wouldn't go amiss,' Lawrence added dryly.

I hung my head. I'd been too exhausted after the long days of work followed by time spent with Pitch and Belle to either get up early or stay up late to wash in private.

'We have high standards here,' he added. 'And that includes personal cleanliness. I'm sure there is a bath night for the stable hands.'

I gulped and nodded. He himself was impeccably clean, his clothes neat and pressed, not a hair out of place in his neat wig. He was clean-shaven too, not a mark or a smudge of dirt anywhere about his person, save a little ink on one finger. I felt suddenly disgusting.

'At least I see you have no fresh bruises. No visible ones in any case. I hope that means you've so far refrained from brawling with the staff here?'

I wasn't completely sure whether he was telling me off or teasing me. His voice was stern, but he didn't look cross, so I risked a grin. I had a reputation to maintain. 'So far, sir,' I said.

'I'm pleased to hear it,' he replied sternly, but slight creases around his eyes told me he was amused. 'Please continue to restrain yourself! I've told Bridges that you're in charge of gentling that stallion. Spend as much time as you can with him. I've also told Bridges he is to teach you to drive a horse in harness. And I'll see . . . .'

We were interrupted by a knock at the door. The footman opened it and an elderly man looked in. He was bent with age, leaning on an ebony cane, but I could see he had once been a tall, strong man. His shoulders were still broad, though stooped. He was dressed in black satin breeches, a fine embroidered waistcoat, and a green velvet coat that looked like it cost a year's wages at least, plus a quantity of costly lace. His eyes, in his lined face, still burned bright and fierce and he wore a very grand, long powdered wig.

The man looked past me at Mr Lawrence. 'I say, John, have you heard that that damned fool . . . Good God!'

The elderly man wrinkled his face in disgust and producing a large lace-edged pocket-handkerchief, held it to his nose. He regarded me over it with considerable displeasure. I could smell the lavender scent it was drenched in from where I stood.

'What the devil is this?' the elderly man demanded.

'Our newest acquisition, my lord,' replied Lawrence. 'This is young Charlie. I'm planning to make him my personal groom once Bridges has trained him up. He has quite a gift with horses.'

'He looks far too young to me! And what the devil is he doing in my house? Can't you speak to him in the stables if you need to give him instructions? He reeks and I daresay he's dirtied the carpet besides.'

'I removed my muddy boots,' I offered, then blushed, realizing I shouldn't have spoken uninvited. 'Sir!' I added belatedly. It was clear to me that this was the master of the house; the owner of all this grandeur.

'You are to address Lord Rutherford as "my lord",' Lawrence informed me. 'He is the gentleman who will be paying your wages.'

There was a slight laugh in Lawrence's voice, but I

didn't dare respond to it. Instead I bowed and said earnestly, 'I'm sorry, my lord.'

'There you are you see,' said Lawrence. 'He's perfectly civilized. And he took his boots off,' He looked amused again, his eyes on me rather than his employer. 'You may go now, Charlie. I daresay I'll see you in a day or so. Remember to spend time with that stallion!'

He nodded to dismiss me, and I slipped thankfully out of the room. The cooler air in the corridor was soothing to my hot cheeks. The old man stuck his head out of the door. 'Make sure you escort him right out of the house,' he said to the waiting footman. 'Keep an eye on him!'

The suggestion that I would steal valuables from the house was deeply offensive to me. But I bit my lip and kept quiet, following the haughty footman down the carpeted corridor and back to the kitchen.

A buxom cook asked me my name on the way out. 'I'm Charlie,' I told her.

'New are you? Here you are then, Charlie,' she said in a motherly way, and pressed a hot bun into my hand. 'I know boys your age are always hungry and you're far too thin!' I smiled and thanked her. There were distinct advantages to being a boy.

I was eating the bun and, mindful of my instructions, heading for Pitch's box to spend some time with him when Bridges spotted me. 'Boy!' he called. 'There's a harness needs cleaning in the tack room. Off you go!'

I hesitated a moment, wondering whether I should remind him of both my name and the duties Lawrence had just given me. The look on his face was forbidding, however, so I turned and made meekly for the tack room instead.

Ben was already in there, soaping the harness that had been used when the gig had been sent into the Bath for supplies. Items such as candles, sugar, oil, and wine had to be bought, but I'd learned that a great deal of the food eaten in the house was grown here on the estate. There was a thriving home farm just across the valley. *The farm my mother wrote her letter from*, I thought.

I picked up the heavy collar and began to soap it beside Ben.

'You didn't get notice then?' said Ben, an impish grin on his face.

'Not this time,' I told him.

'So what did he want to see you for? They don't usually send for us lads. The grooms give us our orders.'

'He just wanted to ask if I was settling in and give me instructions,' I told him, a frown on my face.

'Cleaning tack?' said Ben, perplexed. 'He called you in to the house to tell you to clean tack and muck out?'

'No.' It occurred to me Ben might be able to advise me. 'I'm supposed to be gentling the new stallion,' I said. 'And learning to drive. But Bridges puts me to mucking out and tack cleaning.'

Ben grimaced. 'You're junior, you got to do what he tells you.'

I sighed. 'I think so too. But what happens when Pitch is as wild as be-damned next time Mr Lawrence takes him out?'

Ben grinned ruefully. 'You get blamed,' he admitted.

'Tell me, Ben,' I asked, 'when are bath nights?'

'Saturdays,' said Ben, his face lighting up. 'They draws us warm water and pours it in a tub in the room where we has our meals. The older men gets first wash, but then the three of us boys gets the water. Four now you're here. We have a laugh splashing and making a mess. It's grand.'

He grinned. I tried to smile back, but I wouldn't be able to take part in bath night any more than I could pee in the midden next to them.

We were interrupted by voices in the yard. Ben peeped out, his hands covered in saddle soap. 'It's His Lordship and Mr Lawrence,' he said. 'Calling for riding horses. Now why can't they send an order from the house *before* they come to the stables? 'Cos they don't like waiting.'

Steele called for Ben and two other grooms. Bridges was also out there. It seemed I wasn't wanted, so I kept cleaning. I had finished the collar and began cleaning the bit. I became aware that a shadow had fallen over me. I jumped and looked up.

'As my personal groom-in-training, I would have expected *you* to be saddling up my horse,' he remarked. 'Under Bridges' supervision, of course. There must be other boys who can clean tack.'

I met his eyes squarely and took a breath. 'I think the feeling here is, I should be starting from the bottom and learning the job that way.'

Lawrence looked back at me. 'I see,' he said curtly and left again.

Did he really expect me to insist on precedence in a stable hierarchy where I was both new and extremely junior?

The water in the bucket was ice cold and I had to brace myself as I dipped the rag into it and wrung it out. Shunning bath day was necessary to keep my secret, and this was the only alternative. First I dipped my head into the water, gasping, and rubbed at my short hair, soaping it, rinsing, and shuddering with cold. At least this might ease the itching I'd had over the past weeks. Next I scrubbed my face with the cold water. Then, checking I was still alone in the hayloft, I stripped to the waist and soaped and scrubbed myself, shivering violently. It was late and the night was cold.

My top half clean, I dried myself on some rags and pulled on a fresh shirt. We could have our clothes laundered here; a great luxury. My spare shirt had been washed and had come back smelling of soap and rosemary. Next I repeated the washing process for my bottom half. The dirt on my feet was so ingrained that a bit of cold water made little impression. They needed a soak in warm soapy water. I sighed. And shivered again as I rubbed myself vigorously dry and pulled my filthy breeches back on. I had no spare pair.

My teeth chattering, I crept back down into the stables, emptied the bucket onto the cobbles and entered Belle's loose box. I crawled under the blanket in the corner, shivering.

Belle moved restlessly in her box, looking out over her half-door and then turning back to me. Putting her head down, she snuffed at me. I stretched a hand out and stroked her beautiful face. She lipped at my fingers, hoping for a treat. I felt safest here in her box at night, away from the other boys. It also had the advantage of being open to the yard and the fresh air, while the stalls were enclosed within the stable block and by morning the smell of horse piss was enough to make your eyes water.

Lying under the blanket, my skin tingling from the soap, cold water, and the rough rag, I hoped I was cleaner now. In my mind, I could still see the look of disgust on the old gentleman's face when he smelled me. Lawrence had been more polite, but he must have felt the same way.

I was growing warmer now. Belle's steady presence beside me in the darkness was soothing. Tomorrow, I needed to get up early and spend some time with Pitch. My last thought as I fell asleep was the look of disappointment on Lawrence's face as he left me in the tack room. I wanted so much to please him. I wasn't doing as well as I'd hoped.

CHAPTER FOURTEEN

I touched the fine clothes reverently and looked up at the sewing woman. 'These are really for me?' I breathed.

'Not for mucking out the stables in!' she said. 'They're only to be worn when you accompany any of the family out in the carriage. They'll stay hanging up unless you need them. Mr Lawrence asked that you have another set of clothes made too, for everyday. His lordship likes everyone to be clean and smart. They'll be yours to own and the expense will be taken out of your wages. The livery is not yours. It remains the property of the master; no wages you could earn would pay for it.'

'I should say not,' I said, touching the fine wool. Even as an officer's daughter, I'd rarely, if ever, worn anything so fine. My father had always lived on an officer's pay; it had provided the necessaries of life, but no luxuries.

'Well, go on, try it on then!'

I glanced around me uncomfortably. I'd been measured without being found out as a girl. But stripping off was another matter.

'Lord love you, boy, I'm old enough to be your mother,' the portly woman sighed. 'And you ain't got nothing I ain't seen on a boy before.' Nonetheless, she heaved herself to her feet pulled a folding screen out and set it up in a corner of the room. I slid behind it, clutching the clothes and slipped off my own grubby garments. I was glad I'd washed again last night. It wouldn't do to put such fine clothes onto a filthy body.

The dark-blue woollen breeches fitted perfectly. The linen shirt felt cool and soft against my bare skin. It was made very large, presumably to allow growing room, and hung almost to my knees. I sighed with pleasure as I fastened it and tucked it in. The coat was of blue wool to match the breeches. The cuffs and collar were large and of a pale blue, while the coat was edged and embroidered with silver thread, and silver buttons fastened it. Finally there were fine stockings, garters, and a pair of neat leather shoes fastened with little black buttons.

I emerged from behind the screen to be pushed in front of a looking-glass. I could scarcely believe the reflection in the spotted glass. The clothes looked so fine. I hoped Lawrence would think so too. However, my grubby face and tufty hair ruined the vision before me. I hadn't seen myself in months and was not impressed with the urchin look I'd acquired.

The seamstress clearly thought the same. 'You need a proper wash,' she remarked. 'We have a standard to keep up here. His lordship doesn't buy costly livery for your benefit, but to show the world what a wealthy and important man *he* is. A dirty face is not acceptable.'

'I understand,' I said, my voice low. I *had* washed, but cold water was not ideal for cleaning off the greasy dirt of horses and stables.

'Good. You're wearing your master's livery now. Everyone who sees you knows where you're from. Do you see this dark blue and the pale blue here? They are from his lordship's coat of arms.' She pointed at the arms, which were displayed above the fireplace in the room we were in. Dark blue background; that gives you a dark blue coat. The pale blue chevron gives you the cuffs and the silver is the silver of the stag. You've seen the arms before of course?'

I nodded. 'On the door of the chaise,' I replied, and she nodded, satisfied. 'So there you are then. You understand you're representing the family, and how important that is. Now, here are your new everyday breeches and shirt, and a new waistcoat besides. Put those on now and give me back the livery. I can see I need to adjust the coat in the waist. You're a skinny thing!'

I disappeared back behind the screen and changed obediently. The new clothes were a huge improvement on my brother's old garments, worn to death in the last months.

'Now, before you can try the wig, you need to get that hair shaved off,' said the woman as I emerged once more. 'You've lice in there, and we don't want those in the wig. Steele is the man to see; he will do it for you.'

'Shaved?' I gasped. 'Must I?' I touched my ragged hair, stared at the mirror and tried to imagine myself entirely without hair. It had been bad enough cutting it short.

'Mr Lawrence's orders. You'll be more comfortable that way, quite apart from ridding yourself of the lice,' she said, shepherding me out of the room. 'Off you go now. Come back tomorrow!'

I felt very subdued and forlorn after Steele had shaved

my head. I was now less a girl than ever. Somehow, all my femininity had been stripped from me with the last of my hair. The joy of my new clothes had drained away, leaving me feeling low.

'Hey, that's a haircut!' exclaimed Ben with a grin, as I walked into the yard. I gave him a wavering smile.

'What's the problem?' he asked surprised. 'It'll grow back soon enough.'

I tentatively touched my naked head. 'Oh, I know.' I replied, trying for nonchalance.

Belle put her head over her loose-box door and whickered softly at me. I walked over to her, and felt comforted as she nuzzled my new waistcoat and nudged me. She was most firmly my friend now, though I wasn't officially in charge of her. I longed to ride her, but one of the older grooms had the task of exercising her each morning. I always watched him ride her out of the yard with a jealous eye. I pulled her dark ears gently, talking to her, and rubbed her neck. Her head dropped lower in pleasure, her eyes half-closed.

From this pleasant occupation I was startled by Bridges' voice behind me. 'You're not paid to pet the horses, boy. There is plenty of work to be done.'

'Yes, of course,' I said obediently. Then, aware of my shaven head and the reason for it, I asked, 'Mr Lawrence said you would be taking me out to learn to drive. When will that be?'

'It will be when I've time and when I'm satisfied that you're working hard enough,' he replied sharply. 'Not a moment before. Right now, I need you to polish all the bits and metal on all the harnesses in the tack room.'

I stared at him in astonishment. 'But Ben and I already . . .'

'It needs doing again! His lordship is driving into the Bath tomorrow to fetch his granddaughter from a visit. The harness must look its very best.'

'Very well,' I said reluctantly. Lawrence had hired me for my skill with horses. The work I was doing, mucking out and tack cleaning, could be done by any labourer. I was wasted here.

I stomped off into the tack room, sorted out rags and cleaner and sat down to begin polishing the already-sparkling bits. I muttered to myself as I worked.

When Ben walked in some time later, I had only a scowl for him. 'You done summat wrong?' he asked concerned.

'No, why?' I snapped, hurling a dirty rag onto the floor and picking up a clean one.

''Cos that's the only reason we ever has to polish clean metal all over again,' said Ben.

'I was stroking Belle.' I scrubbed hard at a bit as I spoke.

Ben picked up a bridle and headed for the door. 'It'll sort itself out,' he said. 'Now careful not to rub a hole in that bit!' He ducked out of the door before I could throw something at him.

The light was fading when I finished the last piece. I stood up and stretched my stiff, chilled body. As I bent down to begin tidying up and putting everything back, the door opened and Ben looked in. 'Dinner time!' he announced.

A week later, Steele told me cheerfully that I was to groom both Pitch and Velvet ready for their outing into

Bath. Bridges stood just behind him with a look of deep disapproval on his face.

'And you'll be accompanying them to take charge of the horses while they're there,' Steele added. 'Mr Lawrence's orders. So you'll need your livery.'

'You make sure you behave impeccably,' Bridges growled at me as Steele went off to supervise the chaise being brought out of the coach house. 'Remember you have Rutherford's reputation to guard!'

'Yes sir,' I replied respectfully, before rushing off to fetch brushes.

I groomed the two beautiful horses until they gleamed in the spring sunshine. I was proud that Pitch only tried to bite me once, and it was a half-hearted attempt. When their hooves had been oiled and their manes and tails combed, I left Ben and Joe to harness them and ran to scramble into my livery so that I would be ready before Lawrence and his lordship reached the yard. Mrs Simpkins, the seamstress, had adjusted my coat and gave me a nod of approval once I was dressed. I'd taken extra pains with washing myself last night. The new wig fitted me well, though it felt strange. I would need to get used to it.

I hurried back to the yard where Bridges was inspecting my work critically and running a brush over some imaginary dust on Velvet's hide. There was barely time for a bite of breakfast and a gulp of ale before Ben whispered a warning that I needed to be out in the yard. I emerged, twitching my coat straight, to stand ready as Lawrence and his lordship arrived. His lordship was dressed in a puce coat over a salmon waistcoat, silk clocked stockings, quantities of lace at his throat and wrists, and a powdered full-bottom wig. It was very fine, but I didn't admire his choice of colours.

To my mind, Lawrence was the smarter of the two though he was dressed far more modestly. His coat was brown with a beige waistcoat and breeches to match. He had only a very modest cravat, no embroidery and no jewellery. His wig was a neat tie-wig. Altogether his apparel was unostentatious and proclaimed the gentleman of business rather than leisure. He wore his well-fitting clothes with a quiet dignity and I found I admired him very much. Lawrence gave me a brief nod and a smile as he approached the carriage, signalling his approval of my new attire. His lordship didn't spare me a glance at all. I might as well have been a mounting block or a broom.

'Are we ready to go?' he asked Lawrence, glancing up at the stable clock. 'Let's waste no time.'

Bridges came forward and assisted him into the chaise. The light chaise with the hood let down had been ordered today, as the weather was so fine. I stood at the horses' heads, holding them steady, speaking soothingly to Pitch. I sincerely hoped he would not disgrace us with any bad behaviour today. Lawrence had driven the pair often since our return, but they were fresh today. He climbed into the driving seat, gathered the reins, and made contact with the horses' mouths. Pitch's ears went back flat and he flung his head up, fighting the bit. I talked to him softly, one hand on his nose, until his head dropped once more and his ears came forward.

When he was calm, I looked up and found Lawrence's eyes were on me. 'Ready to go?' he asked. 'He won't stand still.'

'I know,' I said. With a last word to Pitch, I released him, stepped smartly out of his way and ran for my perch at the back of the chaise. The horses plunged and started off with a rush, jerking the carriage forward. I managed to catch hold of the rail and swing myself up, clinging on for dear life as the carriage swept under the archway and out of the yard. By the time the horses slowed for the sharp corner through the gate and headed up the steep carriageway through the park, I was safely on my perch behind his lordship as he surveyed his new half-wild team with remarkable calm.

'Jolly good choice of horseflesh, John!' he said as the horses pulled well together up the long hillside. 'Nice steppers. Good, strong beasts! Fine-looking nags too. What I wouldn't give to train them myself! It's a deuced bore getting old. But thank God I've still got you to pick out my horses. I couldn't abide travelling behind the kind of dull, safe slugs my groom would pick out for me.'

'These two certainly aren't slugs, my lord,' Lawrence replied. 'I told you how Pitch kicked the dashboard of the chaise to pieces at Hungerford. There's a way to go before they're entirely safe.'

'Safety be damned! What's life without the spice of danger?' The old man chuckled and wheezed.

The two men fell to discussing business as we passed through the lodge gates and reached the downs, heading for Bath. I could follow little of it, though I understood what I'd already been told. Lawrence managed his lordship's considerable estate and fortune for him, taking on all the day-to-day work and going out and about on errands. It was also clear that the old aristocrat still took a keen interest in all the details. I listened to Lawrence's respectful tone as he responded to searching questions and strongly-worded advice. He was both tactful and patient.

My attention wandered from the irrelevant discussion in front of me to the beautiful views. The huge trees that graced the skyline in clumps were bursting into brilliant leaf. The new green of the hedgerows was almost luminous in the bright sunlight. The air was both fresh and mild, smelling of damp earth, growing things, and the promise of summer. I stood tall, feeling proud of my smart livery and the fine carriage. I was glad to be alive and to have fallen into such good circumstances. The days of destitution, the loss of my father, and the fear for my own life seemed to have receded into the distance. Though still deeply uncomfortable to think about, the memories no longer seemed so frighteningly all-pervasive and threatening from the safe haven of Deerhurst Park.

Lawrence was quiet as he negotiated the steep hill down from Lansdown into the city. Even the old lord fell silent, merely barking a word or two of advice here and there. It was a difficult hill to tackle with such a highly strung, half-wild pair and I had plenty of chance to appreciate Lawrence's skill with the reins. I wondered how I would fare when it was my turn to learn. I could only hope I would start with more sedate horses.

The old gentleman interrupted my daydreams by breaking into speech suddenly as the hill levelled out and we approached the town. 'This will be a deuced uncomfortable meeting, John.'

'I'm sure you will overawe them with your high-handed manner, my lord.'

'Ha! You think so, do you? Well, there are few brave enough to shout me down, it's true, but all the same. Have I spoiled her, John? Is that it? I've been asking myself.'

The fierce old man in front of me seemed suddenly frail. I looked at the back of his head, at the powdered wig topping the lined face that was upturned almost pleadingly to the younger man's.

Lawrence cast a swift glance towards him, cleared his throat and nodded slightly towards me.

'Oh, ay, but 'tis only a boy, John. You're deaf, aren't you, boy?' the old man said, struggling to turn and glance at me.

'Yes, my lord,' I replied, attempting to cultivate the wooden look that the other servants seemed to excel at.

'Nonetheless, I think this discussion will keep until the port is on the table tonight. With respect, sir.' Lawrence's voice was firm.

'Damned correct, aren't you?' demanded his lordship. 'In my day, servants were so much furniture. Take my word for it, they know everything there is to know about us, whether we speak in front of them or not. Isn't that so boy?' he rapped out, turning to me again.

I was flustered by the sudden attack and blushed fiery red. 'No, my lord!' I blurted out, before I'd thought through the consequences of disagreeing with him.

Lawrence stepped in to protect me. 'The boy is new, sir. Don't terrify him! Besides, we're in the city now, and I must concentrate if I'm to reach the house without mishap.'

He negotiated the narrow, cluttered streets, handling the difficult team with skill, checking Pitch from shying away from a sedan chair with scarcely a pause and frustrating his attempt to bolt over the bridge as we left the city by the South Gate. I looked around me at the other horses on the roads and thought there wasn't another pair half as fine as ours. Pitch and Velvet were magnificent and drew admiring eyes as we drove. I stood tall, aware that they would be looking at me too and not wanting them to find fault.

CHAPTER FIFTEEN

We drew up outside a beautiful old manor house tucked away in a wood on the far side of the city, across the river. It was a quiet, verdant oasis, just a few minutes' drive from the bustling city. When we pulled up outside, a butler threw open the front door, a footman emerged to let down the steps and to assist his lordship to descend, and a groom appeared to take charge of the carriage.

'I'll drive the carriage round to the stables myself and walk up from there,' Lawrence told the groom. 'This is a difficult team.'

He waited until his lordship had descended and then moved off at a smart walk, wheels crunching on the gravel, towards the stables. As soon as Lawrence reined in the horses in the yard, I jumped down and hurried to the horses' heads. He smiled ruefully down at me as he hitched the reins. 'We are likely to be an hour or so, so stall the horses and go and take some refreshment. But bear in mind his lordship won't want to be kept waiting when he's ready to leave.'

'Very well, sir.'

Mr Lawrence jumped down from the carriage, and then came towards me unexpectedly. I looked up at him nervously, wondering if I'd done something wrong. He leaned towards me and added, 'Don't let Pitch disgrace us. And don't you get into any fights, either! The reputation of our house is tarnished enough here as it is!'

'I wouldn't . . . !' I began indignantly, then I realized he might be laughing at me, and bit my lip. 'I'll be a model of discretion,' I promised soberly.

He strode off towards the house, leaving me in the unfamiliar position of directing stable staff I didn't know on how to handle the horses in my charge. I suddenly missed Bridges, but managed to keep Pitch reasonably calm whilst the strange men unhitched him from the carriage. 'You need to keep your distance from this one,' I warned them all. 'He's still wild and not used to strangers.'

I led him off to a stall where I could tether him safely before unharnessing him. On the way, one clumsy young groom barged carelessly past Pitch. Tearing the leading rein momentarily out of my hand, Pitch nipped the groom swiftly on the shoulder.

'No, Pitch!' I said fiercely, regaining my hold on him. I turned to the groom. 'Are you much hurt?' I asked, concerned.

'Damned animal's a menace!' complained the groom, his hand clutching his injury.

'I'm sorry. He's bitten me too,' I said as I led him away. 'Several times.'

I ensured both horses had hay and water before rubbing them down thoroughly. Only when I was completely satisfied that they were comfortable and looking as magnificent and cared-for as ever, did I leave them, in pursuit of my own refreshment. As I walked across the yard, I could see the chaise had been turned about and was ready for the horses to be harnessed again.

There was just time to drink some ale before the chaise was called. 'Carriage for Lord Rutherford!' a footman announced, emerging briefly in the room where I was sitting and then retreating hurriedly again.

'Hurry!' shouted the groom in charge. 'Lawrence won't trust us to bring the horses round; he'll be here in person any minute!' I got to my feet and rushed back out to the horses and began lifting on their collars and buckling on the harness again. A groom harnessed Velvet to the carriage while I struggled with Pitch, who had decided he didn't want to go back into harness so soon and wilfully made my task much harder by throwing up his head, kicking out at me, and trying to bite me.

Two indoor servants emerged into the stable yard, struggling with a huge trunk between them. Lawrence appeared and watched as the trunk was strapped to the back of the chaise and I put the final touches to the harness. I'd learned the task well now and could perform it swiftly. Those difficult weeks at the posting house were standing me in good stead.

We collected a scowling Lord Rutherford from the front of the house. I watched as a golden-haired beauty in a pale blue brocade gown with white lace petticoats came floating down the steps on the arm of a besotted youth. She kissed him on the cheek and bid him a careless farewell. 'Let me assist you into the carriage, Miss Lawrence,' the youth begged, taking her hand as she climbed up beside Lord Rutherford.

I realized at once who she must be. Ben had told me

about Miss Judith Lawrence, Lord Rutherford's grand-daughter, and so I looked at her curiously. She was a handsome girl; fair, with melting blue eyes and a vivid, determined face. Her figure was slender and graceful. A sneaking envy of her beautiful gown and her long, glowing hair caught me by surprise. I'd been so grateful for my present improved circumstances; I ought not to long for more. But it was hard not to compare my shaven head with her feminine good looks.

As I stood on my narrow perch behind her on the chaise all the way home up the steep, narrow roads that led to the downs, I watched the girl charm her grandfather out of his ill-humour. It had been obvious at the start of the journey that he was disappointed in her. She had misbehaved herself on this visit, I gathered. I'd overheard a few muttered comments about Miss Judith sneaking out of the house to meet a secret lover. But she was so sweet and affectionate towards her reproachful grandfather that he failed to remain angry for long. By the time we had passed through the Bath, his lordship had softened considerably and was smiling reluctantly at her playful talk. By the time we were up on the downs he was laughing.

'Oh, grandpapa!' she sighed as we drew near the turning to Deerhurst Park. 'Much as I long to see my dear home once more, I fear it will all seem a little . . . dull after the diversions and liveliness of the city! Am I very naughty and spoiled to say so?'

'Well, my dear. I'm sorry to hear it, certainly. But I have a little something for you, Judith, that I fancy will cheer you greatly.'

'Oh!' Miss Judith clapped her hands and bounced up and down on the seat, causing Pitch to startle and lay his ears flat. Lawrence regained control and then glanced across at her for the first time. Until now he had driven in silence, his eyes and attention on his horses and on the road. 'I must ask you, Judith, to bear in mind that this is a novice team.'

Miss Judith rolled her eyes at his profile and then simpered to her grandfather, tucking her arm in his. 'Grandpapa, I'll be good. Only tell me what you have for me?'

'Ah, my dearest, you'll have to wait! But I promise you, you won't be disappointed.'

The sugar-sweet play between the two, so indulgent on his part, so false on hers, disgusted me. I shouldn't judge her on so short an acquaintance, I knew. But I had another reason to resent her. Belle, the beautiful bay horse I adored, was to be hers. Jealousy wasn't an emotion I was prone to, but in this instance it had me in its toils.

CHAPTER SIXTEEN

Miss Judith squealed with excitement when Belle was led out to be shown to her, making the usually beautifully-mannered mare startle. Then the girl ran and flung her arms around the horse's neck, making Belle back up nervously.

I was leading Pitch into his loose box while this was going on but, with so much excitement nearby, I had to stop and talk him into behaving himself. Once he was bestowed, I rushed to scramble out of my costly livery and back into my ordinary breeches and shirt.

When I returned to rub Pitch down, I found Lawrence in the stable checking the stallion over. As I appeared, he straightened up, stroked the horse's neck, and ran a hand over his shoulder.

'Come on in, Charlie. You're doing a good job with him,' Lawrence said to me. 'He's calmer and more trusting by far. Are you spending a lot of time with him?'

'Whenever I can . . . '

I broke off and bent down to brush some mud off Pitch's back leg, hiding my confusion.

'I'm not stupid, Charlie,' said Lawrence goodnaturedly. 'I realize what's going on. But you are winning Bridges over, you know. He no longer speaks of you

117

with such disgust and once even praised you to me!'

I grinned and continued to work while my master made friends with the stallion. 'Pitch must have been badly broken and treated to have become so difficult,' I observed into the quiet. 'He's only a youngster.'

'That was my assessment,' agreed Lawrence. 'That's why I went ahead and bought him. I hoped he wasn't incurably vicious, but it was a gamble.'

'You love your horses,' I observed, seeing him petting the stallion.

He smiled. 'As do you,' he replied. 'There is an ancient bond between man and horse, forged through the centuries. I feel it and you do too. They are magnificent creatures, are they not?'

I paused to clap Pitch's flank affectionately. 'Certainly,' I agreed. 'Horses have always been my life.'

He nodded. 'Mine too.' He drew in his breath as though he were about to say something, but then let it go again and shook his head.

After a moment's silence, I ventured to prompt him: 'There was something you wanted to say? You had an instruction for me perhaps?'

'No, no, it's nothing.'

I brushed past him in the narrow space, very alive to his presence in the loose box, but trying to be distant and professional; to keep to my role. I moved around Pitch and began working on his other side. 'I hope if you are dissatisfied with me in any way, you won't hesitate to tell me, so I may improve,' I said diffidently as I worked.

'It's not that,' Lawrence reassured me. 'But I do have a . . . request. A slightly unusual one.'

I felt heat flood my face and neck and was glad it was gloomy in the stable. What could he mean? I reminded myself I was in disguise. And I was a mere servant; a lowly one at that. Whatever he wanted from me, it wasn't anything remotely personal. In his eyes, I was a grubby, badly-behaved boy who just happened to have a way with horses. These sobering thoughts helped me overcome my shyness and regain enough presence of mind to say: 'Try me, sir.'

I peeped at him over Pitch's back as I spoke. He was looking at the horse, rubbing his neck absently, a worried frown on his handsome face. I caught my breath and hurriedly resumed grooming.

Lawrence went to the half-door and looked out. Miss Judith was still feeding her new horse sugar lumps. 'You pwetty little thing!' she was cooing in a high-pitched baby voice. 'Bootiful Belle-belle!'

Hearing her, I felt a fierce stab of jealousy and resentment. Belle belonged to Miss Judith, not me, I told myself sternly. She was Miss Judith's horse and I was merely a servant.

Lawrence turned back and stepped closer to me. 'It's this,' he said quietly in my ear so that I could feel his breath on my face. 'Lord Rutherford cares for horses too. He keeps a good stable here; nothing but fine pedigree horseflesh. But he considers them possessions to be proud of, not creatures with feeling. And he has a blind spot.'

His granddaughter, I thought, just before Lawrence said it. I moved away a little and turned to face him, putting down my brush. 'In what way can I help?' I asked him puzzled.

'Just keep an eye on Belle, will you?' he asked softly, cautious of Miss Judith nearby. 'I won't say any more at this stage. Just watch out for her. Consider it as much a part of your duties as Pitch and Velvet. *They* are doing well now.'

I nodded earnestly. 'Of course. I will do so to the very best of my ability.'

'Thank you,' he replied, clasping my shoulder briefly. And then he was gone. By the time I'd recovered from the most inappropriate heart-fluttering caused by his brief touch, it was too late to ask him what exactly I needed to look out for.

I left Pitch and took my brushes along to Velvet's box to rub him down too. Ben had already started, but when he saw me he stood aside to let me take over.

'I got the harness to clean,' he explained. 'So you can finish up.'

I set to grooming once more, pondering Mr Lawrence. I remembered how his presence close to me in the stable had made my hands tremble and my face flush. 'Don't you dare fall for him,' I whispered fiercely to myself. 'You'll only make yourself unhappy. You're a boy now. Behave like one!'

I wasn't sure my heart was listening.

Miss Judith spent the rest of the afternoon running in and out of the stable yard feeding 'bootiful Belle-belle' treats, making a huge fuss of her and generally getting under our feet. I could see such treatment might rapidly spoil a horse, but there was nothing definite I could put a stop to.

Lawrence came and went, taking out Sorrel in the gig on some estate business. He told me he didn't need me to accompany him and took Bridges instead.

After dinner, I played cards with the other stable boys, until Steele complained about the noise we were making and packed us all off to sleep. Mindful of Lawrence's instructions, I went to Belle's box to sleep and found her restless and unfriendly. When I tried to stroke her, she threw her glossy head up impatiently and jerked away from me. I attributed it to Judith's excitement around her. I curled up in the corner, wrapped a blanket around myself and was soon heavily asleep.

I woke suddenly in the middle of the night in pitch darkness, my heart pounding. Something was wrong. I took a deep breath and rubbed my eyes. Why was I awake? I heard a groan and the sound of hooves scrabbling right next to me. Belle was unwell.

I was up in a moment, reaching out to her in the darkness. As my eyes adjusted, I saw she had half fallen against the wall of her box and was stretched out uncomfortably, one back leg trying to kick at her belly. I saw at once that she was suffering a bout of colic.

I felt a chill of horror pass through me. Colic is the main killer of horses. There is little that can be done to help a sick animal. I put my hand on her flank to see how bad she was. She struggled to her feet at my touch, legs flailing, and one hoof caught me on the shin. I cried out and staggered against the wall. As the pain blossomed, I cursed myself for not being more circumspect. The poor horse was in too much pain to know what she was doing.

Belle gave me a desperate whinny as she lay back down, her legs moving almost in spasm. I went to her head. She was sweating, her neck damp. Her eyes were dull and unfocused, her breathing ragged. I ran my hands over her neck. She didn't seem to have a fever which was a relief, but her pulse was fast. Experimentally, I reached across and ran my hand over her belly. It was taut and distended and her reaction was immediate, flinching and scrabbling to get away from my touch.

My own heart was beating quickly and my mouth was dry with fear. Such a beautiful horse; such a loving, trusting creature. Now her life might be thrown away. There was little doubt in my mind it was all those 'treats' Judith had brought her. She'd been thoughtless and selfish, thinking more of her own pleasure in feeding the horse than of what a surfeit of rich food might do to the gracious mare.

Belle wriggled further round with a squeal of pain and tried to roll. In a panic, I hauled on her halter. 'Belle, no!' I cried. 'Get up!'

Belle was beside herself with pain. She fought me, desperate to roll in an attempt to relieve the agonizing pain in her belly. She groaned again. I pulled and pulled. I tried to push her. I even walloped her rump in an attempt to get her on her feet. 'Get up!' I shouted, beside myself with fear. 'Get up, Belle, or you'll kill yourself!'

Belle snorted, struggled to get up, but failed, sweating with pain and effort. I couldn't do this alone. I had to get help.

Hurrying out of the stable, I started to run across the yard to the rooms where the senior grooms slept. On my way, I cannoned into a figure in the darkness. Whoever it was grabbed me. 'What's up, lad?' he asked. 'What are you doing running around the yard at night?'

I recognized the voice. I wouldn't have chosen Bridges to help me right now, but at least he was experienced. 'It's Belle!' I gasped. 'She's got colic and she's trying to roll! I can't get her on her feet!'

He uttered an oath under his breath, and hurried straight to Belle's stall. I scurried after him.

With much coaxing, pushing, pulling, and swearing, between us we managed to get the poor, sick horse up. It seemed to me she had deteriorated even in the short time since I'd left her.

'Open the door!' Bridges ordered me once she was standing. 'We'll try walking her.'

I flung the stable door wide, and between us we led the trembling, snorting mare into the yard. The other horses, aware something unusual was going on, looked out of their boxes at us. Pitch, awake now, disturbed from his slumbers by the commotion, whickered to the mare and then neighed loudly. A flicker of her ears was the only sign Belle gave that she'd even noticed. The pain in her gut consumed all her attention.

Bridges squinted at the stable clock in the moonlight. 'Half past one,' he said. 'We'll walk her for a quarter of an hour and see if it helps. Can you fetch a blanket from the tack room, so she doesn't get chilled? She's in a muck sweat.'

I dived into the tack room, pulled a horse-blanket off the rack, and emerged with it. It was a chilly night, although the days were mild now. Bridges paused so I could throw the blanket over Belle and then we walked on, steadily, slowly, one either side of her head, frustrating her attempts to lie down and roll.

After five minutes, Belle stalled and looked as though her legs were going to go from under her. I stood in front of her, stroking her, speaking to her calmly. Bridges let me be, not criticizing me or pushing me aside as he usually did. I don't know whether it worked, or whether the spasm passed by itself, but the horse grew calmer and started to walk again.

Belle's belly gurgled and growled as we walked and each time it did, she paused, shuddering and writhing in pain. After quarter of an hour, we led her back into her stable.

'Stay with her while I fetch a lantern and a towel to wipe her down,' said Bridges. 'Whatever you do, don't let her roll. We don't want her twisting a gut! But you know that,' he added more to himself than to me. He disappeared into the darkness. I stood quietly, stroking the frightened horse, speaking to her soothingly. I felt she was calmer, but I couldn't be sure.

It was several hours before we were certain Belle was on the mend. We both stayed with her until near dawn, speaking little to each other, but often to the horse. We found ourselves in tacit agreement on how to care for her, and we were proved right. By four o'clock, we were sure she was out of danger so Bridges went back to bed, leaving me in charge. We'd worked well together to tend a sick horse. I hoped it would lessen his resentment of me.

I wrapped my blanket around myself and lay down in the corner of the box. Belle was still restless at first, but after a while, exhausted by suffering so much pain, she lay down and slept. I lay close to her in the darkness, her warmth helping me relax. My relief left me feeling shaken and tearful. 'I love you so much, Belle,' I whispered to her in the darkness. I shuddered to think that if I hadn't slept beside her tonight, we might have lost her.

It was bright light when I awoke, the sun streaming in. The yard was bustling beyond the half-door of Belle's box. I'd slept right through the start of work. I checked Belle. She was still sleeping peacefully. Her temperature seemed normal and her hide was dry. I leaned back against her in relief, yawned, and stretched. A shadow fell on me and I jumped as both Bridges and Lawrence looked at me over the half-door of the box.

'Good morning, Charlie,' said Lawrence. 'I gather we have you to thank that this valuable creature is still alive.'

I sat up, embarrassed to think how dirty and dishevelled I must look after a night caring for Belle and sleeping in her straw with her. I was dog-tired and I hurt all over. 'Er . . . good morning, sir,' I stammered, scrambling to my feet and brushing straw from my clothes. 'Not just me, Mr Lawrence. Mr Bridges was doing a round of the yard anyway and would have found her.'

There was warmth in Lawrence's smile that set my heart racing. 'We're grateful to you both,' he said. He unlatched the half-door and stepped into the box to check Belle over. 'Keep her quiet today,' he instructed us. 'I'll speak to Miss Judith myself. Charlie, how are you feeling after your broken night? Do you feel up to beginning to learn to drive?'

I'd looked forward to learning to drive a horse in harness since Lawrence had first promised it. My tiredness faded in an instant.

'I think the answer is yes, to judge by the boy's expression,' commented Bridges.

'Very well,' said Lawrence. 'Get yourself washed, Charlie. And I mean thoroughly washed. I'm not taking you out looking like that nor reeking of the stables as you do. Livery, please! We have Lord Rutherford's reputation to maintain. And see to it someone harnesses Sorrel to the gig, will you Bridges? Charlie, I'll come and get you in an hour, once I've had my breakfast.'

'You . . . *you're* teaching me?' I stammered.

A smile lit Lawrence's face. 'I'm both more patient and more courageous than Bridges,' he said. 'He'll take over once you're less likely to put the horse and gig in the ditch.'

CHAPTER SEVENTEEN

Lawrence drove the gig out of the yard, negotiated the sharp corner through the gate, and then looked at me. 'Ready to take a turn?' he asked.

'I can try,' I replied nervously.

I'd been allowed a bucket of hot water from the kitchens and had hidden myself in an outhouse to wash thoroughly. My skin was pink and I smelled of soap. I'd even scrubbed my teeth. My new livery smelled of clean, new wool and my wig sat neatly on my head. I hoped I was no longer offensive to sit next to.

Lawrence slid over on the bench and indicated I should move into the central space. I moved closer to him and he put the reins into my hands, showing me how to hold them correctly. Sorrel sensed the change of driver at once, tossing her head briefly and picking up her pace for a moment.

'Can you feel the contact with her mouth through the reins?' asked Lawrence. 'You need to maintain that at all times. Not too tight or she'll fret. Not too loose or she'll be in charge, not you. Unlike riding, the reins are the only contact you have.'

I nodded, trying to remember it all. 'Though Sorrel would probably often do well enough by herself,' I remarked. 'The packhorse trains often used to go ahead of us on the road. They knew their way home.'

'Ah, yes, you've worked the packhorse trains too, haven't you?' asked Lawrence. 'A varied career for one so young.'

'It wasn't for long. I was filling in for Martha's boy who got his leg broken.'

'I see. Keep her going steadily up this hill. She wants to slow down.'

I urged Sorrel to maintain her pace and smiled as she responded. 'It's not so very different from riding,' I observed.

'There are differences,' Lawrence replied. 'You have no leg contact, of course. You need to learn to judge the width of your vehicle, or there are places you may get into trouble. That's something a carriage horse can't do for you. She won't find her way either, as we don't follow a regular route like your packhorses. We'll turn left at the end of the carriageway. I don't think the road down to the Bath is the best one for a learner.'

I drew Sorrel to a halt as we reached the road, to check for other vehicles. Lawrence put his hand over mine to demonstrate how to turn left and to instruct the horse to trot. He then sat back and watched me, one arm resting on the back of the seat. I felt my colour rise under his scrutiny. I concentrated hard on driving Sorrel to the best of my ability.

'So where did you grow up, Charlie?' asked Lawrence at last. 'Who were your parents?'

I cast him a sideways glance, wondering whether it was normal for a man of his status to take an interest in a lowly stable boy. I faced forward and wondered how much to tell him.

'I can't imagine why you're interested,' I said frankly, playing for time.

'It's my job, as Lord Rutherford's steward, to take an interest in all the staff,' Lawrence told me casually. 'Besides, an air of mystery clings to you.'

'A mystery would be far more exciting than the truth,' I told him with a fast-beating heart. 'I'm merely the d . . . son . . . of a soldier who died in poverty and I must make my own way in the world.' I'd so nearly said daughter. How could I be so careless?

'Don't fret the horse,' said Lawrence, his eyes still on me.

My nerves had transferred themselves down the reins. Sorrel had shaken her head and increased her speed. I hated being observed so closely.

Lawrence put his hands over mine and drew Sorrel back to a walk. My hands trembled at the unexpected touch, but he released me again as soon as Sorrel had slowed. Did he suspect something? I felt suddenly unsure of myself. As though my disguise were the most ridiculous and transparent sham ever.

'So where was your father stationed?'

'All over the place. We followed him everywhere,' I said evasively.

'France?'

'Er . . . yes. And the Americas.'

'But you returned to England?'

'My father wished it so.'

'That's unusual,' commented Lawrence. 'Normally the

soldiers who go to the Americas stay. There are better opportunities over there.'

'I know. That's what my brother Robert felt. He chose to . . . ' I bit my lip hurriedly.

'To stay? So you have an older brother.' Lawrence looked keenly interested. Now I might really have put myself, and Robert, in danger. Lawrence and the surroundings of Deerhurst seemed far removed from the squalor and want of London and the horror of my father's murder, but who was to say?

'In what year were you born, Charlie?'

Lawrence fired the question at me unexpectedly and I faltered. I was fairly sure I'd told him I was thirteen, but I couldn't work out quickly which year my birth would be. 'Uh . . . 1708. No, I mean 1712.' I felt a burning flush spread over my face and neck at my own stupidity. Why had I not worked out my new birth date before being asked? I never could do arithmetic under pressure.

'1710, then. I see. Why did you feel the need to lie to me about your age?'

My face was still tingling. I kept my eyes fixed between Sorrel's ears and tried to calm down enough to think straight. Lawrence had led me into talking about myself and then cornered me. Why?

'I could understand it if you'd told me you were older. Why younger? It makes no sense.'

I hung my head. 'I thought you would think me a small, skinny thing, perhaps not up to the work,' I told him, squirming uncomfortably.

'I'd already offered you the job,' Lawrence sounded

more puzzled than angry. 'There was no need to conceal the truth.'

'I know. I'm sorry.'

There was a long silence, during which Lawrence continued to look at me. I felt deeply uneasy. It was hard not to recall those posters in London. Could Mr Lawrence have seen them and made the connection with me? Was I under suspicion? My heart beating quickly with fear, I sought to change the subject, to distract Lawrence from thinking about me.

'I've told you about myself,' I said, rather breathlessly. 'What about you? Have you always lived here? If I'm permitted to ask you, that is,' I added diffidently.

'Of course you are permitted,' replied Lawrence calmly. 'No, I haven't always lived here. I grew up in north Gloucestershire. My father was a navy man, though we didn't follow him as you followed yours. He came and went. He was killed in 1712.'

'I'm sorry. It must have been hard for you to lose him.'

'It was. I was fourteen and my mother had four younger ones to provide for. I was very fortunate to be taken on here. Although I'm related to Lord Rutherford, he was under no obligation to provide for me.'

This gave me a different perspective on Lawrence. I knew he was employed by his lordship, but I'd thought of him as part of the family. Now I could see he might live in the house but he was separate from them; more servant than relation.

As we drove back through the open lodge gates, Mrs Saunders was standing at the door of the lodge house with a curtsey and a greeting. Her eyes were on me, I noticed, not on Lawrence. There was an anxious look in them, almost a look of longing, that made me uneasy all over again. I nodded to her but drove Sorrel on at a steady trot, not relaxing until we were out of sight.

Mr Lawrence let me drive him on his various errands over the weeks that followed. I kept a more careful guard over my tongue and when I sensed he was trying to draw too much out of me, I closed up. He frightened me a little with his curiosity.

When I'd grown confident driving Sorrel, Mr Lawrence had Mustard and Cress, a steady pair of horses, harnessed to the chaise and taught me to drive them too. 'You take a great deal of trouble with me,' I said on our third outing with a pair of horses. 'I thought Bridges was to teach me once you trusted that I was safe with the reins?'

'Who says I trust you?' replied Lawrence lightly. 'I take my life in my hands every time I drive out with you! How could I possibly ask that of Bridges?'

'You're teasing me,' I said uncertainly. 'Why?' My driving was steady, I knew it was.

'Oh, merely for the pleasure of seeing you look so unsure of yourself! You are normally so guarded and self-contained, you know,' said Lawrence, the teasing tone still in his voice. 'If you wish for the truth, you show promise, Charlie,' Lawrence said as we drew into the yard of an outlying farm on the estate. 'It's a great pleasure to teach you. There, does that satisfy your vanity?'

I blushed, both reassured and embarrassed. 'I wasn't . . . I didn't . . . '

'I know,' Lawrence waved a hand as he climbed down from the chaise. 'You weren't asking for compliments. But you are a natural with horses, you know you are.'

That evening, missing my father, I skipped supper and took the package containing his letters out of the hiding place I had made for it behind a post in the stables. I read through several of the letters hoping to feel closer to him. The comfort they offered me was tempered with grief. As the light was fading and I could no longer read the aged ink, I began to place the letters carefully back inside the oilskin. As I did so, the leather pouch containing my father's ring fell out. I picked it up, shook out the ring, and caught my breath as the sun's fading rays fell on the design. It had not struck me until this moment. Until I came to Deerhurst, I hadn't considered that the design upon the ring was a crest. But now it was familiar to me. These days, I saw the stag intertwined with the R for Rutherford every time we hauled Lord Rutherford's chaise from the coach house. Here was the self-same device upon the ring: the crest of the Lawrences.

What was my father doing with a ring that clearly belonged to a noble family? Had he stolen it? Was that why he had to flee and had been parted from my mother? That would account for so much. It could explain why they had gone abroad together, why they had been secretive about their past. It could also explain why the murderer was pursuing my father. Perhaps this ring was a valuable heirloom.

'Oh, Father, what did you do?' I whispered to myself.

'Hey Charlie, what are you up to?' Ben's voice came

out of nowhere. Startled, I stuffed the pouch in my shirt and stood up, the ring concealed in my tightly-clenched hand. 'Why aren't you at dinner, Ben?' I asked.

'Finished. Was that letters? Who learned you to read?' asked Ben.

'Yes, from my mother. She taught me.'

'Your mother, eh?' asked Ben sceptically. 'You sure about that? Not a love note from a secret admirer?'

'Certainly not,' I said, far too primly for a boy.

Ben winked. 'Mr Lawrence seems to like you,' he said meaningfully. 'Always taking you off for long drives. We never knew it were boys he liked, but there's no accounting for taste.'

'What nonsense!' I cried, horrified. 'I'm his groom.'

'Oh yes? You should hear what the others are saying.' Ben threw me a good-natured punch. I hit him back and he grappled with me, shoving me playfully into the wall.

I saw the other boys tackle each other like this all the time and kept my distance. Now, I defended myself, terrified he would grab some part of me that might reveal my gender. 'Stop it, Ben!' I cried, clutching the ring tight, praying I wouldn't drop it. But Ben pummelled me with his fists. He was only being playful, but it was knocking the wind out of me.

'Not more fighting, Charlie?' a voice interrupted us. We fell apart, both shocked to find Mr Lawrence watching us from the entrance to the stables. 'Your bruises from the last time have barely healed yet!' Lawrence complained. 'I can only just take you out in public respectably. You might have a care for the reputation I'll get for beating my servants if you keep fighting!'

His tone was light-hearted, but we both hung our heads. 'We was only larking about, sir!' Ben said.

'Haven't you got work to do, Ben?' demanded Lawrence. Ben effaced himself at once, heading off to the tack room, shooting me a significant look. He left me confronting Lawrence with his dreadful suggestions still ringing in my ears. I shifted awkwardly from one foot to the other, the hand with the ring concealed behind my back.

'You're a troublesome brat, Charlie.'

'Yes, sir,' I agreed meekly.

'I hope you're sorry for it?'

'Of course,' I agreed.

'Charlie, you ride don't you?'

'I do,' I agreed.

'Then I have favour to ask you. Miss Lawrence intends to begin riding Belle tomorrow morning. I have a great deal of work to do and her grandfather is in the gout at present and can't ride at all. I'd like you to accompany her.'

'Me?' I said startled.

'Yes. Her own personal groom left a few months ago and hasn't been replaced yet. When I need you to accompany me, one of the other grooms will go with her, but Steele has better things to do with his time and Bridges would struggle to keep up with her. I'd like you to keep an eye on her. And on Belle.'

'Very well,' I said.

'Thank you. You can ride Merlin. And be warned, Miss Lawrence will do her best to give you the slip. I'm relying on you!'

Lawrence turned to leave and then paused. 'And Charlie? Try and stay out of trouble for a few days, will you?'

I grinned sheepishly in response. Checking I was alone and he'd really gone, I dropped the ring back into the pouch, wrapped it into the oilskin bundle and carefully concealed it all in the gap behind the pillar at the back of the stable block. I stuffed straw around it to hide it completely, but was more anxious than ever about it being discovered. It seemed doubly dangerous now.

I still didn't feel hungry, so I went to visit Belle. She greeted me like a long-lost friend and nuzzled me happily while I scratched behind her ears.

'I don't know what to think any more, Belle,' I confided in her softly. 'Was my father a thief? Surely not! And then Mr Lawrence . . . There's more truth in Ben's words than he knows, from my side at least. I'm sure he doesn't care for me. Not in the way they are suggesting! He thinks I'm a boy, and he called me a troublesome brat, didn't he? But I . . . ' I sighed and stroked the beautiful horse's neck. 'I can't stop thinking about him,' I whispered in her ear. 'I'm a fool.'

Belle snorted contentedly. My secret was safe with her.

CHAPTER EIGHTEEN

'Being accompanied by a groom is stuffy. I'm not having it.'

Miss Judith stared at me mulishly. I kept my face as wooden and expressionless as possible. 'His lordship's orders, miss,' I replied.

'What use will *you* be?' Miss Judith taunted. 'Shouldn't you still be in the nursery having your nose wiped?'

Spoiled brat, I thought to myself. How pleasant it would be to say the words aloud. I reminded myself I was paid to put up with her insults.

'I don't believe you, either. I'll wager it wasn't Grandpapa, but that Gothic John Lawrence who ordered this.' Miss Judith jerked Belle away, jobbing at her mouth in a way that made the mare startle. Dragging her towards the mounting block, Miss Judith settled herself on Belle side-saddle and adjusted her petticoats.

'If you don't like Charlie going with you, miss, I can accompany you.' said Steele. 'Or Mr Lawrence. It's up to you. But we would lose our jobs if we let you out alone.'

Miss Judith tossed her head and didn't reply as Steele helped her adjust her stirrup leathers.

I scrambled up onto Merlin's back and was adjusting my own stirrups, when Miss Judith kicked Belle and shot out of the yard at a slapping pace, leaving me to urge Merlin after her with one stirrup still too long.

After the first half an hour, I understood Lawrence's concern for Belle. Miss Judith rode her with great flair and daredevilry but with no care for her mount's safety. She showed none for her own either, but that didn't impress me. In my view, a rider's primary concern was the safety and well-being of her horse.

Merlin followed Belle's mad flight across the downs gamely, but with far less elegance. My own seat was untidy with my badly adjusted stirrup, and several times I had recourse to grasp a handful of Merlin's mane to stay on his back. I was glad no one could see me. I watched the beautiful mare going through her paces ahead of me and longed to be riding her myself. Every time Miss Judith pulled unkindly on her mouth or risked her legs galloping over rabbit holes, my heart was in my mouth. I would take far better care of her than that.

'Oh. You're still here, then,' remarked Miss Judith looking round with a pout as she reined in at a gate, miles from home. Her face, pink from the exertion and the bracing morning air, was framed by an expensive hat. She looked more beautiful than ever, but she failed to charm me. Belle was sweating, her flanks heaving.

'You can make yourself useful and open the gate,' she told me haughtily. I rode forward past her and took the opportunity to adjust my stirrup before unlatching it.

'You're keeping me waiting, boy,' scolded Miss Judith impatiently.

'Sorry, miss,' I replied. My stirrup done, I unlatched the gate and pulled it open, leaving the way clear for her to ride through. As she passed me, she slashed her whip down on Merlin's rump, then kicked Belle past me into a gallop down the hill beyond the gate.

Merlin half-reared in pain and shock, crashed into the gate, then skittered away from it. I hadn't dreamed Judith would do such a thing and was very nearly unseated. Clinging on desperately, I fought to calm Merlin and get him back under control. By the time this was done and the gate was closed, Miss Judith and Belle were out of sight.

I felt sick with shock and a sense of failure. Lawrence had relied on me and I'd let him down at the very first test. I recalled that he had warned me she would try to give me the slip. Fear for Belle and for the consequences of my failure drove me to push Merlin swiftly after her. I was no hand at tracking, however, and didn't know the area. I was soon hopelessly lost and could find no trace of them.

I asked at a farmhouse, then again at a hamlet, and eventually found my way back to Deerhurst. As I reached the main gates, Mrs Saunders came out to let me through instead of her husband. She reached up and caught Merlin's bridle as I passed.

'Charlie Weaver, isn't it?' she asked. She was looking at me strangely, as she always did. I wondered if she were perhaps a little mad.

'That's right,' I agreed cautiously.

'Where are you from, Charlie?' she asked me. I felt a knot in my belly. Here was another person who wished to know more about me.

'I've lived in many places,' I said warily.

'Who are your parents, Charlie?'

'They are both dead.'

Still Mrs Saunders didn't leave go of Merlin's bridle. She continued to stare at me. 'Excuse me, if you please, Mrs Saunders,' I said at length. 'I have to report Miss Lawrence missing.'

'I'm sorry,' she said, stepping back and releasing me at once. I trotted swiftly on.

When I rode back into the yard alone, the alarm was raised at once. The grooms who knew the area saddled up and rode out in different directions to search for their mistress. I was sent running up to the house with a message for Mr Lawrence. I wasn't allowed beyond the kitchen, but passed the message to a footman who informed me that Mr Lawrence was out.

'I shall appraise him of the situation on his return,' he told me grandiloquently.

'Should I ride and fetch him?' I asked worriedly, unsure what he would want. 'Do you know where he's gone?'

'That won't be necessary,' the footman replied, looking down his long nose at me. He turned and walked through the door in a stately manner, to be swallowed up by the hushed, carpeted house.

'I wouldn't listen to him,' said the same cook who'd once given me a bun. 'He's so full of himself it's a wonder his buttons don't burst right off. Mr Lawrence has driven over to West Farm to look at some puppies. I'm sure he'd want to know at once that Miss Judith has gone missing.'

'Thank you,' I said. 'I know where that is. I'll go at once.'

'Hold on a moment,' she said, catching my sleeve as I made for the door. 'I'm just getting some almond pastries out of the oven. You'll miss your dinner if you go off now, so take one with you!'

'You never give *us* almond pastries, Mrs Bond!' said a young kitchen maid, pausing in her work scrubbing pots in a huge stone sink. 'You're always favouring the boys. We get hungry too!'

'Boys are growing, Susan,' said Mrs Bond sharply as she bent over the oven and extracted a tray of deliciously fragrant pastries. 'And they work hard. They need sustenance. You'll just put on flesh!'

Susan poked her brush at a pot in a disconsolate manner and then gave me a sly smile. There was so much invitation in the look, it took me aback. I was confused for a moment and then remembered she thought me a boy.

Mrs Bond wrapped two of the hot pastries in a clean cloth and put them into my hands. I left the kitchen for the scullery, hurrying to the back door, but Susan was swifter than I. Abandoning the sink, she reached the door first. Once there, out of sight of the other servants, she whipped her hands behind her back and lifted her face to me as I approached, quite clearly asking for a kiss. I paused, astonished at her forwardness. I wasn't going to kiss her, but didn't want to hurt her feelings either.

'Here,' I said impulsively, taking one of the pastries from the cloth and pressing it into her hand. 'Don't tell!' And then, taking advantage of her surprise and delight, I slid past her and made my escape, shoving the second pastry into my waistcoat.

I rode at a slapping pace all the way out to West Farm. Susan and her odd behaviour were quickly forgotten. Merlin had already been untacked while I was looking for Mr Lawrence, and was weary besides, so I'd saddled myself a fine bay gelding called Storm. He was swift and easy-paced with a great mouth and gave me a thoroughly enjoyable ride. I hoped it was allowable to take him. There had been no one senior to ask, with everyone out looking for Miss Judith.

As I reined in outside the farm, patting Storm and praising him, I saw to my relief that the Deerhurst gig was in the farmyard. I slid off Storm and tethered him hurriedly. A buxom woman in a white apron and a cap answered my knock at the door. She had red cheeks and a kindly look on her face. There was no need for her to explain where Mr Lawrence was; I could see him in the spacious farm kitchen beyond her, seated on a low stool, playing with a litter of puppies. On the table stood a cake, several plates and a teapot, indicating he had been a welcome guest. He rose and came towards me when he heard my voice.

'Is something wrong at home, Charlie? His lordship . . . ?' he looked anxious.

'No sir,' I replied breathlessly. 'Not his lordship. It's Miss Judith; Miss Lawrence, I *should* say! I'm afraid she got away from me and she's not back yet. I'm so sorry!'

'Is anyone looking for her?' he demanded.

'Bridges, Steele, and Peter are all out looking,' I told him in a faltering voice. 'But no one knows which way she's gone, because I was lost.'

I hung my head, shamed by my failure, but Lawrence dropped a hand on my shoulder and squeezed it reassuringly. 'I warned you, did I not?' he said. 'What happened?'

I told him and he gave a decisive nod. 'I think I know where she's gone,' he said. 'But it's a devilishly long way from here by road. How did you get here, Charlie?'

'I rode Storm,' I said anxiously, hoping I hadn't acted wrongly, but he looked cheered. 'Capital! I'll wager you were pleased with him?'

I relaxed a little and smiled. 'He's wonderful,' I agreed.

'Good, I'll take him from here and you can drive the gig back home. Do you feel confident to do that?'

'I've never driven alone,' I said dubiously.

'I trust you. Mrs Fielden,' he said turning away from me. 'Thank you for your hospitality. I'm sorry to leave you in such a rush, but I'm sure you understand. Please tell your husband I'll take the puppy with the white foot for his lordship.'

I felt very responsible harnessing Sorrel to the gig and setting out by myself, but I soon relaxed and enjoyed being out in the late afternoon sunshine, the reins in my hands. It was infinitely preferable to mucking out or cleaning tack, the tasks I would be performing otherwise. But worry for Belle disturbed what was otherwise a tranquil drive. By the time I reached the lodge gates, the sun was low in the sky. I'd eaten the pastry on the way and now felt tired and very thirsty.

Mrs Saunders was at the gate once more and opened it as I approached. 'Good evening, Charlie,' she greeted me with a smile. 'You look hot and bothered.'

'It's a warm afternoon,' I admitted.

'Why don't you step down a moment and take a cool glass of milk?' she invited. My thirst warred with my fear and won. Besides I was curious about her interest in me.

'Thank you, that's very kind,' I replied, reining Sorrel in beyond the gate.

Mr Saunders took Sorrel's bridle and hitched her to a ring beside the gate and then disappeared back into his garden. There was a trough of water there and she drank thirstily. I climbed down from the gig and followed Mrs Saunders into the tiny lodge house. It was neat and precise, with embroidered covers hanging over the armchairs and polished brasses above the empty fireplace. Mrs Saunders invited me to sit down at the table and poured me a glass of milk from a jug. She also fetched a pie from the pantry. 'Will you partake of a little pie, as you'll have missed your dinner?' she asked me.

I accepted uneasily, wondering why she was showering me with such kindness. As I ate and drank, Mrs Saunders sat down opposite me. Her eyes were fixed on me. I swallowed, cleared my throat, and met her gaze. It was now or never: 'You stare at me a great deal, Mrs Saunders,' I said. 'May I ask why?'

Mrs Saunders flushed and her eyes filled with tears. 'You look like someone . . . I once knew,' she said.

'Who was that?' I asked, my heart beating quickly, wondering what I might discover. I thought of my mother's letter, written from Deerhurst Park, currently hidden in the stable block.

'My . . . my daughter,' said Mrs Saunders, and burst into tears.

Horrified, I reached out and patted her awkwardly on the shoulder. It only made her cry more. Her apron held to her face, she rocked back and forth. Moved by her distress, I drew my chair over to hers and put my arm around her. 'Please, Mrs Saunders,' I murmured. 'Don't cry!'

After a few moments, she seemed to pull herself together. She lifted her head and looked at me once more with red-rimmed eyes. I drew back from her and watched her anxiously.

'Who are you, Charlie?' she asked brokenly. 'Why have you come to haunt me with the past?'

'I didn't mean to do so!'

'But you do. You're the image of her for all you're dressed as a boy!'

I caught my breath at her words. So, like Martha, Mrs Saunders had seen through my disguise. Would she betray me? I felt danger around me once again, close and suffocating.

'You know,' I said. 'Who have you told . . . who will you tell?'

But Mrs Saunders wasn't listening. She continued to pour out her memories as she wept: 'Ah, my dear daughter has been dead these many, many years. She was in love with a man she couldn't marry. When he abandoned her, she lived a year in sorrow then took her own life.'

I patted the sobbing woman's shoulder. 'I'm so sorry!' I said helplessly.

'But you see, I always doubted it,' wept Mrs Saunders. 'They would have it she'd taken her life, my husband and the Lawrences, but her body was never found. And now you come here, looking just like her.'

'Mrs Saunders,' I said gently. 'What was her name?'

'Her name was Emily.'

I caught my breath in amazement. 'In that case,' I said hesitantly. 'Perhaps she really didn't die? I'm not sure, of course, but I wonder . . . You see, my mother was called Emily . . . And I think . . . that is, I have reason to believe she used to live on the Deerhurst estate. That's why I came here.'

Mrs Saunders turned deathly white. 'My Emily, your mother? It's what's been on my mind since I saw you. But I hardly dared believe . . . My Emily left with nothing, you see. Not so much as a clean shift. We always thought that meant that . . . you know. It destroyed us. Can you imagine how hard it is to live with the knowledge your own child was thrown into such despair that she chose to die *and she did not turn to her own parents for help*? We were to blame for opposing her love, I know. But how could we have guessed? We thought . . . But after she was gone, we gave up the farm and came to live here and . . .'

'The farm? I asked with a gasp. 'Did you live at the Home Farm?' That was the address my mother had written her letter from. It all fitted.

'Yes, we did. But we lost all heart when Emily died.'

'I think perhaps she didn't die,' I said uncertainly. 'Not then anyway. I think perhaps she ran away . . .'

'How can this be? Was your mother Emily Saunders?'

I shook my head. 'No. I don't know what her maiden name was. She was married, you see.'

'But you are Weaver. She didn't know anyone by that name!'

I hesitated. I'd kept my secret so carefully. Was it safe to tell Mrs Saunders? If I didn't trust her, I might never know anything more about my parents. I felt sure I had discovered an important link.

'Can you keep a secret?' I asked seriously.

'Of course,' said Mrs Saunders tearfully.

'You mustn't tell anyone. But my name isn't Weaver. It's Smith.'

I sat back and waited for gasps and explanations. But Mrs Saunders frowned, thought deeply, and finally shook her head. 'She didn't know anyone of that name either,' she said.

'Oh.' I was bitterly disappointed. For a moment I'd thought I was on the brink of discovering my family. 'Perhaps . . . perhaps she ran away and then met my father later?' I asked.

'Or your mother and my daughter are not the same person,' replied Mrs Saunders with a sigh. She took my chin in a trembling hand and looked into my eyes once more. 'And yet . . .' she said. 'You are so like her, my dear. What are you doing dressed as a boy?'

I swallowed hard. 'Earning an honest living,' I said briefly, unwilling to enter on explanations. 'Mrs Saunders, may I ask, would you recognize your Emily's writing?' I asked. 'If I brought you a letter?'

'I think so,' Mrs Saunders agreed. 'Do you have one?'

'I do.'

I was stunned by my talk with Mrs Saunders and could think of nothing else as I drove the gig back to the house. I had come to Deerhurst with some hope of learning more of my mother, but this was beyond anything I'd imagined.

The yard was ominously quiet on my return. I un-hitched Sorrel and tethered her ready for grooming, then went in search of a drink. There was a bucket of well water in the grooms' room. I dipped the ladle into the cool liquid, filled myself a beaker, and drank thirstily. My hands were not quite steady, I noticed as I raised the beaker. It wasn't until I'd drained two cups that I noticed Ben sitting quietly in the corner.

'Ben,' I exclaimed, startled. 'What news?'

He shook his head gloomily. 'Word is, 'is lordship's worried sick and in a towering temper. Miss Lawrence ain't been found. Leastways, no one's back yet.' He sighed. 'And there'll be a mountain of tack to clean when they do get here, and guess who'll get that job?'

'I'll help you,' I promised him. 'If you'll give me a hand putting the gig away?'

Together, we hauled the gig into the coach house and closed the big door. Then I rubbed Sorrel down and sta-bled her, making sure she had fresh hay and water.

As I walked back out into the yard, I caught the sound of clattering hooves. When the riders emerged under the archway, it was Mr Lawrence on Storm and Miss Judith on Belle. I sighed with relief to see them all and went straight to Belle's head. She was exhausted and trem-bling, her eyes dull. Miss Judith sat sulkily on her back until Lawrence dismounted and then allowed him to as-sist her in getting down from the horse. Once on the ground, she turned away from him at once, without so much as a pat or a word of praise for her tired horse.

'Go straight to your grandfather!' Lawrence called after her. 'He'll be in a fret of anxiety!'

Miss Judith flounced off without replying while I made up for her neglect by petting the beautiful bay mare. Lawrence turned to me. There was a furrow of tiredness and annoyance on his brow, but it smoothed away as he looked at me. 'Charlie,' he said. 'You didn't put the gig in a ditch then?'

'Worse! It's in pieces,' I replied. 'I hid the remains in the woods.'

Lawrence laughed briefly. 'I should have known! Charlie, can I leave you with the two horses? I need to go and make sure the volcanic eruption of his lordship's rage and relief isn't too violent.'

'Of course,' I said, biting back the wish that he wouldn't spare Miss Judith too much. In my opinion, it would do her good. I wished I could ask him where Judith had been, but it was none of my business.

I tethered Storm and led Belle to the post for grooming. It was then I noticed that she was limping. I ran my hands over her leg. Her near hock was hot and swollen. That stupid, stupid girl! How could she treat her beautiful horse so? I ran and drew water from the well, dipped a cloth into it and washed down the heated place. I kept washing it, squeezing the cool water over it for a long time. Belle, stiff and sore from being ridden so hard, nuzzled me gratefully and made soft whickering noises. I stroked her soothingly, speaking to her in a long, gentle flow of words that I hoped she found comforting.

Ben had groomed Storm and led him into his stable, the other grooms had returned one by one from their fruitless search, and darkness had fallen before I was done. Bridges checked Belle over and promised to mix a poultice to put on her overnight.

The hock was cooler, though still swollen, as I finally led Belle, now dead lame, to her box. She nosed listlessly at the hay and stood quietly, resting her injured leg. Reluctant to leave her alone, I ran only to grab a drink of water and my blanket, before spending the night in my usual spot in Belle's box.

CHAPTER NINETEEN

The last Sunday of the month was an afternoon off for most of us, and the day dawned bright, clear, and unseasonably warm for late May.

'Let's go to the river,' suggested Ben. 'It'll be cool in the shade there.'

Content that, after a week of lameness, Belle was on the mend, I agreed to go with them. It would be nice to get away from the stable yard and do something different for a few hours.

Ben, Peter, Joe, and I set off once we'd mucked out the stables, been to church and eaten an early cold dinner. The rest of the long summer's day was ours to do as we pleased. I planned to visit Mrs Saunders later in the day, once the heat had faded.

It was a hot walk down to the river, and we were pleased to flop down in the shade and recover when we reached it.

'Who's for a swim then?' asked Ben after a few minutes. He was sitting up, eager for fun and games. 'Charlie?'

I shook my head hurriedly. 'Can't swim,' I lied. 'I'll just paddle in the shallows.'

'Oh come on,' said Ben, stripping off his shirt. 'It's not deep enough that you need to be able to swim!' I averted my eyes as he dropped his breeches and kicked them onto the grass before running naked to the river bank and leaping into the water with a great splash. The other boys soon followed him, leaving me red-faced on the grass, wondering what to do. I'd thought I'd sit on the bank and dangle my feet in the water, but the sight of the three boys wrestling naked in the water was too much for me. I felt as though I was spying on them under false pretences and, really, it wasn't as though I had the least wish to look. I'd grown up with a brother, so I knew as much as I wanted to know about boys' anatomy.

I wasn't left in peace for long. Ben's cry of 'Let's throw Charlie in!' didn't give me enough warning to make my escape. They surrounded me, picked me up and threw me fully dressed into the river. I surfaced, gasping and spluttering at the shock of the cold water, and struck out for the bank.

'Hey, look! He CAN swim!' yelled Pete.

'What were you so afraid of, Charlie-boy?' demanded Joe.

'Doesn't want to get his tool out in front of us and that's the truth, I reckon!' shouted Ben. 'Ain't that right, Charlie? That's why you won't join us for bath night either, hey? Terrified we'll see how tiny it is!'

'On the contrary, Ben,' I said with a grin. 'I don't want to make you feel inadequate.'

'Oh, Charlie, you've asked for it now!' said Ben.

'Asked for what?' I said, realizing too late my bravado had been disastrously ill-judged.

'Strip him, lads!' shouted Ben, splashing into the water

next to me, churning up the water, mud, and weed. 'Let's see the truth of this!'

All three lads converged on me, laughing uproariously. It was a game to them; they had no idea. Terror gave me a strength and speed I didn't know I had. I leapt through the water to the bank and clawed my way up through the mud, the three boys close on my heels. At the top of the bank, Pete threw himself at me, bringing me down full length with a painful bump, my face hitting a stone.

Half stunned and convinced all was over, I gave myself up. But just as the three boys piled onto me, a girl's voice cried out from the trees: 'Oh, what are you rough boys doing to poor Charlie?'

Susan, the kitchen maid, was standing in the trees with two of the other maids. The sight of them made the naked stable boys holler with shock and leap back into the water. As soon as they backed off, Susan rushed forward towards me, putting a hand on my wet, muddy shirt and bending over me solicitously. 'Are you much hurt, Charlie?' she asked tenderly. 'There's blood on your face!'

At that moment, she was my saviour. I smiled up at her, light-headed with relief. 'I'm well enough, thank you Susan,' I told her. 'I think I hit my head.'

'You're so brave,' she sighed admiringly. 'Why don't you come with us? We're walking further down the stream to paddle and pick flowers.'

'Thank you, I will,' I replied, scrambling to my feet. It was an unexpected helping hand and I didn't hesitate to take it.

We spent a very pleasant afternoon wading in the shallows, plucking wild flowers, and chatting. Susan made a great deal more fuss than was necessary cleaning up my muddy face with her pocket-handkerchief. I had a cut across one eyebrow that had bled a little. It stung as Susan cleaned it gently.

The girls shared their lunch with me, since mine had been left behind with the boys. After lunch, I helped them weave flowers into their hair. I felt a little wistful, as my own hair was still only mere fuzz on my scalp. I kept it very clean now though, hoping there would be no need to shave my head again too soon.

'You're so good at this, Charlie,' said Susan, smiling up at me. 'Wherever did you learn it?'

'Oh, I have sisters,' I said quickly. It had been so pleasant to enjoy female company again that I'd forgotten myself. Luckily my glib explanation seemed to satisfy her.

'Oh, sisters! That explains why you're so nice to talk to too. Not like the other boys, all rough and shouting.'

I had the grace to blush.

As the heat of the afternoon faded, we walked up to the Home Farm and bought a pitcher of cool milk for a farthing, which we shared sitting under an apple tree in the garden. Much refreshed, we walked back down to the house, in time for the evening meal to be served. Parting at the back of the house by the door to the kitchens, Susan stood on tiptoe to kiss my cheek and then fled with her two friends, giggling.

As I turned away, shaking my head, I saw Lawrence striding towards me from the stables in riding dress, whip in hand. I realized he'd witnessed the little scene and that a frown creased his brow.

'I hadn't taken you for a ladies' man, Charlie,' he said with a definite note of disapproval in his voice. 'Aren't you a bit young for that? I hope you can conduct yourself with propriety and not get any of our maids into trouble.'

I fixed my eyes on the ground. 'Oh n-no, sir,' I stammered awkwardly.

'And you've been fighting again,' he said despairingly.

I touched my brow lightly, realizing it had swollen.

'N-not exactly,' I replied. 'It was all in fun, sir.'

He shook his head and sighed. 'Get some ice on it,' he said curtly. 'I need you to accompany me out tomorrow morning without looking like a prizefighter. Be ready in your livery at nine o'clock sharp!'

Lawrence nodded a curt dismissal to me and I made my way back to the stable yard feeling unaccountably low. It took an hour of grooming and petting Belle to restore my peace. The gentle mare had a restful presence.

Later, I braved the kitchen and Susan's attentions once more to fetch ice for my bruises. In the cool of the evening, I walked up to the lodge gates to speak to Mrs Saunders, with one of my mother's letters tucked into my shirt. But before I reached the lodge house, Mr Saunders walked towards me, with no friendly expression on his face.

'Good evening,' I began, uncertainly. 'I've come to call on your . . .'

'I know why you're here,' he broke in. 'And I won't allow it. Why can't you leave her alone? Coming here, raking up the past, just as she's found some peace! You have no idea what she's gone through! Take your lies and your false hopes away, I won't listen to them!'

I fell back, astonished and hurt. 'But please, I just

wanted . . . ' I pulled the letter from my shirt, but he pushed it away without so much as a glance.

'No! Go! And stay away from my wife!'

I hesitated a moment, wilting under his fierce, angry stare. Realizing there was no point arguing, I turned sadly away, tucking the letter back into my shirt. Shaken and dispirited, I walked back down the hill through the park. I spent the night in Belle's loose box once more, sleeping up against her warm flank, soothed by her breathing, which was steady and rhythmic in the darkness.

The following morning, I accompanied Lawrence down to the city, where he had various commissions to perform. He didn't speak a word to me, which was unusual. I was surprised to find he was annoyed with me over something apparently so trivial. My cut scarcely showed this morning and the bruise had only darkened a little. I seemed to have the trick of angering everybody at the moment.

In the city, I took charge of the horses at the White Hart inn. Lawrence had left orders for me to be served a meal while he was gone, so once Pitch and Velvet were comfortably bestowed, I sat in a quiet corner of the taproom and enjoyed some ale and stew.

Left with nothing to do for once, memories overwhelmed me. I missed my father and thought longingly of the days when my parents were still alive and my family together. Those seemed like golden days to me now; a distant land where life had been perfect. Now, by contrast, everything had fallen apart. I recalled the horrific sight of my father's body, once so handsome, but wasted by poverty and worry, murdered and left to lie on the floor of that sordid lodging room. As a result, I lived in hiding, in fear of my life. What was worse, Mr Saunders was furious with me and even Mr Lawrence, in whose company I took much pleasure, was distant and displeased with me.

Tears began to steal silently down my cheeks. As my back was to the room, I let them fall unchecked. Perhaps the company of the maids the day before had triggered memories of my mother, for I could almost smell her scent and feel her warm embrace as I sat forlorn. I missed my family so much that it ached.

When Lawrence joined me at the table sooner than I'd expected, I jumped, embarrassed to be caught shedding tears. 'Crying Charlie?' he asked, sitting down opposite me. 'Not troubles of the heart, I hope?'

I lifted my arm to wipe away the tears. 'Not your sleeve, Charlie,' said Lawrence, catching my wrist. 'That is costly livery you're wearing!' He pulled out a pocket-handkerchief and handed it to me. 'You'll find this is perfectly clean,' he promised me.

I wiped my tears fiercely away and blew my nose. A little restored, I gulped and looked up, sure that my eyes must be red and my face blotchy.

'Do tell me what's wrong!' invited Lawrence. 'No, I really don't want that handkerchief back now, please. Keep it in case you have need of it again!'

I nodded and stuffed the damp linen square into my sleeve.

Lawrence had a look of concern on his face. I had no idea what to say to him.

'So?' he prompted kindly.

I shook my head. 'I can't very well say it's nothing,' I said in a voice still choked with unshed tears. 'But it's nothing I want to talk about.'

'So it's not Susan the pretty, plump kitchen maid?'

I shook my head vehemently. 'No, indeed! I don't care for her except as an acquaintance!' It seemed important to tell Lawrence that.

'I don't like to see our dependants unhappy,' said Lawrence at last, when it became clear I would say no more. 'I hope if I can ever be of assistance, you won't hesitate to come to me?'

I nodded, touched by his kindness.

'Come,' said Lawrence, rising. 'I gave the order to have the horses harnessed before I came to find you, so we can leave now.' I gulped and followed him, ashamed to have betrayed such weakness.

'I'm sorry I was so silent on the drive down,' said Lawrence as Pitch and Velvet pulled the chaise smartly out of the city and then slowed for the long, steep climb. 'I was much preoccupied. I have some very weighty matters on my mind; some business for Lord Rutherford that concerns me very closely too. I suspect there is something gone awry and I'm greatly troubled by it.'

'Yes, of course,' I replied, wondering what that could be. 'I'm sorry to hear it. And, of course, I am here to serve you, not to be entertained.'

Lawrence glanced briefly at me over his shoulder. 'I know,' he said. 'And of course it would be ridiculous to think that my silence had anything to do with your upset.'

'Yes, that would be ridiculous,' I agreed firmly.

'We've done an excellent job between us reschooling this pair, you know, Charlie,' said Lawrence, changing the subject and nodding to Pitch and Velvet who were trotting beautifully together. 'I think we can sell them on soon. How are you at choosing horses? Would you like to accompany me to an auction? I rather fancy a team next. I like a challenge.'

'I've a fair eye for a good horse, I believe,' I said, greatly cheered both by the prospect of choosing new horses and by the idea of accompanying Lawrence. The summer sun shone on my face and a light breeze cooled me, drying the last traces of tears from my face. Despite the great grief I carried inside me, life was not so bad after all.

CHAPTER TWENTY

Miss Judith began riding Belle again some weeks later. At first she behaved herself well enough. She accepted my escort without complaint, she rode with reasonable moderation, and she was only rude and unpleasant every second outing.

'That's enough sugar for one day,' I said to her one afternoon when she'd come to the stables yet again with her pocket full. 'You'll make Belle ill.'

Miss Judith narrowed her eyes at me. 'Whose horse is Belle-belle?' she demanded. 'Let me see . . . um, yours? No, stable boy. Wrong. You don't own her. Mine? That's right; she's mine. My horse. So get back to mucking out her manure, for that is what you're paid to do. It's all you're fit for. Leave me to enjoy her company!' She pulled more sugar out and fed it to an eager Belle.

I turned away quietly, smarting at her words. Every one of them was true. I cared nothing for that, except where Belle was concerned. Belle I wished to protect, indeed I had been asked to try and do so. But Judith could always hurt me by reminding me I had no right to. My jealousy was a red-hot knife twisting in my belly.

I had a quiet word with Steele, who sent Miss Judith away. 'She's bored, so she overfeeds her horse,' he said to me when she'd gone. 'When there are visitors in the house, she doesn't come near her. You did right to tell me.'

Belle was not my horse, but mine was the pain of watching over her all night, edgy and uncomfortable when Miss Judith had allowed her to gorge herself. 'Oh, Belle,' I whispered to her, stroking her velvet nose as she paused from moving restlessly about the loose box, keeping me awake. 'If only you had the sense not to eat it! It's all very well for Miss Judith. She's sleeping soundly in the house and doesn't see the state you're in.'

Judith always rode down towards the city on her longer excursions, and dawdled past a particular house, looking up at the windows. Several times, a man's face appeared and once the figure waved.

Given the gossip at the house at the Bath she had been a guest at, it was not difficult to guess that there was some clandestine romance in train. Miss Judith was certainly in a better humour if she'd seen the mystery face at the window. If there had been no face, no wave, she rode back dangerously fast and was much too free with her whip. Poor Belle arrived home trembling and sweating and Merlin and I were hard-pressed to keep pace with her.

'Having you trailing after me is so tiresome, you flea-bitten gutter-scraping,' she snapped at me on one such occasion. 'Why can't you break both legs and stay at home? Belle and I don't want you.' Then she kicked Belle into another gallop, leaving me to follow as best I could on Merlin, my stomach somersaulting with fear for Belle's legs.

*

'She'll ruin that poor horse,' I told Lawrence earnestly as we drove to an outlying farm on business. 'Belle's already far more difficult to handle in the stable than she was. She spooks so easily, we are all at risk of being stepped on when we approach her.'

Lawrence was silent for some time. I bit my lip, wondering if I'd overstepped the mark by speaking so frankly. I was driving Pitch and Velvet well up to their bits. They were going beautifully and I was rather pleased with my handling of the reins.

'It won't be the first time. Miss Judith has ruined a number of good horses, I'm afraid,' he said. 'Lord Rutherford is the only one who could do anything about it, but he will not.'

I looked up at him, thunderstruck and lost my concentration for a moment. Velvet dropped to a walk while Pitch tried to keep trotting, jolting us considerably. Lawrence took the reins from my hands. I relinquished them and moved over.

'There, you see how essential it is not to lose focus for a moment when driving difficult horses?' said Lawrence. He demonstrated how to get the pair back under control and going smoothly again, and then spoke once more: 'I know you've become attached to Belle. Perhaps I've been unfair to allow that to happen, though it's difficult to see how I might have prevented it. The fact of the matter is, Miss Judith gets whatever she wants. She does not remain contented with a horse for long. When she is discontented or unhappy, she treats them badly.'

A chill gripped me. 'What . . . what happened to the other horses?' I asked, dreading the answer.

'Two recovered enough to be sold on. Her last was shot on her grandfather's orders.'

'No!' I cried faintly. I felt sick with horror, my stomach churning at the thought of Belle doomed to such a fate. Mr Lawrence underestimated my affection for the beautiful bay mare. I hadn't merely grown attached to her; she was the centre of my world.

'That's why her last groom left the position,' said Lawrence grimly.

I swallowed hard. 'Is there nothing to be done? Surely you must have some influence: with Lord Rutherford if not with Miss Judith?'

Lawrence shook his head. 'Nothing I can say will make any difference. Money is no object to his lordship where Judith is concerned. He is not greatly concerned about how many horses he has to buy her.'

'That's monstrous!' I objected vehemently. 'This is a horse's life! A beautiful, valiant, trusting creature. There must be something you can say? If you . . .'

'I've tried,' Lawrence interrupted me. 'Charlie, I may live in the house and eat at their table. I may be a relative, but I am a poor one. When it comes to it, I am an employee like you, utterly dependent on their goodwill. I have very little influence.'

I stared bleakly out over the horses' glossy, black backs as they made their way down the hill ahead of us, the weight of the chaise in their collars.

'Why are you telling me this if there's nothing we can do?' I asked miserably.

'I'm asking you whether you can think of something,' said Lawrence after a pause. 'This is the only reason I'm raising the matter with you. I need not tell you I should not be discussing this with you. But I really cannot bear to see yet another beautiful horse destroyed so wantonly and I know you feel the same way.'

I nodded. To lose Belle would break my heart.

'Think about it for me, Charlie,' Mr Lawrence said, before handing the reins back to me.

It was hot that night and I couldn't sleep. The sun had beaten down on the roof of the stables all day; the first really hot spell of the summer. The building had absorbed the heat and was now radiating it like a hot fire in winter.

I lay in the corner of Belle's loose box with no covering, sweating and uncomfortable. I could scarcely breathe. Belle was restless. My mind was running over the conversation with Lawrence earlier in the day and making me jumpy.

As the clock struck one, I could no longer bear the thought of lying still. There were still too many hours of discomfort to endure before morning. I pulled on my shoes, got up and went to the open half-door to breathe the sultry night air. I could hear light snores rumbling from the stables. Clearly the other boys were not suffering with the heat as I was. Or perhaps their minds were easier.

I stepped out of the stable, fastening it behind me. It was cooler in the yard, though still hard to breathe. Belle whickered softly to me, her tail twitching from side to side. I patted her damp neck.

'I wish I could take you for a ride!' I whispered to her. She nuzzled me and blew out through her nostrils. It wasn't possible to take her out. The gates to the stable yard were all locked at night to keep the valuable horses and equipment safe from thieves. 'But it would be pleasant to walk out together,' I sighed, imagining bareback riding through the park by moonlight. Together we could ride as far as the stream and wade in the water, or climb to the high downs and breathe the cooler air. The thought made me even more restless and discontented.

I decided even though I couldn't take Belle out, I would escape the confines of the yard myself. Fetching the spare key, which was kept in the shed in case of emergencies, I unlocked and opened the small door within the larger one and stepped through it, out into the gardens behind the house. This area was strictly off limits to the stable staff unless we had a very specific reason to go there. However, at one in the morning, I couldn't imagine there would be anyone to be troubled by my presence.

Walking out into the garden, I cast a glance up at the back of the great house. Countless dark windows stared down at me. There was not one light so late. Only a single window high up in the house was open. I wondered if it was any cooler in there.

I pulled off my boots and stockings, feeling the grass cool and damp against the soles of my feet. I wandered through the shrubbery and headed to the left, through a stone archway out into the cultivated, formal gardens beyond. I hadn't realized how beautiful it was here. I'd seen the gardeners coming and going with barrows, spades, and scythes, of course. And on a Sunday we were allowed to troop through the shrubbery to reach the church next to the house. But I had not, until now, gone deeper into the gardens.

Roses grew in profusion, carefully pruned and nurtured, their colours indistinguishable in the darkness. Over every gateway into the next hidden garden, honeysuckle or jasmine was trained, falling in cascades, filling the warm night air with heavy fragrances. There were trees too, though none were tall as yet. The gardens were all still as new as the house itself. There was a clear view of the star-studded sky above me. It was all breathtaking. It was as if I'd walked into an enchanted place. Its very stillness seemed magical.

From beyond the next archway, the faint sound of trickling water broke the stillness and silence. It was a welcome sound, and I walked on, eager to find the source. Ahead I saw a gleaming surface of still water. A large rectangle of stone walls sunk into the ground and filled with sparkling, clear water from a trickling waterfall. This pool must surely be especially for bathing? Had the family used it today, in the heat of the afternoon? I would have done so if I were them.

I knelt beside the water and dipped my hand below the silvered surface. It was deliciously cool. I cupped my hands and scooped up water to splash in my face and to pour over my short hair. It was refreshing, but my body was still sticky and uncomfortable in my hot clothes.

I glanced around, but there was no one here but me. Family and servants alike, everyone was asleep. Did I dare?

After a few moments' hesitation, I slipped off my clothing, unwound the scarf from my breasts and slid into the dark water. I gasped at the sudden cold, and

166

struck out for the far wall, swimming carefully, so as not to splash. I didn't want to be heard. Bathing in Lord Rutherford's private gardens was certainly not allowed.

Gradually, I adjusted to the temperature. The water no longer felt cold and I floated lazily on my back, gazing up at the stars. They winked down at me, complicit in my naughtiness. It was such a relief to cool down. I was committing an act of defiance; taking something that was not for me, and enjoying it anyway.

I swam for a long time before hauling myself out of the water onto the grass. I shivered slightly as I sat at the edge, waiting to dry so that I could put my clothes back on. I ran my hands over the short, spiky fuzz that was my hair, pleased to feel how much it had grown.

The swim left me inexpressibly weary. I knew I would be able to sleep now. Pulling my clothes on, I hurried back though the gardens and slipped as quietly as possible back into the stable yard where I fell swiftly into a deep and dreamless sleep.

CHAPTER TWENTY-ONE

July came before I saw Mrs Saunders alone. I knew that, despite her husband's warning to me, she was waiting for me. Her eyes told me so every time she saw me. But whenever I passed through the lodge gates, it was in company with Mr Lawrence or Miss Judith. The only times I was alone Mr Saunders was there, a forbidding frown on his face. I didn't dare disobey him deliberately by walking up from the house.

By the time Bridges sent me into Bath with the gig to collect a new gown and hat that had been made for Miss Judith, I'd almost given up hope of speaking to Mrs Saunders. Nonetheless, I hurried to slide one of my mother's letters into my shirt once more, just in case.

Luck finally favoured me. When I returned, the band-box and hatbox stowed safely in the gig behind me, Mrs Saunders was alone at the gate. 'Won't you come in, Charlie?' she asked.

I tethered Sorrel and entered the cottage. Mrs Saunders hurried to put a kettle onto the fire and then sat down at the table, her hands clasped tightly together. 'You've brought it?' she asked me.

Without hesitation, I drew the letter out of my shirt and laid it before her on the wooden table. Her hands shook as she reached out to take it.

'Oh,' she breathed, as she spread the yellowed sheet out and saw the writing. She turned it to look at the signature and tears filled her eyes once more.

'It's her,' she faltered. 'Her very hand; her signature! This is from my dear daughter! My Emily!' Mrs Saunders looked up at me, her eyes sparkling. 'This was indeed your mother?'

I nodded. 'It was,' I agreed. 'I'd know her hand anywhere. She taught me to read and write.'

Mrs Saunders put a trembling hand to her. 'Then she did not die when she left us! And . . . you really are my granddaughter?'

'I think I must be.'

Mrs Saunders embraced me, a scent of wood smoke, home-baked cake and soap enveloping me: the scent of my grandmother. I was so moved to have found her I wept a little myself. I was no longer alone in the world. Unlikely as it seemed, I'd found my mother's family.

The door opened and Mr Saunders stepped in. He stood silently in the doorway, as Mrs Saunders released me. I felt my heart quicken with anxiety. He would be furious with me for coming here.

'What's this?' Mr Saunders demanded, pushing the door shut behind him with a snap. His wife went to him with tears in her eyes.

'You may not be angry, my dear Bill,' she said. 'For it is as I thought; this really is our grandchild! Emily did not die when she left us!'

Explaining everything in a breathless, emotional voice, she put the letter into his hands. Contrary to my expectations he examined it, noting the date, the address, and reading the first lines. Meanwhile, Mrs Saunders questioned me eagerly about my mother: how she lived, what she was like, when she died.

'Do you see?' Mrs Saunders asked at last, turning back to her husband. 'Do you see from the letter that she was planning to run away, not to take her life?'

'This is not proof,' growled Mr Saunders. 'Anyone could have got hold of this letter. It proves nothing! Except that Emily was still in love with . . .'

Mrs Saunders came to me and took my face gently between her hands, turning it to her husband. '*This* is all the proof I'll ever need!' she exclaimed, interrupting him. 'Just *look* at the dear girl! Isn't this the image of our own Emily?'

'Girl?' asked Mr Saunders bewildered.

Mrs Saunders laughed shakily and rolled her eyes. 'Oh, you men never see further than your noses. This is Charlie! Is it your real name, my dear? Is it short for Charlotte?'

I nodded dumbly.

The kettle was boiling on the fire by now and Mrs Saunders hurried to make a pot of tea, which she set upon the table with cups. 'Sit down, Charlotte,' she said to me. 'You must tell us who your father was. This is all so extraordinary! You have brought joy into my old age!'

Mr Saunders looked less delighted as I slid into a seat and accepted a cup of tea. He still stared at me suspiciously, his lower lip jutting out. 'Forgive me if I'm cautious,' he said at last. 'I'm slow to accept new ideas.' He looked at the letter again and at his wife. 'She wrote to *him!*' he said to her. 'Look; it's addressed "Dear Andrew". Did you have any knowledge of this?'

'No, not until I saw this letter,' Mrs Saunders replied.

Mr Saunders turned back to me. 'Your father was Andrew Lawrence?' he asked with a frown.

'No!' I exclaimed, taken aback. 'My father was Andrew Smith. He wasn't a grand gentleman at all!'

'Smith?' Mr Saunders asked dubiously. I nodded.

Both husband and wife looked at me. 'Emily didn't know a Mr Smith,' said Mr Saunders.

'Perhaps she met him later. Bill, do not lose sight of the fact that this is our *grandchild*! That our Emily did not die when she left us! Can you not take pleasure in that? It seems to me to matter very little whom the child's father was. Only that she found love and happiness again.' Mrs Saunders wiped a tear from her eye.

I looked at Mr Saunders' doubting face and made a helpless gesture. 'I quite understand that you won't take me on trust!' I said. 'And the truth be told, I am puzzled over my parentage myself. There are . . . many things I don't understand. For example . . . ' I hesitated, unsure how much to tell them. I was sure I could trust them with *my* identity, but what of the mysterious ring that might incriminate my father in a crime? And what of his murder?

'Gate!' came a cry from outside.

I jumped to my feet, startled. It was Mr Lawrence's voice.

'Please!' I begged Mr and Mrs Saunders. 'Do not tell him, or anyone yet, of what we suspect! There are reasons why . . . '

Mr Saunders looked suspicious again at once, but Mrs Saunders embraced me. 'Of course! You wish to keep your place here. But come again as soon as you can, Charlie. Bring the other letters and we'll puzzle it out between us.'

'I will,' I promised.

Mr Saunders stepped outside. 'I see you have Sorrel and the gig here,' I heard Lawrence say to him. 'Do you also have my errant stable boy? Miss Lawrence has been waiting these several hours for her new gown and hat and gave me no peace until I came to look for them.'

I took a deep breath and stepped outside too. 'I'm sorry, sir!' I apologized to Mr Lawrence. 'I felt a trifle faint in the heat and Mrs Saunders kindly offered me a cup of tea.'

Mr Lawrence looked at me closely. 'You look very pale, Charlie. Let me drive you home. We can tether Storm behind the gig.'

He dismounted at once and led Storm to the gig. I felt guilty for lying to him and putting him to so much trouble. I climbed meekly into the gig beside him and sat quietly as he drove me back down to the house.

Out of sight of the lodge, Lawrence cast another searching look at me. 'You look as though you have been crying again rather than ill, Charlie,' he remarked, once again showing uncomfortable acuteness. 'I've asked this before; is there anything I should know about?'

I shook my head. 'I'm perfectly recovered now, I thank you,' I said. 'I'm really sorry to have put you to trouble on my account.'

'A mysterious tearfulness that has now communicated itself to Mrs Saunders,' mused Lawrence with yet

172

another glance at me. I could feel the colour rising in my cheeks. 'What is the mystery, Charlie? What are you hiding from me?'

'Nothing,' I assured him, feeling guilty about the lie.

'And yet Mrs Saunders has scarcely been able to take her eyes off you since the day you arrived here, has she?'

I caught my breath. Mr Lawrence noticed so much more than one imagined. 'I remind her of . . . someone she once knew. That is all,' I told him. Mr Lawrence frowned, irritated by my reserve.

'Very well, we'll leave it at that for now,' he said. 'Meanwhile, I would like to leave for London the day after tomorrow to attend an auction. Will you be well enough to accompany me?'

'The day after tomorrow?' I asked, biting my lip, thinking of my promise to Mrs Saunders.

'If that doesn't interfere with your many social engagements, of course,' remarked Mr Lawrence with heavy irony.

I flushed. 'No, of course not,' I replied.

Ben poked his head into the tack room the following evening as I was soaping a saddle. Bridges was on the other side of the room checking over the carriage harness.

'Message from Mr Lawrence,' Ben told me. 'He'll be leaving for London in the morning and you're to go with him, Charlie. We're to harness Mustard and Cress to the travelling chaise for the first stage. They'll be sent back from there and you'll hire horses the rest of the way.'

'Thanks, Ben,' I said.

'Oh, and Susan's looking for you. Shall I send her in?'

'No, please do not!' I cried in alarm. Ben disappeared and I could hear him snorting with laughter. Susan walked into the tack room a moment later. She'd washed her face and tied a ribbon in her mousey hair. She hesitated when she saw Bridges but, surprisingly, he smiled at her. 'Don't mind me!' he said.

'Charlie!' Susan said, turning to me with a coquettish smile. 'I never seem to see you these days.'

'I've been busy,' I replied, thinking ruefully of the many times I'd concealed myself recently to avoid her.

'I've got an hour free later. Would you like to walk out with me? When you've finished your work, of course.'

'I'm sorry, I have to finish cleaning this tack and then groom Mustard and Cress ready for tomorrow,' I said.

'That's all right, lad,' said Bridges mischievously. 'Ben can do that. We can spare you for half an hour.'

I sent him a look of heartfelt reproach and he turned a sudden snort of laughter into a cough. It seemed the entire stable staff wanted to set me up with Susan.

'I really can't leave it to Ben,' I said to Susan, feigning regret. 'Mr Lawrence's orders. Why don't you ask Ben, Peter, or Joe to walk with you?'

Susan pouted, hurt that I should suggest someone else. 'Certainly not,' she said. 'I shall watch you work and we can talk instead.'

As good as her word, she hung on the door of Mustard's stall while I brushed him down and checked his hooves. 'How strong you must be to make such a great horse pick up his foot,' Susan sighed admiringly.

'Not at all,' I assured her truthfully. 'I daresay I'm not much stronger than you!'

'Oh, you are!' Susan breathed.

'It's all in the technique. Look: I lean on him until he shifts his weight onto the other foot. And then it's easy enough to pick up.' I demonstrated, cleaning out the mud from Mustard's hoof while it was lifted.

'Charlie,' she asked as I worked. 'If you're busy today, will you walk out with me this Sunday instead?'

I bit my lip. 'I can't. I'm sorry, but I'm going away with Mr Lawrence tomorrow for a week.'

Susan's face fell ludicrously. 'Oh! Must you go?'

'Yes, indeed I must. I am his groom, you know.'

She nodded sadly. 'I shall miss you.' Her voice dropped to a whisper: 'You can kiss me if you like. There's no one looking.'

I edged further back into the stable and put Mustard's bulk between us.

'No, I can't. Really, Susan, I . . .'

'Come now, Susan, do you not have work to do?' Mr Lawrence's voice made Susan jump out of her skin. She blushed scarlet and fled. I drew a sigh of relief.

Lawrence frowned at me. 'You need to keep that damsel at a distance, Charlie,' he said. There was irritation in his voice.

'Indeed, I wish you might tell me how to do so!' I exclaimed.

Lawrence's brow cleared and he laughed. He shook his head at me. 'A personal groom is supposed to be almost as discreet as a butler, you know,' he said. 'Yet you brawl and flirt at every opportunity. My fault, I suppose for employing you so young.'

'You misunderstand me, sir,' I said, a little hurt, but I didn't argue any further.

'You got my message about tomorrow?' Lawrence asked. When I told him I had, he nodded. 'Good. Meanwhile, saddle Storm for me, will you? I find I'm obliged to ride across to West Farm to collect his lordship's new dog. He should have had him a week or so ago, but was in the gout again and couldn't face it. I must fetch the creature before we leave for London.'

I left Mustard with a pat and a word of affection and went to lead Storm out of his box. He'd managed to lie down in his own droppings after he was groomed this morning, so I was obliged to sponge him down and brush him off swiftly before tacking him up. Lawrence stood and exchanged conversation with Bridges meanwhile, and I was pleased to see them both smiling. That meant there were no complaints about me.

When Storm was ready and I led him across, Lawrence said, 'Bridges tells me Belle has not been out for a couple of days. Saddle her too, Charlie, and you may accompany me.'

Flushing with delight, I handed Storm's reins to Mr Lawrence and rushed to do his bidding. I'd never ridden Belle, though I'd longed to do so. I petted her as I brushed her quickly down and lifted a saddle onto her back.

Belle went like a dream for me. I'd ridden several fine horses since I'd been at Deerhurst. As Lawrence liked to say, it was the greatest perk of the job. But Belle was better than any of them: smooth-paced, responsive, and so light on her feet.

'You look as though you're enjoying her,' called Lawrence with a smile as we pulled up from a canter across a meadow.

'Oh, yes!' I exclaimed enthusiastically, bending forward to clap her burnished neck and praise her. 'She's the finest horse I've ever ridden!'

'I thought you would like to say farewell to her,' said Lawrence. 'Just for the week!' he added hastily, as I turned an alarmed face towards him. 'There's nothing sinister in store for her, I swear! Bridges has promised to ride out with Miss Judith and keep a close eye on her while we're away. Besides, Judith will be away herself for several days at a house party.'

Returning from West Farm with the puppy on Lawrence's pommel, we passed a herd of cows being taken in for milking. Belle grew out-of-reason nervous and became hard to control. When a dog appeared at her heels out of nowhere and barked, she shied, then bolted.

I clung on to Belle's mane and lay low over her neck. She was in full flight, mane and tail high, with the bit between her teeth. She had torn across a field and crashed through a hedge before I was able to gain some measure of control. I circled her and she slowed up, sweating. I kept speaking to her soothingly and gradually she came to a trembling, snorting stop. I praised her and encouraged her to turn, and walk gently back. Once I was sure she was not going to snatch the bit again, I patted her.

'Brave Belle,' I told her. 'There was no need for that panic, my beauty. It was just a sheepdog.'

Storm and Mr Lawrence came thundering up to me.

'Are you hurt, Charlie?' asked Lawrence. There was real concern in his voice.

'I'm fine,' I said calmly. 'It's Belle that's spooked. She would never have behaved like this a few months ago.'

'I know. What does Judith do to upset her so?'

'I'm not absolutely sure. I know she uses her whip far too freely. She rides recklessly and has dreadful hands; I've frequently seen her job Belle in the mouth both by accident and in temper.'

Lawrence nodded. 'I've seen all that and more. Perhaps she treats her even worse when we're not by. I've known her tease her grandfather's dogs most cruelly at times. Come, let's get this poor fellow home.' He indicated the puppy that he now cradled in one arm. The tiny thing wagged his tail and wriggled, trying to lick Lawrence's hand. 'I fear he got a little crushed when we followed you!'

We rode home steadily, giving Belle an opportunity to calm down, but she was still damp with sweat when we rode into the yard. To my consternation, both Lord Rutherford and Miss Judith awaited us there.

'I told you, grandpapa!' Judith piped up, as the horses' hooves clattered over the cobbles. 'That groom's been stealing my horse again! He's always sneaking off with her. He can't ride properly and he's ruining her!'

'What's this, Lawrence?' asked Lord Rutherford gruffly as we pulled up beside them. I slid down from the saddle directly, but Lawrence remained seated.

'I asked the boy to accompany me,' he said calmly, stroking the puppy wriggling in his arms to soothe it. 'Belle had not been exercised for several days and Judith was otherwise occupied.'

'How dare you take my Belle-belle?' demanded Miss Judith furiously, snatching the reins from me so that Belle startled and threw up her head. 'You've galloped her into a sweat too! Grandpapa, it's too bad! The boy should be dismissed!'

Lord Rutherford cleared his throat. 'John, did you indeed give the boy permission to ride the horse?'

'I did, my lord. I thought she needed exercise. I'm sorry if you consider I did wrong.'

Miss Judith was feeding Belle sugar and cooing at her. Belle was accepting it, but warily. She looked poised to dodge out of the way at any moment, her ears laid back. 'Look what he's done to her! Galloped her into a lather and frightened her!' said Miss Judith.

'I hold you responsible for this, John,' said his lordship sternly. 'You're not to take Judith's horse without permission again.'

'Ever!' added Miss Judith fiercely, sending him a look of dislike.

'Yes, my lord,' Lawrence replied.

I thought how dignified he was, sitting calmly and accepting the unfair reproaches without embarrassment and managing to hold on to a restless puppy at the same time. As for myself, I was flushed and shaking, feeling slandered but fearing I might lose my position if I defended myself. I kept my eyes on the ground, and tried to make myself as small and insignificant as possible.

'Won't you dismiss the dirty, arrogant boy, grandpapa?' Miss Judith coaxed. From the corner of her eyes she darted me a look of hatred. I felt sick with fear.

'Not today, Judith, m'dear. But he's on a warning. Do you hear that, boy?'

'Yes, my lord,' I mumbled.

'Bring the dog to the house, would you, Lawrence?' added Lord Rutherford.

He turned to leave. Miss Judith followed him, her concern for her horse seemed to have disappeared and Belle was handed casually to Bridges without so much as a pat. As soon as the two had left, Bridges handed me Belle's reins again. 'Rub this horse down, will you, Charlie?' he said with a wink.

Lawrence dismounted quietly and with a brief, 'See you at six tomorrow morning, Charlie,' he left, handing Storm over to Bridges.

We worked in silence, Bridges very properly not deigning to discuss the incident with someone as junior as I. Lovingly, I rubbed Belle down, until her bay hide gleamed in the evening sun. I was dreading parting from her the following day. We were the last in the yard when I finally led Belle to her box. I stood for a few moments, stroking her in peace and quiet before following the others in for dinner.

CHAPTER TWENTY-TWO

The roads, as we set out for London, were quiet so early in the morning. The day was deliciously cool with a promise of hot sun later. We passed cows returning from milking, sheep being driven to market, a carrier's cart loaded high with goods, and a lumbering wagon. Once we'd reached the main road from Bath to London, we saw trains of packhorses heading for the capital loaded with wool, but none were Martha's horses.

Lawrence drove in silence for the first couple of hours. He was rarely talkative early in the morning, which suited me well. At Chippenham, we stopped for some refreshment and Lawrence arranged for the return of Mustard and Cress to Deerhurst. He mounted the box seat again with hired horses harnessed to the chaise. I stood watching the ostlers rushing about and smiled to myself. I was very glad that particular job had been such a short episode in my career.

As the new horses stepped smartly out of the yard, I swung myself up onto my perch on the chaise as it passed me, in what was now a practised manner. 'Climb over and sit beside me, Charlie. I get a crick in my neck talking to you when you're standing behind me,' Lawrence requested as we drove out of the town.

'Will it not look odd?' I asked dubiously.

'Not if you are driving. Besides, I don't have a great position to maintain, nor do I care as much for appearances as my titled relative.'

'He might wish you to care, as we are sporting his crest and his livery,' I remarked. Lawrence shrugged and gave me a quick grin over his shoulder.

I submitted, scrambling over the back of the seat, taking care not to get my dirty shoes on it. Lawrence handed over the reins and I drove the horses along the main London road. At first I was silent, for the horses were hard-mouthed and difficult to drive and the narrow road was busy. It took all my concentration. We passed a pike and Lawrence paid the toll.

'Mistress Martha used to go round that one,' I said with a grin, indicating the toll-gate. 'There's a path over the hill.'

'All the packhorse trains do so where they can,' acknowledged Lawrence. 'In a chaise, we have no choice but to pay.'

'What did you wish to speak about?' I asked Lawrence as we left the gate at a trot. He was sitting with a relaxed attitude, one arm thrown back across the seat behind me, watching me handle the reins.

'Firstly, I wished to mention that you drive a pair very competently now.'

'Thank you.'

'And secondly . . . Oh, nothing in particular. This will be a long journey and I wish to be entertained. Tell me about America!'

I must have looked surprised, for he chuckled. 'I've

never been out of England,' he said. 'It must be very different to here.'

'You wouldn't believe how different,' I agreed. 'It's a vast, wild country. And there are huge areas with no people at all, only endless forests or, further north, grassland. It's hard to imagine riding for four or even five days and seeing no sign of civilization at all, not even a house or a ploughed field.'

'Not even natives?'

'Yes, sometimes. Often we saw tracks or the remains of a fire.'

'And were you never afraid?'

'I was rarely alone. I was travelling with the regiment, you see, and all the wives and other followers. But it *was* dangerous at times, which is why my parents used to dress me . . .'

I stopped in confusion, realizing how I'd been about to give myself away. There was an awkward silence.

'Yes . . . ?' Lawrence prompted me. There was a sudden frown on his face.

' . . . in shabby clothes, so I didn't look as though I were worth robbing,' I finished lamely. I searched my mind for a change of topic, desperate to draw him off. 'So . . . so, did you never consider going into the army?'

'Oh, yes, occasionally!' said Lawrence, apparently successfully distracted. 'Isn't every boy tempted by that dandy red uniform? But my father, as I told you, was a navy man, so mainly I dreamed of a blue coat, not a red one.'

'What changed?' I asked curiously.

'My dear boy, do you have *any* idea what commissions in the army or navy cost? I imagine you must, since your father served. Quite literally a small fortune.'

'Yes, indeed. They are beyond the pockets of all but the wealthiest,' I agreed. 'It's a scandal, seeing raw rich-boy officers coming in and taking control of experienced troops. Then getting them killed as often as not.'

'But was your father not an officer?' asked Lawrence with a faint smile.

'He was a major. But by promotion, not purchase. He worked and fought hard for his rank.'

Lawrence nodded and sent me another of those sideways looks. 'Tell me some more about him,' he invited.

'Oh, there's nothing much to tell. He was a good man,' I said uncomfortably. Lawrence asked about my family too often for my liking. Instead, I began describing the scenery in the Americas, or at least what I had seen of it, while remaining vague about where I had been.

'I see I missed a great deal in relinquishing my child-hood dream,' Lawrence said after many questions. 'But I love the work I do on the estate.'

'Yes, you are fortunate. What will happen when Lord Rutherford dies? Will you still have the position? I have heard that Miss Judith's father is dead. So who is heir to the Deerhurst estate?'

Lawrence's mouth closed in a tight line and he frowned out over the backs of the horses. They pulled us steadily along a gravel road as it wound its way up a hill.

'Does Lord Rutherford have other children? Who is next in line?' I persisted.

Lawrence was silent for so long I thought he wasn't going to reply. Finally he said, 'You haven't heard the gossip then? In the stables or the kitchen?'

'No, I've heard nothing,' I replied.

'I suppose you associate mainly with the younger servants and it was before their time.' He took a deep breath. 'There was another son. An elder son, in fact. *He* was the heir, not Judith's father who was the second son.'

'But he died too? How sad.'

'Not exactly. I'm not supposed to speak of this. Lord Rutherford has forbidden all mention of it; of him.'

'Really?' I asked. 'He's forbidden mention of his own son?' I recalled my own parents' love for my brother and me. I was certain nothing we could have done would have induced them to ban all mention of us.

'There was a disagreement,' Mr Lawrence told me. 'The son wished to marry some quite inferior woman on the estate; one of Rutherford's tenants. Lord Rutherford refused to countenance such a union.'

I gasped. Lawrence noticed but misconstrued the reason. 'It may seem strange to you,' he explained. 'But this was more than twenty years ago. Marriage was, still is, a way of increasing land or wealth, of achieving alliances. For the heir especially, a good marriage is of the utmost importance. If he had chosen to marry a girl with no dowry, it would have been considered bad enough. But a farm girl was not even of his class; it would have meant social disgrace. Lord Rutherford would not allow it.'

I was silent, frozen with shock at his words. I could feel my hands turn ice cold and numb on the reins as

Lawrence's words sank into my brain. I remembered Mr Saunders' words after he had read my mother's letter . . . *Emily was still in love with* . . . He had mentioned an Andrew Lawrence. The inferior woman Lawrence was talking about . . . That must surely have been my mother? My brain seethed with possibilities. When I tried to speak, my voice didn't sound like my own: 'So he didn't marry her?' I asked faintly.

'He did not. But Lord Rutherford had no joy from his victory. His son disappeared. He's thought to have run away, but no one's ever seen or heard a trace of him since. For all we know he could be dead.'

My heart was beating so quickly I could scarcely breathe. Sensing my inattention, the horses dropped to a walk. I forced myself to concentrate and urged them into a trot again.

'And the young woman?' I asked. 'What became of her?'

'I believe she is generally thought to have taken her own life. It all happened long before I came to Deerhurst.'

I swallowed hard. 'Mr and Mrs Saunders' daughter,' I said faintly. 'It was her, wasn't it?'

'Ah, so you have heard the story? Yes, she was their daughter. They never recovered from the sorrow of losing her.'

'It's so sad,' I whispered. Was this my mother's tale? She was forbidden to marry the man she loved and it broke her heart. But she had not died. I knew she'd loved my father with all her heart and soul; I'd witnessed their affection for each other every day of my childhood.

But my father couldn't have been a Lawrence. No, surely not. His name was Smith. Had my mother recovered and found love again? But the ring . . .

The puzzle had many more pieces now, but they still would not fit together for me. Why had my parents kept such secrets from me? It was all so confusing.

'A very sad story indeed,' said Lawrence beside me. He was looking into the distance, the frown still on his face. 'Lord Rutherford still grieves for his son, although he will not show it. He is too proud. He threw himself into rebuilding his house and landscaping his park to distract himself. But still,' he sighed, 'I do not believe he has learned from it.'

'He will not let Miss Judith marry as she chooses, you mean?' I asked. I bit my lip at once, realizing that I should not betray my understanding of the family in this way. It was none of my business.

'I apologize,' said Mr Lawrence a little stiffly. 'I've been indiscreet. I ought not to speak of the family to you in this way.'

'I won't say a word, I swear,' I promised him. I slowed the horses as a wagon approached. The road was narrow and it would be tricky to pass.

Lawrence watched in silence while I negotiated the manoeuvre successfully. When we had passed it and the horses were trotting again, I asked: 'But Mr Lawrence . . . to come back to my original question. If the eldest son is dead, who inherits the estate?'

There was a long pause before Lawrence replied. A shadow passed across his face. 'Unless the son is found, I do,' said Lawrence.

CHAPTER TWENTY-THREE

My thoughts and conjectures following the conversation with Lawrence occupied me for many days. No matter how much I puzzled over the story, I could not make sense of it. I needed to see Mrs Saunders again and I wanted to read my parents' letters more carefully, but I had left them behind at Deerhurst.

Other than this, the long journey to London passed very pleasantly. Lawrence treated me more like a friend than a servant. I sat beside him in the chaise most of the way, driving or being driven. We ate our meals together in the taprooms of the inns in the evenings. We talked a great deal and I often needed to guard my tongue, so as not to be drawn into betraying myself. Only at night was our accommodation quite separate. Lawrence took a room in the inn. I had been allocated shared rooms with other male servants, but I chose to sleep in the chaise, wrapped in my father's cloak.

As Lawrence drove the horses into the inn yard in London and reined them in, I recognized it as the Castle and Falcon, where Martha stayed with her packhorse train. On one wall I saw that the wanted notice with my face on it, which I had once removed, had been replaced. The new one was larger and hung there for all to see, but had faded and curled at the edges. I shivered a little. If I needed a reminder that I should not have come to London, there it was.

I looked around me and for a moment forgot the notice. To my delight, I spotted Magpie being unloaded by Jason. Unbuckling the pack from Sparrow was Martha herself. Quite forgetting my duties, I leapt down from the chaise the moment it stopped and ran to Martha.

'Martha!' I cried. 'Oh, Martha, it's so good to see you!'

She turned and stared at me blankly for a moment, her weathered face registering no recognition of this clean, well-fed boy in fine livery and a wig.

'It's me! Charlie!' I cried excitedly.

Her face cracked into a grin and she pulled me into a hug. 'I've been that worried about you!' she said. 'I went looking for you at the John of Gaunt and they would tell me no more than that they'd let you go. But I can see you've done well for yourself. Just look at you!'

She stood back to admire my livery and my grey wig with a broad smile. 'That'll be Lord Rutherford's colours you're wearing? However did you get yourself a place there?'

Her words recalled me to a sense of my duties, and with a hasty 'I'll hope to see you later,' I hurried back to Lawrence who had stepped down from the chaise and was watching me. The ostlers had already unhitched his horses and led them away.

'I'm so sorry, sir,' I said contritely. 'I worked for Martha before I went to the John of Gaunt.'

'Yes, I remember. I have some acquaintance with Mistress Martha.'

To my surprise, Lawrence invited Martha and Jason to join us at our table in the coffee room of the inn for the evening meal. Lawrence asked Martha about life on the packhorse trains over stew and potatoes and a large jug of ale. He was relaxed and friendly with her, despite the fact that he was dressed in fine wools and soft linen while she wore a muddied woollen gown with a far-from-clean neckerchief, her red short-cloak thrown over the bench beside her.

Jason was yawning and rubbing his eyes so, the moment he had finished his food, Martha packed him off to bed. While Lawrence was ordering another jug of ale, she took the opportunity to lean over and whisper in my ear: 'Where do you sleep? Not with the grooms? And not in *his* room, I hope?' She nodded towards Lawrence.

'No, in the chaise,' I whispered back.

She shook her head and pursed her lips disapprovingly. 'You come and share my room tonight,' she whispered, then turned with a ready word and smile for Lawrence who had finished speaking to the waiter.

I accompanied Martha up the stairs to her room when we all turned in for the night. Jason was sleeping in the stables, so it was just the two of us.

'He seems a good master,' she said. 'Asked questions about you when you went out to the latrine, he did. He don't suspect you're a girl?'

'Not as far as I know,' I replied. 'Did it seem to you as though he might?'

Martha shook her head. 'No, but he gave little enough away. So what's it like living in such a fine household?'

'I'm very happy there. The hours are long, but the work isn't strenuous. Nothing like the John of Gaunt! I've been treated well.'

'Lawrence is a good man. I've heard nothing but praise of him. But the old lord is another matter. Plenty of talk about *him*. Didn't he drive his own son away?' asked Martha.

'Something like that,' I agreed. 'And he's very bad tempered when he's in the gout, I'm told.'

'Oh, good Lord, child, they all are!' Martha exclaimed. 'I've heard that granddaughter's a wild piece and all.'

I nodded. 'Cruel to her horse, too.'

'You can tell a lot about a person from the way they treats their animals,' replied Martha. She pulled the shutters closed and climbed into bed, lying down heavily beside me with a sigh. I pulled off my wig and laid it carefully on the chest.

'Eh, they've shaved your hair right off!' exclaimed Martha.

'Oh, it's grown a good deal already!' I assured her, rubbing my head. 'Martha, what did Mr Lawrence ask about me?'

'This and that,' Martha rolled over to look at me in the gloom. 'You're not in love with him, are you?'

I didn't answer and was glad the semi-darkness hid my burning cheeks. Martha groaned. 'There's no future in that but heart-break, child,' she said shrewdly. 'He may be a steward but he's gentleman born; he'll not marry such as you. The old lord is as stiff-necked as they come. He'd never allow it in a thousand years! Lawrence is his family.'

'I know that, Martha,' I said softly. 'I knew it even before he told me how close he stands to the inheritance.

I'm not stupid.' I thought of my mother. She too had loved a man who was forbidden to her.

'All girls in love are stupid,' Martha said roundly. 'You're no different! You keep your sex quiet or there's no saying what might befall you. There's no trusting the gentry! He'll get you with child and then pack you off without a penny. You and me are barely human to such as he!'

'Did he really seem so depraved to you?' I asked, my face burning.

'Take it from me, Charlie: in your situation, you can't be too careful,' warned Martha.

'You're right, of course,' I agreed, hoping very much that she was wrong. I changed the subject, preferring to keep my feelings to myself. 'But in fact, Martha, the real danger to me at Deerhurst is a kitchen maid.'

I told Martha about Susan and she roared with laughter. 'Promise me one thing, Charlie,' she said before we fell asleep. 'If you're ever in any trouble, and I don't just mean the family way, any trouble at all, you'll come straight to me. Don't you hesitate! I'm not farther away than you can walk in a day. You come to Martha and I'll help you out if I can. You understand?'

'Thank you, Martha,' I said gratefully. 'You have the kindest heart.' There was danger pressing in on me from all sides; my virtue was the least of my troubles. But it was good to know I had a friend.

'Bless you, child. I know more of poverty and hardship than I care to remember,' said Martha. 'And I hope more than you will ever experience. Sleep now; it's an early start in the morning.'

CHAPTER TWENTY-FOUR

I rose quietly before dawn the next morning and crept down to the yard to remove the poster once more. But when I got there, it was gone. The coincidence was uncanny and sent a chill of fear down my spine. Had someone recognized me? Perhaps it was chance and someone had happened to remove it. I tried to shake off an intense feeling of unease and went softly back to bed for an hour.

The auction yard was busy, even though we arrived early. I'd spent two days hanging around the stables of the Castle and Falcon while Lawrence conducted business in the city. He hadn't invited me to join him and I didn't ask what he'd been doing. Whatever it was, it had put a frown on his face and made him thoughtful and distracted.

On the day of the auction, Lawrence seemed to have thrown off whatever was troubling him and was cheerful once more. People looked over the horses, checked their teeth and hooves, and watched as they were trotted out to show their paces. I stayed close to Lawrence and resisted the urge to clutch his sleeve as we walked through the bustling crowd. I was dressed in my own breeches, shirt and waistcoat, as Lawrence didn't want us to be known to everyone by my livery. 'The price might go up,' he'd said with a grin.

I knew he was here to look at a specific team that he'd heard were for sale. But the matching chestnuts, when we inspected them, disappointed us both. 'Showy rather than sound, I'd say,' said Lawrence quietly in my ear. 'What do you think, Charlie?'

I ran my hand over one horse's leg and paused over a small lump on the pastern. The horse flinched very slightly. 'There might be a problem here,' I said, straightening up. 'Or it may be nothing.'

'I'll swear that one has a touch of laminitis forming, too,' said Lawrence with a frown. We stepped back to observe the horses at a distance again.

'They look good together, I have to admit,' said Lawrence. 'Finely matched. But I think two are a trifle short in the back. I'm not convinced they're a good buy.' He sighed. 'It was a long journey for disappointment.'

'There's a great deal of interest in them too,' I pointed out, looking at the crowd milling around. 'Will that not drive the price up?'

'It may. It's always difficult to tell.'

I took the auction list from Lawrence's hand to glance down it. 'There are some match bays,' I said.

Lawrence shook his head. 'No. They're too old. I want to invest in some younger animals.'

'There is a team of greys for sale too,' I said, pointing at the item on the list. 'Should we have a look at those?'

'Greys? I hadn't noticed. Yes, by all means. I didn't know you could read, Charlie. A young man of hidden talents.'

I shrugged. How unusual was it for a stable boy to be able to read? Extremely unusual, I supposed, but not so unusual for the son of an officer.

The greys turned out to be four beautifully matched young horses in fine shape. There was a great deal of praise for them until they were driven out as a team. They went poorly together and were a handful. One kept shying and none responded properly to commands. Several potential buyers turned away, shaking their heads, but Lawrence's eyes gleamed. 'Just what we were looking for, Charlie!' he said quietly so as not to be overheard. 'As far as I can see they are sound and full of potential. But there's plenty of work to be done to get them pulling well as a team!'

The bidding began at two o'clock. The single horses came up first: hacks, hunters, and some carriage horses. We discussed each one as they were brought forward and trotted out for the crowd. I was enjoying myself. I'd never been to a big auction before and everything was new to me: the speed of the bidding, the way the auctioneer called out the lots and took bids, and the noise and excitement of the crowd when buyers fought to outbid one another.

Lawrence bid on a hunter but pulled out when the price rose too high. He succeeded in buying a nice-looking roan gelding for a good price and looked quietly pleased with himself.

'I didn't know you were planning to buy him!' I remarked once the hammer had struck the gavel and the auctioneer had announced: 'Sold to the gentleman in the blue coat!'

'Call it a sudden impulse,' said Lawrence with a smile. 'I've been considering buying myself a horse for a while. I looked him over earlier while you were admiring that temperamental Arab mare. The price was too good to resist.'

The greys were one of the later lots. Lawrence held back for the first rounds, waiting to gauge who was interested in the team. Bidder after bidder dropped out, and finally only Lawrence and one other were left. I could scarcely breathe for excitement, hoping against hope that he would succeed in purchasing the team.

I looked across at the man bidding against us, who wore a drab coat over an embroidered waistcoat. I wondered how high he would think it was worth going. A face in the crowd caught my eye and instantly I became oblivious to everything else. My heart missed a beat and the blood froze in my veins. It was my father's killer and his pale eyes were looking straight at me.

I had no idea whether he'd recognized me, but his eyes were narrowed as he stared appraisingly at me and then flicked over my companion. I couldn't look away; I was transfixed and horrified until the hammer fell. The man turned away and vanished into the crowd. I stood rooted to the spot, scarcely aware that Lawrence was speaking to me.

' . . . to collect the horses and arrange payment. Charlie? Charlie, are you listening to me?'

His hand on my arm brought me back to the present and I looked up at him, dazed and shocked. 'Are you unwell, Charlie? You look as though you have seen a ghost!'

'I do feel unwell. I'm sorry. It's . . . it's all the excitement.'

'Here, why don't you go back to the inn and order yourself a glass of something?' said Lawrence reaching into his pocket and pulling out a shilling. 'I'll join you when I'm done.' He offered me the coin, but I shook my head numbly.

'No, please . . . I'd much rather stay with you.'

Lawrence looked searchingly at me and replied: 'Very well then, if you're sure.'

I stayed as close to him as I decently could as he completed his purchases, producing bills and signing various papers. All the time I kept looking out for the murderer, though I could see no sign of him. I couldn't stop shaking and it was hard to breathe.

Throughout the summer at Deerhurst, I'd thought myself safe. The memories of that dreadful day had faded along with the paralyzing fear. I'd believed my flight and my disguise had been successful; I thought I'd left no trace of myself behind. Now I was secure no longer. Either the murderer had tracked me despite all I had done, or this was the unluckiest mischance imaginable. If only I'd stayed away from London! I was so easy to trace now. If the murderer had seen me with Lawrence, it would be no difficult task to discover his identity. He could bide his time and pounce at any moment. I thought of my papers, still concealed in the stables at Deerhurst Park. Why did he want them so desperately?

Lawrence arranged for the five horses to be taken to the Castle and Falcon and then hired a hackney cab and took me straight back there. We went into the coffee room and he called for a glass of claret for himself and some tea for me.

'Sit down, Charlie,' he ordered me, pushing me into a seat. 'And tell me what the devil is wrong. No more stories of excitement or tiredness. Either you are ill, or something happened.'

I shivered despite the warmth of the day. 'I can't,' I said, my voice low and almost lost in the hubbub of conversation around us. I cast a wary look over the people nearest us. Any one of them could be a spy, working for that fiendish man. 'Not here,' I mumbled. 'I can't talk here.'

When the waiter brought our drinks, Lawrence picked up his wine and sipped it. Then he leaned back in his seat watching me. He looked concerned. 'Wait here a moment,' said Lawrence suddenly putting down his glass and rising to his feet.

'No, please!' I exclaimed grasping his sleeve, forgetting all need for deference and obedience. 'Don't leave me alone!'

Lawrence put his hand comfortingly over mine, looking down at me strangely. After a moment he seemed to come to himself and firmly removed my hand from his sleeve. 'Charlie, don't be foolish. I'm only going as far as the bar to order the horses to be put to as soon as they arrive. I won't even go out of sight. Drink!'

I sat back, ashamed of my outburst and sipped my tea while I watched him speak to the inn servants. When Lawrence joined me again, he explained that we would leave within the hour. He said he hoped to put some twenty miles behind us before we stopped for the night.

I was relieved to hear we were leaving London almost at once.

'Will you ride the new horse, Caspar, for me?' asked Lawrence. 'I'll need to drive the team; they'll be a handful. I can only hope they won't repeat Pitch's shameful display of temper at Hungerford.'

Chatting peaceably, he distracted me from my terrors until the horses were ready. I would have preferred to be in the chaise with him rather than riding beside it, but the murderer could scarcely attack me on the highway in broad daylight.

By the time we pulled up at the Black Boy in Slough, the after-effects of the shock had begun to wear off. I was relieved to hear Lawrence tell the ostlers we would be staying overnight and order a private parlour and a supper for two. 'Bring a bottle of burgundy up,' he added.

An aloof landlord showed us into the parlour, clearly considering it both reprehensible and demeaning that my master wished to dine with his groom. I stood discreetly in the shadows while the meal was placed upon the table. When the wine had been uncorked, Lawrence dismissed the waiters and beckoned me to the table. 'Sit down and get some food in you,' he told me. 'Then we'll talk.'

I could scarcely eat a thing. My stomach was in knots and it was hard to swallow. I sipped very cautiously at the wine. Used only to weak ale, I was afraid it would make me drunk. Even the small amount I took gave me a feeling of recklessness.

'So,' said Lawrence, wiping his mouth on a snowy-white napkin and leaning back in his chair. He poured some more wine into his glass and looked up at me. 'Tell me, what happened at the auction? I presume you accept it is safe to do so here?'

'Yes, thank you,' I said gratefully. But to be certain, I rose, tiptoed to the door, opened it, and peeped into the corridor. It was deserted. My fears were making me look mad.

I sat back down and allowed Lawrence to pour a little more wine into my glass. 'To tell the truth, I do not understand it myself,' I said. I dared not reveal my father had been murdered. If I did, and Lawrence had read that dreadful notice in the yard of the Castle and Falcon, he might realize who I was and guess that I was a girl. He might hand me over to the authorities, or to the magistrate. I was terrified it was the same thing. The whole world seemed to be against me.

I drew a deep breath. 'There is someone after me,' I said, simplifying the tale. 'He tried to kill me once before but I fled. Today, I saw him at the auction.'

'Did he recognize you?'

'I can't be sure. But he was looking straight at me.'

'Then we must assume that he did. Calm down, Charlie. No one can hurt you here.'

I bit my lip, trembling. I was no longer certain I was safe anywhere.

'Why does someone want to kill you, Charlie?' asked Lawrence. 'Did you steal from him? Harm him in any way or otherwise break the law?'

I shook my head vehemently. 'No! I've done nothing wrong!'

'Do you know who it is?'

I shook my head. 'I only know his face, not his name.'

'We should go to the authorities,' said Lawrence with a frown.

'No!' I cried before I could stop myself. I took a breath and calmed myself as Lawrence looked at me, startled. 'No!' I repeated more calmly. 'I can't prove anything. It will make everything worse!'

Lawrence looked at me puzzled and worried. 'Lord Rutherford will not be pleased if he finds he is harbouring a fugitive,' he said.

I shook my head. 'It's nothing like that, sir.'

'Charlie, this is important. You *must* tell me what you know! No secrets now!'

His voice was stern and I quailed. I swallowed hard. 'I swear I don't know why he is trying to kill me,' I said truthfully.

There was a long silence. Lawrence sighed with exasperation. 'I wish you could find it in yourself to trust me, Charlie,' he said. 'I think it would benefit us both.'

'It's not that I don't trust you . . . ' I said in a small voice. But of course that was precisely the problem. I trusted no one.

Lawrence drank the rest of his wine and poured another. He offered me more, but I shook my head. He remained sunk in thought a moment longer, then said unexpectedly, 'Charlie, I cannot possibly let you sleep in the chaise tonight.' A wry smile crossed his face. 'It would be most inconvenient for me to lose my stable boy. I'm going to have a truckle bed set up in my room for you to sleep in. I hope you will agree that this is a sensible safety measure?'

The relief that filled me, knowing I would be safely

behind a locked door tonight, outweighed any concerns about my virtue. Lawrence believed me a boy, after all.

'Thank you,' I said.

Lawrence nodded. 'Very well. And Charlie?'

'Yes?'

'I will not push you to tell me more at this point,' His voice was still stern and entirely devoid of his usual humour. 'But I'm losing patience. Please think seriously about when you will tell me whatever it is you are hiding from me.'

CHAPTER TWENTY-FIVE

I barely slept that night nor the next, which we spent at an inn in Reading. I lay awake, heart beating quickly, my fears crowding in. When I dropped off for a few seconds, the nightmares that haunted me were terrifyingly real.

In the end, afraid of waking Lawrence, I wrapped myself in my sheet and sat up against the wall. I listened to the rise and fall of Lawrence's breathing as he slept on the other side of the room and it filled me with unutterable sadness. He was so kind, so good. He had taken me from the gutter and installed me at Deerhurst in comfort and safety, surrounded by beautiful horses.

And now it was all over. I couldn't remain in Lord Rutherford's service. I was no longer safe there. I needed to disappear without trace; to go to a different part of the country and seek a new life. I shed tears just thinking of leaving. I'd grown to love the place. I adored Belle and worried for her future. I wanted to be there to watch over her. And now this was the end, I could finally admit to myself that I'd fallen in love with Lawrence. I looked at his sleeping form in the semi-darkness of the inn room and longed to go to him; longed to stroke his shoulder, which had escaped the sheet. I wanted to run my fingers through his short hair, now bare of its wig in sleep. But that could never be.

I must seek my fortune elsewhere. I must leave as a boy with no farewell. Lawrence would never even know that I had cared for him. It was the only way. As soon as I reached Deerhurst and retrieved my letters and ring, I would go.

Towards morning on the second night, exhaustion claimed me and I sank into a deep slumber. Lawrence was up before me. I woke as he leaned over me, one hand on my shoulder.

'Charlie,' he said as my eyes opened and looked sleepily into his hazel ones. My heart flipped over. 'What are you doing out of bed?' he asked. 'Why are you sleeping sitting up?'

'Nightmares,' I replied simply. His hand tightened on my shoulder in sympathy. 'You look exhausted,' he said. 'I'm sorry to have woken you, but we must go.'

He stood up and rang the bell for his shaving water. He'd pulled on his linen shirt that reached to mid-thigh, but was otherwise quite naked. I averted my eyes hurriedly, threw off my sheet, and got to my feet.

'Have you been sleeping fully dressed, brat?' demanded Lawrence sitting down and looking at me in the mirror. 'What an urchin you are!'

I gave him a small smile and hurried to pack my few things together so that I would be ready to leave as soon as Mr Lawrence was.

We breakfasted in the coffee room together in silence and then I ran back upstairs to our room to collect our bags and take them out to the chaise. Lawrence's wasn't closed properly and as I picked it up, the things on the top slid out onto the floor. Embarrassed to be handling his personal belongings, I picked up his shaving gear and his clean cravats and shoved them quickly back into the bag. Then I froze, seeing something else had slipped out. It was crumpled and faded, but unmistakable: it was the poster from the yard at the Castle and Falcon. I smoothed it out with trembling fingers, my eyes skimming over the hateful words accusing me of my father's murder; naming me not as his daughter but as his servant. So it was Lawrence who had taken this poster down. Why? Had he recognized me and made the connection? If so, why had he said nothing? Once more I felt danger closing tightly around me. I hesitated, wondering whether to destroy the sheet, but decided it was safer to pretend I hadn't seen it, so I pushed it deep into his bag.

My thoughts during the last stage of our journey were dark and fearful. In my mind, I kept seeing that poster in Mr Lawrence's bag and wondering why he had taken it.

It was almost dusk as we passed through the lodge gates. Mr Saunders respectfully welcomed Lawrence. As we passed by, I smiled at him, but the look he gave me in return was more puzzled than friendly. My heart sank still further. Mrs Saunders might accept we were related, but he apparently did not.

As we descended the long drive through the park at Deerhurst, we passed a herd of deer, grazing in the meadows. The shy, graceful beasts melted swiftly into the trees at our approach. The whole park lay in beautiful, harmonious peace, so different to the dreadful turmoil inside me. Though I was glad to be back, I had to remind myself that it was no longer my home. I needed to tear myself away again as soon as possible.

'Good to see you back, sir,' said Bridges with a welcoming smile as Lawrence drew up the new team in the yard. He ran his eyes over the new horses and admired their points. Wearily, I pulled Caspar up beside the chaise, patted him and slipped down from the saddle. I was stiff, sore, and longing to sleep. But there was work to be done. My livery needed to be changed for working clothes and there were five horses to be unharnessed, groomed, fed, and stabled. Lawrence disappeared, striding off towards the main house, clearly considering me safe now we were home. I wasn't quite so sure, though it was good to be back.

I'd barely finished grooming the new team, with Ben and Steele's help, when Susan came tearing around the corner, petticoats flying, and would have flung herself into my arms had I not forestalled her by picking up a bucket of water that Joe had drawn to sluice down the yard, and clutched it to my body in self-defence.

'Hello, Susan,' I said cautiously, glad that Lawrence was not here to witness this. I backed away slightly towards the stable.

'Oh, Charlie, I missed you so much!' she said, twisting her apron in excitement. 'Will you walk out with me this Sunday?'

'Perhaps,' I said thinking it was only Tuesday today and that by Sunday I would be gone. Susan bounced up and down on her toes and then planted a kiss on my cheek that I couldn't avoid, though I spilled water down my breeches attempting to dodge it.

As soon as my work was done, I went to Belle's box. She hadn't looked out at me since I returned, which was unusual. I leaned over the half-door to see her beautiful glossy bay rump facing me. At first I thought she was eating her hay, but then I realized she was merely standing facing the end wall with her head drooping.

'Belle?' I called quietly, worried by her listlessness. Belle startled as though I had cracked a whip behind her, crashing into the wall and cowering there, trembling.

Seriously alarmed, I unlatched the door and stepped carefully into the loose box with her. 'What's wrong, girl?' I said approaching cautiously. Normally the sound of my voice would bring her eagerly towards me, eyes bright and ears pricked, nosing for a bit of carrot or a pet. Instead, she cringed away from me. Her whole body shook as I approached.

'Charlie,' said Bridges voice behind me. 'I'm sorry. Belle . . . I did my best.'

'What's happened to her?' I asked feeling sick. I looked at Belle's hunched, unhappy shape in the box. I'd left her only a week ago, fit and well. 'Miss Judith was going away! And you promised, you *promised*, you'd watch over Belle the days she was here!'

I glanced at Bridges and thought how old and exhausted he looked, pale with dark shadows under his eyes. His skin looked papery and his movements stiff.

'She didn't go on that visit after all,' said Bridges in a defeated voice. 'A message came that there were measles in the house and she should stay away. She's been out riding every day; galloping that poor creature in the heat, jumping her until she refused.'

'Why didn't you stop her?' I demanded. I moved closer to Belle gradually and reached out to her with great care. At first her skin twitched at my touch, but then she submitted, trembling. I could tell she was poised for flight, every nerve strung out. The slightest sudden movement from me would turn her into a wild animal, fighting to protect herself.

'I tried, Charlie! But she'd have none of it. I was a fusty, stuffy old man who didn't know his place. Going to his lordship for a word had no effect. He said Miss Judith was a slapping rider, game as a pebble, and that she knew better than I what her horses could do.'

Slowly, carefully, with many words of reassurance, I began to stroke Belle and then run my hands over her, checking her. She broke out in a sweat of fear and distress, despite my soothing words and gentle, careful movements. 'Why is she in such a state?' I asked Bridges.

'Miss Judith was jumping her in the woods. She made her jump the stream. It's a bad landing on the far side and a real risk to the horse's legs. Once Belle had had one taste of that, she wouldn't take it again. Refused dead. Miss Judith was too free with the whip and Belle bucked her off right into the stream.'

He paused and shook his head. 'What a figure she looked when she pulled herself out: covered in mud, streaming with water, her riding habit quite ruined. But she was in the devil's own temper. She used that whip on her. I took it off her, but not before she . . . '

As he spoke, Belle turned her head towards me and

the full horror was revealed. All down the fore side of her neck and shoulders were cuts and weals, some oozing fresh blood, consistent with vicious slashes from a whip. Worst of all was the cut across her face. The whip had missed her eye by a whisker, but the swelling had closed the eye, which now leaked tears and mucus that streaked her burnished mahogany hide.

'Oh Belle,' I whispered brokenly. 'You poor girl. What has she done to you?'

'It will heal, Charlie,' said Bridges. 'I've done everything I can to treat it.'

'I'm sure you have. But what then?' I whispered, running my hand soothingly over Belle's uninjured shoulder. 'What will she do to her next?'

I wished that Belle were my own horse and I could take her away from this, so that she need never be subjected to Miss Judith's cruelty again. But I was only a servant without power or means. All I could do was stand by and watch helplessly. I felt little better than a traitor to Belle.

CHAPTER TWENTY-SIX

I had wanted to flee Deerhurst that very night. But I couldn't leave Belle alone, injured, and frightened. Instead, I took my blanket to her loose box as usual so I could dress her hurts again in the night.

'Poor Belle,' I said softly. 'No one should treat such a valiant beauty so badly. You deserve so much better.'

Belle whickered softly to me, the first positive response I'd had from her since I returned from London. I stroked her velvety nose and fought the wave of despair that crashed down on me. What was I to do? How could I flee in order to save my own skin, leaving her here alone to face such cruelty?

I reapplied ointments to Belle's cuts when the stable clock struck midnight. She was less afraid now and I managed to tend her without waking Bridges for help. When I'd finished, I stopped and stroked her and she nuzzled me affectionately as she used to. I leaned against her, breathing in her warm scent of sweet hay. 'You can trust me, Belle,' I promised her in the darkness. 'I'll never hurt you and I won't abandon you either. I don't know yet what I shall do, but I'll think of something.'

After a while Belle seemed to fall into a peaceful doze. I was hot, uncomfortable and had too much on my mind. Questions about my parents and my fear of the murderer gave me no peace. Despite my weariness, I was unable to either lie or sit still. My legs kept jumping and my skin crawled.

Eventually, I slipped quietly out of the stable into the yard. Even here there was little relief to be had. I walked up and down restlessly; it was another hot and sultry night. I sighed with temptation for the cool pool in the gardens. But I knew I was safe here in the locked yard. No one could get in without keys. That would not be the case if I wandered beyond the door. Although the gardens were walled and gated too, they were far less secure than the stable yard. Did I dare? Worry for Belle had driven my own danger from my mind for several hours, but the threat was very real.

I imagined slipping into the cool water, finding relief from the heat and the fears and doubts that tormented me. It was too tempting to resist.

I locked the yard door softly behind me and stepped out into the gardens. The moon was full and the sky clear, making it almost as bright as day on the open lawn. In the corners and under the trees and bushes, long black shadows reached out to me like claws.

I scurried along the paths, staying out of the grasping, creeping shadows as far as I was able. At first, I was convinced I would be pounced on at any moment. But the fear receded as the gardens proved to be tranquil and empty. An owl raised his quavering voice in the distance and another replied mournfully near at hand. They would not do so if violence and death were lurking.

When I reached the pool, it gleamed like black glass

in the bright moonshine. My skin, prickling with heat, thirsted for the coolness of the water. I threw cautious looks around me, but there was no sign of another soul. Sighing with pleasure, I threw off my breeches, boots, and stockings. Tonight I kept my long shirt on, feeling too insecure to be comfortable naked. But underneath the loose shirt, I unravelled the scarf that constrained my breasts and dropped it on the pile of my clothing.

I slid into the pool with barely a ripple, gasping as the cold water caressed my skin. It was wonderful; divinely refreshing after the hot, dusty days spent travelling. I swam some lengths, careful not to splash, then ducked right under, scrubbing at my hair and my face to remove any lingering dust from the road and the big city.

Feeling fresher than I'd felt in days, I paused by the side of the pool, leaning against the cool stone. I was glad I'd come. How stupidly timid it would have been to have fancied it too dangerous.

I'd barely had that thought when I heard a light footfall behind me. I whipped around with a splash feeling utterly exposed, terror filling me. There was a tall, slender figure standing beside the waterfall watching me.

Raw panic is a horrific thing. When you most need to flee, it freezes you, turning your limbs to lead and clamping an iron band around your lungs so you can barely breathe. I just hung there, unable to move, turned to stone for what felt like an eternity. The unknown silhouette stood there staring back. Somehow I unfroze my limbs. With a strangled whimper of terror, I turned and struck out for the far side of the pool, desperate to get as far away from the figure as I could. Vaguely, I thought I heard my name called. But then he knew my name, didn't he, that man who had snatched my father's life away?

There was a splash behind me and strong arms caught hold of me in the middle of the pool, clamping my arms to my side. I went under, struggling frantically against the grip. It was futile. I was dragged through the water to the side of the pool. The grip on me loosened and I gasped, turned away from my captor, and tried to leap out of the water and away.

'Charlie, don't be ridiculous, it's only me,' said a familiar, calm voice. Lawrence's voice. 'So you are the secret night-time bather! Don't be in such a hurry to run off now.' As he spoke, he caught me around the chest and pulled me back down into the water.

Though I realized in that moment that I was probably safe from murder, my relief was tempered by the realization that my secret was now uncovered.

Lawrence released me abruptly. I turned in the water to face him, braving it out, and saw the confusion in his face as he backed off. There was no possibility that the thin fabric of the shirt had disguised my breasts under his hand. A dawning astonishment replaced the confusion of his expression.

'You're not, you're . . . ' he stuttered, his habitual calm deserting him for once.

I stayed quite still, waiting for his reaction, wondering what he would say, what he would think. A part of me was glad that he knew now, whatever the consequences.

'Good God!' Lawrence rubbed a dripping hand over his face. 'I don't know what to say. You're a girl?'

'I am,' I admitted.

'You've deceived me!'

'Would you have employed a girl as a groom?' I asked defensively. 'I didn't set out to deceive you. I didn't even know you. I dressed like this to hide.'

'From the man in London?'

'Yes, from him.' In my mind, I saw again the poster folded and concealed in Lawrence's luggage. How much had he guessed? How much more likely would he be to make the connection between the information on the poster and me now he knew I was a girl?

But instead of questioning me, Lawrence stepped closer and reached out a hand to me. I flinched, trying to dodge him, anxious about what he intended, but he only took my chin and tilted my face this way and that, exposing it to the moonlight.

'I see now,' he said wonderingly. 'It all makes sense. You always looked odd as a boy. But you make a very pretty girl.'

I blushed and tried to turn my face away, but he made me look up at him. The droplets of water on his face and in his short hair were gleaming in the moonlight like miniature diamonds. He looked far younger without his wig, just as he had done in his sleep. Just a youth, when all was said and done.

'How did you dare?' asked Lawrence at last, releasing me. He stood beside me, his loose shirt floating about him in the water as mine was. 'How have you managed the work? How have you coped being surrounded by men and boys?'

'It's tricky,' I admitted. 'Keeping such a secret; finding opportunities to wash. And the work at the inn was too hard for me. That was partly why they dismissed me. But not here. I could manage it all here.'

'And Mistress Martha, did she know?' he asked wonderingly.

'Oh, yes. She knew from the first, though she did not tell me so until later. In fact, she cut my hair short for me.'

'Good God, and I made you have your head shaved! Did you hate me?'

'No!' I laughed shakily, some of the tension going out of me. I'd feared anger, recriminations; I wasn't quite sure what, perhaps even instant recognition and to be hauled before a constable. But it seemed Lawrence was still my friend. 'My hair will grow again,' I said with a shrug. 'It already has. Although I admit I was unhappy to lose it at the time! You won't . . . tell anyone, will you? That I'm a girl, I mean.'

'I'll keep your secret,' said Lawrence. 'So this has been the mystery? The reason you haven't trusted me?'

I nodded, relieved that he felt this explained everything.

Lawrence reached out and ran his hand over my short hair. His hand felt warm against my scalp and I caught my breath. His closeness made it difficult for me to breathe. My heart was pounding in my chest, making the blood pulse in my veins. His touch was light, almost caressing.

'I still cannot believe it,' he said. 'Somehow my mind won't quite take it in.'

'It's not so strange to me,' I said shakily. 'My parents often dressed me as a boy and pretended they had two sons. It was safer. I nearly let that piece of information slip out, do you remember? On the way to London.'

'I do. How did I not guess then?'

'The baggage train of the army is no fit place for a grown girl, my father used to say,' I told him, relieved by how calmly he was taking the revelation. My own courage was rising once more. 'And yet my parents could not bear to part so that my mother, brother and I could live somewhere settled. Not even for a few months.'

'They loved each other so much?'

'They did. When my mother died, my father was a broken man. He never recovered.'

'I'm sorry.' He paused, looking at me closely again. 'No wonder you concealed your age. Did I guess it correctly? You're fifteen?'

'I've turned sixteen now. It was my birthday in June.'

'Sixteen! I suppose you had to lie about that to explain the lack of a beard!' He laughed, pinching my chin, but then stopped abruptly as another thought struck him: 'And your name? Of course, it isn't Charlie?' He sounded sad, but I smiled.

'Indeed it is,' I said. 'It's short for Charlotte.'

An answering smile lit his face. 'That's something. Charlotte . . . This explains many things that were puzzling me: your need for privacy, your difference to the other boys, your tendency to blush and to cry . . . my . . . my strange attraction to you that I couldn't explain to myself.'

My heart began to thud painfully again. He'd found me attractive? Even grubby and scruffy as I'd been? I could feel myself flushing, whether with awkwardness or excitement I couldn't tell. I was glad of the moonlight that bleached all colours from the world, leaving only shining shades of silver and grey.

We both looked away, shyness overcoming us at the unexpected intimacy of the situation. I was painfully aware of my nakedness under my long shirt. The impropriety of being alone with Lawrence in this secluded place in the middle of the night struck me. Martha's words of warning rang in my ears. But at the same time, I was close to the man I loved. I'd always thought it was a hopeless love, doomed to remain forever undeclared. But now here he was, in the water with me in the middle of the night, speaking of attraction.

'I made you share my bedchamber,' said Mr Lawrence abruptly. 'No wonder you slept in your clothes! It puzzled me. Good grief, I hope I didn't embarrass you by undressing . . .'

'I didn't look!' I told him hurriedly and we laughed awkwardly.

He stared at me some more and shook his head. 'How brave you've been to deal with so much. I'm all admiration.'

'Now you're teasing me,' I said, flushing again.

'Not at all. But you were always brawling. Did you not get hurt? Why would a girl fight?'

'I never did!' I assured him, a laugh escaping me. 'Each time it was either an accident or I was attacked and came off worst. You assumed I'd been fighting and I let you.' I laughed again. 'You had such a disapproving face every time I had new bruises!'

'And Susan?'

'Oh, Susan,' I said more soberly. 'I haven't known what to do about her. She would be so mortified if she knew!'

'I felt cross and jealous every time I saw you flirting with her!' exclaimed Lawrence. 'I couldn't understand myself!'

'You did?' I asked shyly, my eyes falling before his. 'Really?'

'Really. Look at me, Charlie!'

When I raised my eyes, Lawrence looked deeply into them and this time I didn't look away. He moved towards me, the water swirling softly about him, ripples spreading out across the pool. He drew me slowly, gently into his arms, his body tantalizingly warm against mine through the thin layers of our drenched linen. 'Charlie, Charlotte, stable boy and vagabond,' he said. 'So brave; so beautiful.'

Lawrence looked down into my eyes a moment longer and then bent his head and brushed his warm lips against mine. Trembling, I held myself quite still, feeling his breath on my face. He drew back and looked at me again, a question in his eyes, as though he were asking permission to continue. In reply, I twined one arm around his neck and drew his head down, lifting my face for his kiss.

I'd never been kissed before. I hadn't imagined it to be as it was; so close, so intimate, so passionate. I was chilled in the cold water now, but Lawrence's embrace sent a fire sweeping through me that left my very fingertips tingling with warmth. His mouth and his tongue were hot and sweet against mine and he wrapped his arms around me so that I felt enclosed in him for the long, lingering moments that it lasted.

When he lifted his head to look down at me again, I was breathless, all my senses alive. Gently he stroked one hand over my cheek and my hair, whilst still cradling me in his other arm.

'Dear Charlie,' he said. He pressed his warm lips to my forehead. I shivered. 'You're cold,' he said. 'Come, you should get out of the water.'

'He vaulted out of the pool with ease, the water streaming in a silver, moonlit cascade from his wet shirt and breeches. He'd jumped into the water fully dressed. He turned to offer me a hand but I shook my head.

'Will you turn your back please?' I asked him bashfully, aware that my shirt might not cover me as I climbed out. 'I'm not . . . decent.'

He smiled and turned away obediently, looking up to the back of the house. I clambered inelegantly out of the water, shivering a little, and retrieved my breeches. It was difficult to pull them onto my wet legs but, once I'd buttoned them up, wrung out my wet shirt and pulled it down over them, I felt less exposed.

Lawrence took my hand, led me to the bench beside the pool, and sat down with me there, drawing me back into his arms. I nestled against him with a sigh of contentment, resting my head on his shoulder, not thinking of anything beyond the happiness of the present moment. 'How did you know I was here?' I asked.

'I was awake and sleepless, concerned for Belle and for you. My room is on one of the upper floors; I can just see the far end of this pool from my window. I could see someone was in the water. I saw you once before, or at least I thought that it was you, and guessed you had been bathing.'

'So you expected it to be me, then, when you came down tonight?'

'I hoped it might be.'

'I thought you were . . . that man who has been pursuing me,' I said with a sigh. 'I was terrified.'

He kissed the top of my head soothingly and then rested his cheek against it. 'I'm sorry,' he said. 'But I'm sure he won't come here. Why would he?'

I shrugged, not knowing what to say to account for my apparently irrational fear that someone as insignificant as I should be the target of a killer. Lawrence drew me closer and we sat still for a moment without speaking.

One by one, birds started to twitter in the bushes around us. We both realized the dawn was near. 'Back to sleep with you,' said Lawrence, straightening up. 'If you wish to keep your secret, it would be better for us not to be seen here.'

As I got up to follow him, his words threw a dark shadow over my happiness. For an hour, I had allowed my feelings to run away with me, but it could go no further.

Lawrence accompanied me back to the door into the stable yard. There, before we parted, he drew me into another long, loving kiss. Aware that this could be farewell, that I must leave Deerhurst soon, I held nothing back, kissing him as freely and tenderly as he kissed me.

I crept back into the stable to find Belle asleep. I stood watching the rise and fall of her breathing, my heart tearing in two. Belle, Mr John Lawrence; I loved them both and I longed to stay here with them. But at any moment, Lawrence might make the connection between me and the girl on the poster. If he did, could I be sure he would believe I was innocent? I knew it was time to leave, while everyone still slept. I would slip away at once and find Henry in Dorset.

I took my waistcoat from the nail it was hanging on and pulled it on over my still-damp shirt. Then, feeling ready, I went to the main stable door and eased it open to fetch my satchel and to retrieve my papers. As I crept across the aisle to the cupboard, Ben yawned and sat up, straw sticking out of his tousled red hair.

'Mornin', Charlie!' he said sleepily. 'Is it time to get up?' The words were scarcely spoken before the stable clock began to chime five and the other boys began to stir. I would have to wait until tonight.

 CHAPTER TWENTY-SEVEN

The following day seemed unreal to me. Sleep deprived, I stumbled clumsily through my duties.

'Whatever's up with you?' demanded Ben over breakfast. He punched me lightly on the arm to get my attention. 'That's three times I've spoke to you already today and not a word have I had back.'

'I'm sorry,' I said and smothered a yawn. 'I didn't sleep well. I had to tend Belle.'

'Belle indeed!' cried Peter. 'Up dreaming of his lady-love he was!' He put on a high-pitched, mocking voice: 'Oh! Miss Susan, I can't wait to walk out with you on Sunday!'

'I never said so,' I objected.

'You might not have done, but *she* talks of little else,' Joe sniggered. 'You're in with a chance there, Charlie! If you ask me, she can't wait to throw herself at you. Taking her into the woods for a bit of you-know-what, are you?' he said with a wink.

'You are wide of the mark indeed,' I replied, my lip curling. I was faintly disgusted with his crudeness and feeling all the inappropriateness of being linked with poor Susan in such a way.

It was just after noon when the order came from the house to harness the new team and don my livery to accompany Mr Lawrence on an errand. I pulled the smart clothes on and the wool prickled against my skin. It was another hot day; even more sultry than the day before. Being out in the sun would be unpleasant, but at least I would see Lawrence one last time.

When Lawrence arrived, he gave me a nod. The stable was bustling with staff, so he gave me no more sign of what had passed between us last night than the faintest of smiles that just creased the corners of his eyes. As for me, I scarcely had the courage to look at him. I kept my eyes downcast, dreading that I might betray myself by blushing.

I held the first pair of the team while Lawrence climbed into the driver's seat and gathered the reins. I was just awaiting orders from him to 'Let 'em go!' when Lord Rutherford came through the archway from the main house, leaning on his cane.

'Hello there, John,' he called out. 'So this is the new team?'

He walked forward, moving much more briskly than usual, barely seeming to need his cane. I deduced from this that his gout was rather better at present.

Lord Rutherford walked around the team, running an aged hand over their necks and checking their points before looking up to Lawrence. 'A fine team, John! How do they go together?'

'Oh, that leaves a great deal to be desired, my lord! But where would be the challenge or the profit in a perfect team? They are not as unpredictable as the previous pair. No stallions among them.'

'Where are you off to today?' asked the old gentleman.

'I need to speak to Phillips about letting his cattle graze across Symonds' land. You know how it is with those two!'

Lawrence was fretting a little, eager to be off. His impatience communicated itself along the reins to the horses, who stamped and pawed the ground, jingling their harness.

'Tell you what,' said Lord Rutherford unexpectedly. 'I'll accompany you! I'd like to see these fellows in action. You, boy!' he turned to Ben who was lurking in the shade by the tack room. 'Run and take a message to the house for Miss Lawrence that I've driven out for an hour or so!'

He turned back to Lawrence. 'Judith won't miss me. She's practising her pianoforte!'

Bridges assisted Lord Rutherford to climb into the chaise. I watched gloomily as he settled himself beside Lawrence, reminiscing on the teams he himself had driven as a young man and how pleasant it was to get out behind some decent nags on such a fine day. 'For I don't mind telling you, John, being in the gout is no fun. No fun at all! Life is scarcely worth living.'

I let the horses go, and as I leapt up onto my perch behind the chaise, they swept smartly through the arch and out of the yard. Once they'd pulled us up the long drive, Lord Rutherford took the reins himself and sent the team along the road across the downs at a brisk trot. His conversation ran on the excellence of the horses, anecdotes of teams he and his acquaintance had owned in the past, and advice on how to cure this team of their various quirks and bad habits. All of this Lawrence responded to with his usual quiet politeness.

Once we had turned around, driven back along the downs and taken the lane to the village of Doynton, Lord Rutherford handed the reins back to Lawrence and sat back. 'They were a deuced good buy, my boy! They'll make us a pretty penny once you have those little tricks ironed out, by Jove so they will! Well done. I'll let you take them from here, however. You lose your precision of eye with age, you know, and this is a narrow lane for a team.'

He then fell silent for a few minutes. I looked at the back of Lawrence's head and wished desperately that Lord Rutherford had not chosen to accompany us. My regrets were abruptly interrupted by his lordship's next words.

'Damned shame, given your skill with carriage horses, John, that you cannot do better choosing a horse for Judith! Every one turns out a dud! Whatever happens to you? Do your judgement and wits go begging?'

I felt a surge of anger flood me and was hard put not to cry out what a perfect horse Belle was. I bit my lip and stayed silent.

Lawrence was silent too. I guessed he was gathering his thoughts. Probably he hadn't expected this sudden attack any more than I had. When he spoke it was in a restrained, measured tone: 'I believed, indeed I still believe, Belle to be an outstanding horse, my lord. Beautifully put together, highly trained, and with the sweetest of tempers.'

'Sweet tempered be damned! She did her best to savage my poor girl!'

'You'll remember, my lord, I spoke to you about this yesterday and have done in the past . . .'

'I know what you said! But you weren't there, were you, John?'

'No, my lord, but . . .'

'Then how can you know what happened? Judith was there and she told me! The damn horse bucked her off and then tried to savage her!'

'With the greatest respect, I don't believe that is quite what happ . . .'

'Are you accusing my granddaughter of lying?' interrupted Rutherford furiously.

'No, my lord, merely suggesting that her version of events is . . .'

'Damn it, you are! How dare you? This is not the first time you've made insinuations about Judith and I won't stand for it!'

Lord Rutherford was red-faced and shaking with anger in defence of his beloved granddaughter. I could see why Lawrence had said it was difficult to speak to him.

'My lord, please! I insinuate nothing. I merely wish to suggest that it is not a coincidence that Judith has problems with *all* her horses.'

'You hope to get my favour by slandering my closest surviving relative! Well, you are wasting your time! If you continue, I shall have something to say about the way you select dangerous and unsound horses for her!'

'I understand you, my lord,' said Lawrence quietly. He attempted no further representations and, after a short silence, finding himself unchallenged, Rutherford added: 'The horse will be destroyed. It's a shocking waste of money, but it's clearly dangerous and therefore I cannot in conscience sell it on.'

A strangled squeak escaped me. Lawrence turned slightly so that I could see his frown and faint shake of the head. He was warning me to stay silent and he was right. No words of mine would convince his lordship. I put my hand to my mouth and bit down hard on my knuckles to stifle my distress.

'Brookes is coming over in the morning to put a bullet in her and that will be the job done,' continued Lord Rutherford brutally. 'I'll commission someone else to select her next horse.'

Lawrence bowed his head slightly. 'I hope both you and Judith will be better pleased with the choice,' he said.

Lawrence took a left turn from the village to get to the farmhouse near Doynton. He said no more. As we lurched over the rough surface, I had to cling on tightly to the rail and couldn't prevent a tear or two trickling slowly down my face, gathering silently on my chin, and dripping onto my livery.

When we drew up in the farmyard, I jumped down from my perch and took the heads of the first two horses, keeping my face averted from my employers. Lawrence hitched the reins and assisted his lordship in climbing out of the chaise and gave him his arm to the house. He returned to me after a moment.

'Don't be distressed, Charlie.' he said softly. 'There's still time to think of something.'

'Think of what?' I demanded in a voice that shook. 'How do we find a way to convince him by tomorrow? It's impossible!'

Lawrence bit his lip, his eyes downcast, silently admitting the truth of my words.

'Poor Belle!' I exclaimed passionately. 'She's done *nothing* to deserve this!'

'I know,' Lawrence replied. 'I'm so sorry there's no opportunity to speak today. This wasn't at all how I'd planned this trip.'

'I know,' I said, my voice low. But at least I'd discovered the truth. I was forewarned. If I'd not heard this conversation, I would have left tonight, unwittingly leaving Belle to her fate. This way, I had the chance to do something. I just didn't know what yet.

'Drive the horses into the shade over there, would you?' Lawrence asked me. 'They mustn't stand in the sun and nor should you. We won't be more than an hour.' Glancing over at the house to check no one was observing us, he swiftly caught one of my hands in his and pressed it lightly before releasing it.

With a heavy heart, I mounted the chaise, climbing up into the box seat and gathering the reins. In the confusion, Lawrence had quite forgotten that I'd never once driven a team. But I only had to drive the horses some twenty feet; how hard could it be? I found I was right. The principle of driving a team was not fundamentally different to a pair, though I struggled with how best to hold so many reins.

In the shade of the beech trees, my troubles continued to plague me. Belle was sentenced to death in fewer than twenty-four hours. I searched my mind for ways to rescue her from her hideous fate. I pictured myself trying to persuade Lord Rutherford, but I knew if I actually tried to speak to him I would merely stutter uselessly and become tongue-tied under his fierce gaze. Could I persuade Judith to speak for her horse? No, that too was a lost cause.

When the two men returned, I held the horses as Lawrence helped Lord Rutherford climb back into the chaise, then jumped lightly in after him. I swung onto my perch as the carriage pulled away. I noticed Lawrence slowed the carriage for me, a courtesy he had never shown before he had discovered I was a girl.

No sooner was the chaise underway than Lord Rutherford interrupted Lawrence's talk of the tenants they had just visited to speak of Miss Judith again.

'I've taken a decision, Lawrence!' he announced. 'Judith must have a London season this winter! I daresay I shall dislike it greatly, but it must be done. I've put it off too long. She must be brought out in form and given something other than her horses and unsuitable young men to think about. I thought she would find a husband at the Bath, but I was mistaken. Nothing but octogenarians, half-pay officers, and fortune hunters! We need to go to London. I won't have history repeating itself! I'll leave it to you to supervise the opening up of the town house and engaging of servants, if you please.'

'Yes, my lord,' Lawrence replied.

'I daresay this whole thing will cost me a fortune, but nothing I can't afford. I'll buy Judith a new horse myself when we get to London! Until then, she can ride that new gelding you brought back from the last auction.'

'I bought Caspar for myself, my lord. With my own money. I will be riding him.'

'If you won't lend him, I'll buy him from you, damn you!' cursed Rutherford.

I bit my lip, appalled at the old man's autocratic ways. Would Caspar now go the same way as Belle? I waited to hear what Lawrence would say to this.

'He is not trained to side-saddle, my lord. I could not advise it.'

'Pooh, I'm sure . . . ' began Rutherford.

'He's not for sale.' Lawrence's tone was firm.

Lord Rutherford's hands clenched and unclenched in his lap a few times but he said nothing.

'Have you considered the possibility that it might be better for Judith's romance to be allowed to run its course?' asked Lawrence cautiously. 'That if she were allowed to see the young man regularly in company, she might quite naturally discover for herself that she is not as in love as she thought? If she were . . . '

'Are you giving me advice on raising my own granddaughter?' demanded Lord Rutherford, turning an interesting shade of purple. I looked at him curiously, wondering if he would suffer an apoplectic fit one of these days with such rages. 'It's the outside of enough, coming from a poor relation I've rescued from poverty! You're suggesting I allow my only grandchild to consort with indigent officers who have nothing to live on but their pay? Perhaps you believe I should actually consider allowing her to marry such a lowly fortune hunter? You must be out of your mind, John!'

'I simply fear that confining such a high-spirited girl, and denying her the one thing she wants above all others . . . ' began Lawrence.

'Silence!' shouted Rutherford. 'Good God, you are suggesting I allow her to disgrace not only herself but also me and our family name? Unthinkable! I would disown you if *you* made a marriage half as shameful! You will drive me home without another word.'

Lawrence flinched, but did as requested in tight-lipped silence, driving the team up to their bits at a smart pace. A heightened colour had crept into his face at such a verbal lashing, but he bore himself with his usual quiet dignity.

It seemed I had guessed correctly the root of Judith's unhappiness and periodic escapes. She was thwarted in love. Not that this excused her cruelty in the slightest, of course. But I could see that perhaps she was venting her deep frustration and unhappiness on her horse.

We were about halfway down the carriageway through the park when I noticed a figure walking down the hill ahead of us. The sun was in my eyes making it difficult to see but there was something vaguely familiar about him; the set of his shoulders and his slight stoop. I watched him pause, open a snuff box, and take a pinch. A prickle of unease ran up the back of my neck.

As we drew level with him, Lawrence drew the horses to a halt. 'Why, Mr Johnson,' he said. 'How do you do? It's good to see you! Can we take you up?' He reached down a hand and the other man looked up and shook it. As he turned, I caught a glimpse of his face and my unease turned to terror. It was the magistrate from London.

CHAPTER TWENTY-EIGHT

Lord Rutherford moved over to make room and the man climbed up beside him. I stood behind them rigid with horror. I was now absolutely certain I'd been recognized in London and this man had come after me. So far he hadn't so much as glanced at me, but I dreaded the moment he did. Through a haze of fear, their conversation reached me. 'So how is our matter going on, Johnson?' Rutherford was asking.

'I've done as you instructed, my lord. I'm afraid the business hasn't prospered so far. But I'm hopeful there may be some better news soon.'

'That's capital! I look forward to hearing more. You will dine with us, of course?'

'Your lordship is too kind.'

We reached the yard and Lawrence reined in the horses. Feeling as though I was caught in a nightmare, I jumped down and ran to the horses' heads. The magistrate, or Johnson, whoever he really was, climbed down from the chaise and reached up to assist Lord Rutherford. As he did so, his eyes met mine and I knew that he knew me; that he'd expected to see me. His eyes were as hard as stones.

I watched the three men walk off together. The most

insane conjectures ran wild through my mind. How did they all know one another? Were they plotting together? What kind of scheme was this? *I've done as you instructed.* Could Lord Rutherford be implicated in my father's death? And what of Lawrence? *Good to see you!* he'd said. An appalling thought struck me. What if it was *Lawrence* who had told him to follow me here? Had all his sympathy and kindness towards me been a lie? But what about last night? I shivered, my mind in turmoil.

'Come, Charlie, don't stand around!' called Steele impatiently. 'We have a team to see to!'

I set to work in a daze. Numbly, I helped unhitch the team and lead the horses away one by one. I ran to change out of my livery, hanging it carefully on a hook on the wall before racing back down to help groom the four horses.

I glanced at Belle's box as I worked, but she wasn't looking out over her half-door at me. I longed to run straight over and check on her. Her warm, comforting presence would help soothe my worst terrors. I also wanted to reassure her that I wasn't going to let them hurt her. Terror for myself had not made me forget Belle's danger for an instant.

My last horse stabled at last, I ran to Belle's box. But as I unlatched the door, I realized the box was empty. 'Where's Belle?' I cried out, fearing the worst at once. 'Where have they taken her?'

'Belle?' asked Steele, bemused. 'Why, she's there, in her . . . Oh!'

Losing all sense of my proper place, I grasped his arm and shook it. 'Have they shot her? Have they! Tell me at once!'

'Shot her? No! Why would they?' asked Steele, astonished. He shook himself free of my hand. 'Have you lost your mind, Charlie?'

'But where is she?' I demanded.

'Bridges has been in charge of the yard this afternoon while I took Storm to the farrier. Let's ask him. He's in the tack room.'

'Belle?' Bridges asked bewildered. 'Isn't she in her box?'

'Her saddle is missing!' I said, pointing to the empty space on the wall where the side-saddle normally hung. I looked across and saw that the hook for the bridle was also empty. Relief swept through me. It didn't seem likely that anyone would have saddled and bridled a horse to shoot it. She must have been taken out. But there was only one person who would have taken the side-saddle.

'Has Miss Judith ridden her out?' I demanded. 'Belle is not fit enough to be ridden! Her eye!'

Bridges looked concerned. Steele's eyes were running along the walls. 'Two saddle-bags are missing,' he said, indicating an empty shelf. He looked back at us. 'Why would she take saddle-bags? Has she run away for real this time? How did this happen?'

Bridges sank his head in his hands with a groan. 'She sent me up to the lodge about two hours ago with a message for Mrs Saunders . . . And like a fool, I fell for it! If she's eloped, I'll never forgive myself.'

'Charlie, run across to the house and ask them to give an urgent message to his lordship and to Mr Lawrence,' ordered Steele. 'They'll want to send out a search party. Ask if . . .'

He was interrupted by a sudden clattering of hooves in the yard. We all rushed to the door hoping to see Miss Judith on Belle, both of them safe and sound. But Belle came cantering into the yard without a rider, stirrups flying loose, banging her sides. Her eyes were wild and she was lathered in sweat. Red-flecked foam dripped from her bleeding mouth and the reins dangled, broken.

'Dear God, what's happened?' cried Bridges hoarsely.

'That dratted girl . . . !' said Steele. He shut his mouth hard on the unwise words and stepped forward to catch Belle's bridle. Startled at his approach, she dodged him, reins flying.

'Let Charlie catch her,' called Bridges. 'She trusts Charlie! Ben, you run to the house! Tell them Belle's come back riderless and we think it was Miss Judith as took her out!'

'Blimey!' exclaimed Ben, running off at once, leaving the carriage horse he was grooming. I walked slowly towards Belle, speaking softly to her, but she was badly frightened and skittered away from me as she had from Steele. It took me ten minutes to catch her, and by that time Ben was back.

'We're to get horses ready for a search,' he said.

'Ride Merlin up to the lodge,' Steele ordered him. 'We need to know if she went that way.'

As Ben clattered out of the yard on Merlin, I stroked Belle soothingly and tethered her ready for grooming. I was still shaking with the double shock of seeing that man walking boldly up to the house and finding Belle missing.

I worked steadily, gently washing Belle's hurt mouth, reapplying ointments to her injured face, then rubbing her down, calming both of us a little in the process. I urgently needed to decide what I should do, but my mind still wasn't working rationally.

'That's enough on Belle now, Charlie,' Steele told me, breaking in on my thoughts. 'Stable her!'

I did as I was told and, from the gloom of her box, I watched Ben come back with no news and Lawrence arrive in the yard. I didn't show myself. I no longer trusted anything he'd ever said to me.

Lawrence rode straight off on Caspar, who was saddled and waiting for him, to search for Miss Judith. He took the route towards the Bath while Steele rode in the direction of Bristol. Bridges set out to search the rides across the downs. It was all panic and bustle. Once they had all departed, an uneasy peace fell and I could draw breath at last. I carried Belle's muddied saddle and bridle into the tack room, where Ben was working.

'How do we repair this?' I asked Ben, holding up the broken rein. It felt unreal to be discussing everyday things. Ben looked at the rein.

'Fetch me the box off the shelf up there and I'll do it,' he said. 'I daresay Miss Judith will want to replace it. You won't catch her riding with patched-up tack! But it'll do for now.'

As I lifted the box down from the shelf, I experienced a spell of dizziness and nausea so acute that I almost fainted. My hands, suddenly numb, lost their grip, and I dropped the box on the floor. It burst open, showering needles, threads, awls, finger guards, and other equipment all over the floor of the tack room.

I sat down heavily on a bench, my head clutched in my hands, gasping for breath as the dizziness gradually receded.

'You all right, Charlie?' asked Ben. He squatted down beside me, one hand on my shoulder, looking up into my face. 'You look as sick as a parrot!'

'I'll be well enough in a moment,' I managed to say. Everything was slowly coming back into focus. I could see the mess I'd made. 'It's just the shock on top of all these days of heat, I think.'

Ben looked sympathetic and began to gather up the things I'd spilled. 'Lid's broke,' he observed. 'They'll take it out your wages.'

'I don't care,' I responded wearily. There would be no more wages for me in any case. My time here was done. But what could I do about Belle? I couldn't run away, leaving her here to be shot.

I sat watching Ben fit the broken ends of the rein into the small stitching pony that protruded from the wall like a small wooden arm. Carefully, he made holes with an awl ready to stitch the leather back together. As I watched, my mind cleared and it struck me there was a solution that solved all my troubles in one blow: Belle. I could escape on Belle.

Why had this not occurred to me before? I knew the answer to that. It would be theft. The fact that she was sentenced to death would not weigh with a judge. If I were caught with a valuable stolen horse, I would hang for the crime. I already knew that I was going to do it anyway. I *had* to run away. If I were to take Belle with me, it would have to be by day while the stable yard was unlocked; in fact, it had to be right now.

Ben had threaded up two needles and was pushing them through the leather in an experienced manner, stitching the torn pieces back together. 'Feeling better?' he asked with a glance at me.

'Yes, thank you. Ben, I've suddenly remembered something.' I got to my feet.

'Course,' Ben shrugged. 'Off you go. Don't worry 'bout leaving me with all the work.'

I summoned up a grin for him. Running to the stables, I grabbed my satchel from the cupboard it was stored in and snatched up my blanket and my cloak. I retrieved my father's papers and ring from their hiding place thinking of the address inscribed on my father's note to me: *Henry Palmer, Sea View Cottage, Studland, Dorset.* Henry was a good friend. He would be willing to help me for old times' sake. Well, now at last I would go to him.

With the papers tucked inside my shirt, I emerged into the yard. I was in luck. Ben was heading to the latrines. With everyone else out looking for Miss Judith, the yard was deserted.

Dropping my bulging bag into Belle's box, I slipped quietly into the tack room, picked up Belle's newly repaired bridle and an old saddle. I also picked up a halter, a leading rope and a bag of oats. It was a long way to Dorset from South Gloucestershire.

Belle seemed surprised to be saddled again so soon, but was patient and co-operative with me. I slipped the bit very gently into her sore mouth. 'I'm sorry, Belle,' I whispered. 'Believe me, the alternative is worse.'

The yard was still empty as I emerged, leading Belle to the mounting block. I'd just climbed into the saddle and was adjusting my stirrups when Ben emerged from the latrines and stared at me on Belle's back.

'What you doing?' he asked, puzzled.

'I've had an idea where Miss Judith might be,' I said, improvising hurriedly. 'I'm going to look for her.'

Ben's eyes ran over the full satchel slung on my back and his face went so pale his freckles stood out. 'No, you're not! You're cutting your stick. Charlie, they'll hang you if you go an' steal that horse! And likely as not me too, for letting you do it!'

I leaned down and grasped his shoulder. 'Ben, they're shooting her in the morning.'

Ben looked from me to Belle, his face a picture of shock and indecision. 'They'd never . . . ?'

'They will. I heard Lord Rutherford himself say so. I've gone looking for Miss Judith, remember? Or better still, you didn't see me at all. Take care!'

I urged Belle forward and we trotted briskly under the archway and out of the yard. I followed the carriageway a short distance up the hill, hoping there were no eyes watching me from the house, then struck out across the park, avoiding the lodge house. I was distressed to leave without a word to Mr and Mrs Saunders . . . my grandparents. My sudden disappearance would be a new grief to Mrs Saunders. There were still so many questions unanswered about my connection to them and to Deerhurst. However, I couldn't take the risk of saying farewell. Perhaps I would never know the truth now.

Belle cantered across the smooth turf to the edge of the park. There we passed through a gate and struck out southwards, leaving both the house and our old lives behind us for ever.

CHAPTER TWENTY-NINE

It was almost dark when I pulled Belle up in a small wood miles from Deerhurst. She'd kept going valiantly with only short breaks to drink from a stream or mill-pond, but she was flagging now.

Concealed among the trees, I unsaddled her and wiped her damp hide down with a cloth, praising her efforts. She'd barely recovered from Miss Judith's savage beating and I'd asked a great deal of her.

'This is to save you, you beautiful, brave-hearted horse,' I told her, patting her neck. She nosed me wearily and I remembered the oats in the saddle-bag. Dipping my cupped hands into them, I held some up for her to eat, which she did eagerly.

I covered her with my blanket and tethered her loosely to a tree, leaning against her warm body in the darkness. It seemed unreal that we had run away together. Like a dream. Perhaps I would wake up tomorrow in Belle's stable at Deerhurst and all would be well. How I wished that could be so.

'There's no one I'd rather run away with than you,' I assured her.

An image of Lawrence rose in my mind, his hazel eyes looking into mine, but I pushed it firmly away. I was very afraid he was not the person I'd thought him. And even if he should be innocent of all blame, there was no possible future for the two of us together. I must try to put him out of my mind and be glad that I'd escaped and saved both my own life and Belle's.

I woke in the night, cold and stiff from sleeping on the ground, to the sound of Belle grazing beside me. She was cropping the grass hungrily with little tearing sounds. I opened my eyes and saw her head close to mine, little clouds of steam around her nostrils. It was the first cool night in weeks. I sat up and yawned, wishing I'd thought to bring food for myself as well as for Belle. It was time to move on.

After that first afternoon, we rode through the night to avoid being seen. I was too distinctive a figure, a working boy astride a valuable horse. Anyone spotting us might well remember me if asked, and I didn't want that. So we used the darkness as cover and slipped unseen through countryside and villages.

Belle was tired the first night so I rode her slowly, picking our way through woods and across fields, avoiding the roads wherever I could. Every now and then, I would join a road to pick up my bearings, then I would leave it again for the onward ride.

I risked leaving Belle tethered in a copse on the second day while I went into a small market down to purchase a map and food for us both. I was terrified all the time I was gone that she would be discovered or even stolen, but thankfully she was waiting for me, ears pricked eagerly, when I returned. I hugged her in relief and fed her the carrots I'd bought for her.

We found an empty barn to hide in for the day. I slept a few hours and then we moved onwards before dusk, riding with the setting sun on our right. Belle was alert and willing, perked up by the oats I'd fed her and by the day's rest.

Jumping a small hedge into a field, we almost landed on a fox on the far side. Startled, the fox leapt away from us and disappeared into the hedge with a flash of his white tail. Belle threw up her head and whinnied indignantly. I laughed for the first time since our mad flight began.

Belle's injuries were healing and she was growing leaner and fitter day by day. As I stroked her neck and shoulder, I felt the firm muscles bunched under the skin. Her stride grew in power and speed as we covered the long miles.

As the nights passed, Belle grew to understand and in-terpret the lightest command from me, changing speed and direction fluently. She was a joy to ride: calm, trust-worthy, and willing. The flow of communication passed unspoken between us. I knew when she tired and I eased the pace at once. She sensed when I was anxious and moved more quietly or more swiftly in response. Once, as we hid in a copse from some men who'd frightened me, she stood as still as a carved statue, not twitching so much as a nostril, until I breathed freely again and told her with a pat that they had gone and we might move on.

'You're a queen among horses, Belle, my beauty,' I told her, feeding her oats from my cupped hands after a long night's ride. In reply, she blew down her nostrils into the oats, showering them onto the grass. I laughed, letting her eat them from the ground instead, nibbling the fresh summer grass at the same time. I leaned my head against her shoulder and sighed. 'We've escaped,' I told her. 'We're well and truly away from Deerhurst. All we have to do now is conceal ourselves so they never, ever find us.'

The following evening, Belle woke me at dusk, nuzzling my face and blowing her sweet, grass-scented breath over me. I opened my eyes, fending her off, realizing I'd overslept. Belle nudged me forcefully, as if telling me to get up and resume our usual routine. I sat up, yawned, and stretched. Once more I was grubby and probably smelly, if only I knew it.

'When we reach our destination, I shall bathe in the sea,' I promised myself aloud. 'And you can see how you like the salt water too!' I told Belle. 'Not far now.'

I prayed I would find Henry where my father's note told me, and that he would be willing to help us. No matter how carefully I'd watched my small store of coins, they'd diminished frighteningly quickly on the journey. The few items of food I'd bought for us had cost far more than I'd expected. I squared my shoulders and pushed the anxiety away. No point worrying until I was sure there was a need.

That night we climbed some high downs under cover of darkness. Belle took the slope steadily, pacing herself, but towards the top she was pulling hard, puffing with effort. I slipped out of the saddle, pulled the reins over her head and walked beside her. The grass was sparkling with dew in the moonlight. There was a chill in the air and I could tell the long summer was drawing to a close.

We reached the top of the down where the wind was fresh. At long last I could smell the sea. I breathed deeply, excited, knowing we were close to our destination now. A few steps more and the ground sloped away ahead of us, the view of the distant sea bursting upon us, shining vast and silver in the moonlight.

I halted and Belle stopped beside me as I gazed down at the English Channel, drinking in the beauty of the silvery sea. The landscape spread out at our feet was so different to Deerhurst; the hillsides were criss-crossed with dry-stone walls and dotted with sheep, the grass was rough and interspersed with dark gorse. Belle stirred restlessly beside me. When I didn't respond she butted me.

'I know, I know,' I told her. 'You want your breakfast and a rest. You can have both, as soon as we get down off this hill and find a stream and some shelter. Meanwhile, what do you think of this place?'

She whickered softly in response and I rubbed her nose affectionately. 'I quite agree. It looks a wild but beautiful country for both girl and beast.'

After sleeping the day and most of the evening in a barn and refreshing ourselves at a stream, we set forth the next night to find the village of Studland. It was cold and the ground was damp with evening dew. 'Here's hoping we get a welcome from Henry, Belle!' I exclaimed, shivering. 'Autumn is almost upon us.'

We followed the cliff path along the shore to the east, the sea shining far below our feet in the late evening sunshine. The coastline was varied and dramatic; the village further than I expected.

By the time we reached the village of Studland, the night was fading, but even in daylight I was unable to find the cottage named in the letter. I had to forgo the discretion I'd so far maintained and ask for directions. I stopped a farmer, driving his cattle back to pasture after milking.

'Sea View Cottage? You want the coastguard?' he asked, sending us a darkling look from under his brows. 'You sure about that?'

'I'm looking for a Henry Palmer.'

'Aye, he lives there all right.' The farmer turned and spat deliberately onto the grass. 'He's a Preventer. Still want to find him?'

I nodded dumbly, with no idea what he was talking about. I was relieved to know that Henry was still here, close at hand.

'Go back along the coast a step, past the village and out onto the cliff road. It's a white cottage overlooking the sea.'

I thanked him, but he scowled and turned away.

I turned Belle about and we wearily retraced our steps. 'Good grief!' I said to Belle as the cottage drew in sight. 'We came past here! I must have missed it.'

The sun was rising as I hooked Belle's reins over the fence at the front of the cottage, opened the creaking gate, and walked up the short path through the neat little garden. I'd knocked twice before a window opened above me and a sleepy, night-capped head poked out. 'What do you want?' asked a voice groggily.

'I'm looking for Henry Palmer,' I said, peering up, trying to make out the face above me.

'Well, you've found me!' The face looking down into mine became more alert, his eyes focusing on my upturned face. 'Charlie?' he said uncertainly. 'Is that really you?'

I felt tears prick my eyelids in sheer relief as I nodded. The window banged shut, there was a pause, presumably while he dressed hastily, then he came thundering down the stairs. The front door flew open and Henry grasped my shoulders, giving me a little shake.

'By God, Charlie, you're a sight for sore eyes! A friendly face in this hell-hole! I've been waiting and waiting to hear news from your father! But what are you doing dressed as a lad?'

'I know, I know,' I laughed and cried all at once. 'It's such a long story! I'll tell it all, but do you have breakfast for me and my horse? We're famished!'

Henry looked past me to where Belle watched us with bright, curious eyes, her ears pricked forward. 'That's a beauty of a horse!' he remarked, limping down the path to take a closer look at her. 'She's been in the wars a bit, though, hasn't she?' he remarked, pointing to her injured face. 'However did your father afford her, Charlie?' He paused and then gasped. 'Did he prove his claim?'

'What claim?' I asked puzzled.

He looked sharply at me and then shook his head. 'It can wait until breakfast.' He turned back to Belle. 'What a fine creature you are!' he praised her as he patted her. Belle took his attention calmly, pricking her ears forward endearingly.

'How is your leg, Henry?' I asked him.

'Oh, it'll never heal. But I can get about and it doesn't pain me too much any more.'

'It seems a lifetime since Newfoundland. So much has happened.'

'It has, Miss Charlotte, and that's a fact. Would your horse be happy turned out in the paddock with my nag? There's a good bit of grass and he'll be glad of the company.'

'She'd love it! You have a horse of your own?'

'I'm the Riding Officer now. My work is mostly at night, which is why you caught me napping just now. It wasn't easy for a cripple like me to find work at all. I wasn't wanted anywhere as a groom, so this seemed an honourable calling; working for King and Country as I was used to.'

Henry unhitched Belle as he spoke and led her away down the path. She went with him willingly, sensing the hand on her bridle was both kindly and experienced. I followed as he continued to speak.

'It was a way to remain on horseback too. But that was before I came here to work this stretch of the coast. I assure you, Charlie, they are scoundrels the lot of them! If they aren't smugglers themselves, they're in league with them, lending their horses or their barns. I tell you, no brandy, wine, or tea used around here has paid a penny in duty, bar what you'll find in my house! I'm hated so that no one will even give me good day. All for trying to do my duty!'

'That's bad,' I agreed, thinking this explained the farmer's hostility. 'But surely the vicar and the squire at least must support you?'

Henry gave a bark of mirthless laughter and looked at me from under his brows. 'You'd think so, wouldn't you?' was all he said.

Unsaddled and turned loose in the paddock, Belle kicked up her heels for joy. She headed straight for the muddiest patch in the field and rolled vigorously. Scrambling to her feet when she was done, she cantered once about the paddock, her dark head held high, her glossy black tail streaming behind her in the sea breeze. Finally, she touched noses with Henry's horse, Cloud, a strong grey gelding, and then jumped away playfully squealing. The two horses danced around each other, before settling down to crop the grass sociably side by side.

I waited to tell Henry my own story until we were sitting before the open fire in his cottage, some buttered bread, eggs, and ale inside me.

'Come then, Charlie,' Henry said. 'You have a tale to tell. You're looking far too skinny, and you've cut all your hair off, so I'm guessing something's not right. I'd expected to hear from you and your father long before now. Indeed, I'd expected to see you in quite a different situation to this. Do you have a message from your father?'

I shook my head, wiped my sleeve across my eyes, and gulped. 'No, Henry. I don't. Father has been dead these six months. Murdered in our lodgings in London. I've been on the run from his killer.'

Henry gasped and grasped the table for support. The colour drained from his face, leaving him grey. I clasped his arm anxiously. 'Oh, I'm so sorry!' I cried. 'I'm thoughtless to throw it at you like that! You see, I've grown used to it, and I didn't think . . .'

Henry took hold of my hand and patted it, drawing a breath. Then he limped over to the dresser and poured himself a shot of some strong liquor. Downing this in one, he sat down heavily. I watched as a little colour returned to his face.

249

'Oh, Charlie. Poor Andrew! He survived all those years of battles, fevers, and ship voyages to far off lands. For this! It breaks my heart! And just when I thought he was returning to sort out . . . Lord, he never told you, did he?'

'Told me what?'

'We can discuss it later. First, tell me all what happened.'

As I told him the tale, I wept, pulling Lawrence's pocket-handkerchief from my pocket to wipe my tears. Henry's grief made my loss all the more poignant. When he heard the circumstances of my father's death, Henry became distressed. 'Oh Lordy, Lord, he went about it wrongly, I fear.' He wiped tears from his eyes.

'You know something?'

'I do. It's nothing to shame your father, Charlie, so don't look so afeared. I wish . . . Tell me again, you're quite sure it wasn't a common burglar who turned violent because he was discovered at his work?'

'I don't believe so. He knew my name. He threatened to follow me. And I believe he did, Henry, for I saw him again.'

'It's a bad business. A sad, sad business. But before we talk more of it, tell me what became of you.'

I recounted the rest of my tale. Henry was a good listener. He shook his head and tutted when I told of my destitution, he laughed when I told him of my work with the packhorse train, and he nodded wisely over my description of the rigours of work in a posting inn. It was when I reached my tale of Deerhurst Park that his jaw dropped and he looked thunderstruck.

'Deerhurst Park? You have the name right? In Gloucestershire?'

'Yes, indeed. You've heard of it, have you?'

Henry's face was serious. 'I should say I have! Are you honestly telling me you've been working for Lord Rutherford? The old lord?'

'Strictly speaking, I was engaged to serve as personal groom to his steward and agent who is also a relative. I was being trained to take over from Bridges who is finding the work too much. But yes, I was on Lord Rutherford's payroll. Yes, he's very old. And cranky.'

Henry snorted. 'That's polite, my dear.'

'You know him then?'

'Worked for him myself once. But finish your tale!'

I wasn't surprised to hear this. Somehow it all fitted. I began to realize that Henry was about to help me fit the last pieces of the puzzle together and I even began to guess what they were. But I was patient and told him the rest of my story, omitting that moonlit bathe in the gardens. Henry frowned over the fact that I'd stolen Belle.

'I'm truly sorry if I've brought trouble on you,' I said contritely. 'I was quite desperate to save her and had nowhere else to go. And I couldn't help wondering if father had left your address for me on purpose.'

'I don't blame you for a moment, Charlie. The only thing is, I'm so hated here, I fear someone might lay information against me . . . Even so, I wish you'd come sooner, Charlie. Far sooner!'

'I had no way to do so, unless I'd walked all the way from London with no food,' I pointed out. 'I had no means of travel and no money unless I worked.'

'Why ever didn't you write to me? You've had enough money for that these past months.'

'I was so afraid of revealing my whereabouts! Recollect that I have no idea who is pursuing me or why, or how powerful they might be. The murderer was in league with the magistrate! I haven't dared put my name to paper and write to Robert either, for the same reason. I feel dreadful that he doesn't even know that our father is dead.'

'He will know soon enough,' said Henry. 'He's on his way back to England.'

'What?' I cried. 'He must not! Who knows if it is safe for him here?'

'His company was recalled. I had a letter from him in May, telling me to expect him. I imagine he will be arriving soon if he is not already in the country.'

'Oh, it's good to know he's well. But I wish he were not returning right now!'

'Perhaps it's for the best. Miss Charlotte, there's something you should know.'

'When you call me Miss Charlotte instead of Charlie, I always know it's serious,' I said with a grimace.

'Wait here,' said Henry, rising from his chair with an effort.

He climbed the stairs and returned with a fat package, which he dropped onto the table before me. 'I'm guessing you took your father's papers with you when you fled?' he asked soberly.

'I did, but there was almost nothing left. He used to have more!'

'That's why,' said Henry, nodding to the package. 'Before we parted, he asked me to keep them safe for him.

I think you should look through it all and then ask me whatever questions you have.'

He began to clear the table and wash the dishes. I opened the package, spread out the crackling sheets of paper, some of them yellow with age, and began to read. Here was everything that had been missing when I took the papers from my father's hiding place: my birth certificate, my brother's too, my parents' marriage certificate, and their own papers. I stared at them, willing my brain to make sense of it all.

'But Henry . . . ' I said.

He stacked the last of the dishes and turned back to me, wiping his hands.

'Yes?'

'Our surname . . . all the way through! Only his enlistment papers bear the surname Smith!'

'That's right, Charlie. The name Smith is false and always was.'

'It had crossed my mind,' I faltered. 'When I talked to Mr and Mrs Saunders . . . that perhaps . . . that perhaps father had used an assumed name. For they assured me that mother had known no one called Smith. But it seemed too incredible that he could actually be . . . '

'That he could be Andrew Lawrence? But he was, Charlie. He was the eldest son of old Lord Rutherford. If you've lived and worked at Deerhurst, you understand what a momentous thing he did, turning away from his inheritance for love.'

I nodded. It was as if I'd known it somewhere inside me for a while, but it had seemed too far-fetched to be possible.

'You've been working as a stable boy for your own wealthy grandfather when you should have been living in luxury in his house!' exclaimed Henry. 'How is that for irony? I worked for your grandfather and father for over twenty years. So no one knows better than me. I've been with him since before he and Emily ran away to get married. You guessed, didn't you?'

I nodded dumbly. 'I couldn't believe it. But there was this . . . ' I paused, drew the leather pouch from my shirt, and shook the ring out. Henry sighed when he saw it. 'I'm so relieved to see that ring safe!' he said. He picked it up and showed me the engraving on the inside: ASL. 'Andrew Stephen Lawrence,' he said.

'I wondered, when I realized the design was the Rutherford crest, whether he had stolen it,' I admitted.

'Far from it. This will be your proof, along with these papers, of who you are.'

'Did he ever regret it, Henry?' I asked. 'Leaving all that wealth?'

'Never. Your mother was a wonderful woman. I was a junior stable-hand at the time it all happened, as you've just been. I accompanied your father when he ran off. Andrew and I joined the Army together and became close friends. Emily joined us later, just before we set sail for France and later she came with us to America. I'm his witness, if you like, and now yours, having watched you and your brother grow up. My elder brother still works at Deerhurst and will know me, even after all these years. You know Bridges, you mentioned him earlier.'

I gasped with shock. 'He's your brother? You don't look much alike! So your surname is false too?'

Henry smiled. 'He is. And it is. You see, it was your father's intention to claim his inheritance. He said it was all very well remaining far away and obscure while his dear Emily was alive; he wouldn't have his family shame him by refusing to acknowledge her or treat her with proper respect. But when she died, he returned for your sake and for your brother's. He told me you shouldn't be poor, when a whole estate would one day be rightfully his.'

'We consulted a lawyer in Portsmouth on our return. I thought from the beginning that he should go straight home. But he wouldn't; too proud, or too unsure of his father's reaction. A bit of both perhaps. Instead, he wrote him a letter. Then I took up the post here while he went to London to await a response from his father. And then something must have gone terribly wrong. I confess I've been worried sick, hearing nothing from him and seeing nothing in the papers.'

'Do you think his murder is connected to the inheritance? That someone wished to prevent him from making his claim as the rightful heir?' I asked sadly.

'It looks uncommonly like it, doesn't it?'

'But who . . . ?'

'I've not the faintest idea,' Henry admitted.

'The murderer was in league with the magistrate. I saw them, Henry. *I saw them talking together!* Later, when I saw that same magistrate walk up to the house at Deerhurst, I fled. He was welcomed by Lawrence and Lord Rutherford and taken inside. I was so afraid! I didn't understand *what* was going on. He was transacting some business for them. Could that have been murder?'

'It seems unlikely that they are both in it together. Perhaps the business is unconnected with the claim,' said Henry.

I sat, puzzling. 'Lord Rutherford could well have plotted against his own son. He's evil enough for anything, Henry! He wished to shoot Belle just because his granddaughter complained of her!'

'That's bad, Charlie, but it's a big step from there to having your own son murdered in cold blood! No, I don't see his motive. They were estranged, he and your father, it's true. They didn't agree about his choice of bride. He was an autocratic, fierce man, but I never knew him to be evil.'

I rested my chin in my hand, frowning. I could see his point.

'What about Miss Judith's father?' Henry asked me. 'He would have a great deal to lose from his elder brother's return.'

I shook my head. 'No. He's dead and Miss Judith has no brothers.'

'Then who . . . ?'

'No. Oh, no,' I whispered, a cold, sick feeling knotting itself around my stomach. 'No, it cannot be . . . ' But it wasn't the first time I'd been suspicious.

'Who is the heir now, Charlie, aside from your brother? Bear in mind nothing may yet be known of his existence. The person who killed Andrew may have no idea he had a son.'

I swallowed hard, dread flooding me. 'Mr John Lawrence is the heir,' I said. 'He's related to Lord Rutherford and is also his steward. He lives with the family and is next in line, though he's only a fairly distant relative. He told me so himself.'

Henry sat back in his chair. 'Then there you have it,' he said. 'The perfect motive.'

I remembered seeing Lawrence greet him. *Good to see you*, he'd said. Was it possible that Lawrence had ordered the death of my father? The thought that this might be true filled me with horror. If it were true, the man I'd fallen in love with had been my enemy all along.

CHAPTER THIRTY

Henry and I argued back and forth all that day and the following one about what we should do. He wished to find a magistrate who would be willing to serve a writ and arrest Lawrence on suspicion of murder.

I fell silent when he urged this course of action, but wouldn't tell him why. The words stuck in my throat. 'The magistrate in London had been bought,' I said at last, when I had enough control to speak. 'Who is to say any other we go to won't be bribed just the same, once the plotters discover what we are attempting? We could be putting ourselves in mortal danger.'

'It's not likely, Miss Charlotte,' said Henry uncertainly.

'It's more than likely! These are powerful people.' I sighed in frustration.' They are wealthy, influential! And who are we? A riding officer and a stable hand! What chance do we have of being believed against men who own half a county?'

'I take your point,' Henry said reluctantly. 'However, you're forgetting the papers, and the fact I knew your father. That makes you as important as them.'

'No, it doesn't!' I cried. 'It makes my brother Robert a claimant with a case still to prove. And we've no money to buy anyone's services.'

Henry sighed heavily, but didn't want to give up.

'The papers will do us no good if we're dead and they are stolen, Henry! That was the plan, you know. What's to stop it succeeding another time?'

Henry took a turn about the room. 'So how about this,' he began, and I knew what was coming, for I had heard this before. 'We ride straight up to the house and confront the old man. Tell him who we are. Call Bridges in to identify me.'

I shook my head, my throat tight. 'If he doesn't believe us, we are no further on, except we have put ourselves into danger. We cannot be sure he'd care about my father's fate. They were estranged.'

'But Miss Charlotte!' Henry exploded. 'You cannot just remain here and do nothing!'

'Oh yes, I can,' I said sadly. My feelings were too complex and tangled to explain. If it were true that I was granddaughter to Lord Rutherford, then I was well-born enough to marry Lawrence after all. But if he were guilty of ordering my father's murder, I wouldn't want to.

'We must wait for your brother to return,' said Henry with another heavy sigh.

'Even my brother returning doesn't solve anything,' I pointed out. 'Lord Rutherford may refuse to acknowledge us. He may live twenty more years! And while we wait, if it really is Lawrence who seeks to remove us from his path,' I paused, choking on the words, 'then he has every opportunity to do away with us!'

Henry fell silent.

'To tell the truth,' I told him, 'I don't care about inheriting or my "rightful place", or any of that balderdash.

Being wealthy doesn't seem to have made any of the family happy. The whole lot of them are horrible people! I'd rather stay with you and Belle and earn my bread myself somehow. Perhaps we should even go back to America with Robert and stay far away from it all.'

'But someone took your father's life. It's not right that we leave his murder unsolved, Charlie.'

I couldn't argue with that, so I went out to check Belle. She was completely well now, eyes bright and coat glossy. She was enjoying the company of Cloud and all the attention she got from me now that I had no other work to do.

The following evening Henry went out as normal, leaving me alone in the cottage. 'I shall go to the post office and see if there's news from your brother before I begin my patrol,' he promised me.

Before darkness fell, I went out to the paddock to see Belle and then walked back along the cliff path. The sea crashed on the rocks below my feet and white horses rode upon the waves. The wind whipped through my hair, and I thought how much longer it had already grown. Not long enough to be a presentable girl yet, but approaching it.

Back at the cottage, sitting by the fire in the kitchen, I must have dozed a little. When I jerked suddenly awake, disturbed by some noise or other, the kitchen was in darkness. I bent and woke the fire, stirring the embers and adding another log. I lit a tallow candle and noticed a sheet of paper lying on the flagstones by the front door.

Thinking it must be a message for Henry, I went to pick it up. The candlelight fell on the paper, and I was shocked to see that it wasn't addressed to Henry. Instead, the name scrawled across it was *Charlotte Smith*. The sight of those words sent a chill of fear through me. How did anyone know I was here?

I opened the note and tilted it towards the candlelight. The wind whistling through the gap under the door made the flame flicker and dance, casting shadows on the page.

Bring me the Papers.

Come Alone or the Horse dies.

South Beach in One Hour.

My scalp tingled with horror. Had he taken Belle?

I raced out of the cottage into the darkness and along the lane to Cloud's field. The gate was open and the field was empty. 'Belle!' I shouted desperately, running into the field and straining my eyes to look into every corner in the darkness. 'Belle, where are you?'

There was no friendly whinny, no elegant bay mare trotting out of the shadows to greet me. Feeling sick, I ran back to the cottage as fast as I could. Still gasping for breath, I scanned the scrawl again.

I'd eluded the killer for months, but now my luck had run out. But if there was any chance Belle was still alive, I needed to do as I was told. Perhaps if the man got the papers, he would leave us both unhurt. I could plead with him. The slender chance of an unwanted inheritance didn't seem to me to be worth Belle's life. Nor was it worth a lifetime of running and hiding in fear. I would let the papers go.

CHAPTER THIRTY-ONE

Taking the candle, I ran up to the tiny bedroom in Henry's cottage where I slept, lifted my mattress and retrieved the papers and the leather pouch I'd hidden beneath it. They were all in one place now, both those that I had carried with me for so long and the ones Henry had kept safe for me. The note hadn't mentioned the ring. It was possible the murderer didn't know of its existence. I shook it out of the pouch into the palm of my hand.

Downstairs, I pulled a lace from Henry's second-best boots and threaded the ring onto it, tying it securely around my neck inside my shirt. This ring, at least, I would keep safe. The note I left lying on the kitchen table for Henry to see, in case anything happened to me. Blowing out the candle, I tucked the papers into my shirt, pulled my cloak around me and stepped out into the night.

The wind buffeted me as I strode quickly east along the path that led to South Beach. Clouds covered the moon, and I found my way with difficulty in the darkness, staying away from the cliff edge until the land dropped towards the beach.

A long, dark path led through a wooded hollow to the sea. I stumbled blindly along it, cursing that I'd not thought to bring a lantern.

I could orientate myself better once I stepped out onto the sandy beach itself. At first, I could see no one; the beach appeared deserted. Black waves crashed onto the sand and what light there was from the overcast moon glowed on the surface of the water. I picked my way cautiously along the shore. I saw a brief flash of a lantern ahead. Was it the man I'd come to meet? Or a party of smugglers? Henry had warned me that they could be extremely danger-ous if seen at their work. But I would almost rather face a gang of cut-throat free traders than the man who had murdered my father and was now holding my horse to ransom.

'Stop there!' a voice called out suddenly to my left. I froze. A beam of light flashed out of the darkness, daz-zled me for a moment, and then was shuttered, leaving us in near-darkness. 'Have you got them?'

'Yes. They're yours if my horse is safe.'

'It's not your horse, though, is it?' The murderer's voice was horribly familiar, smooth and educated as I re-membered it. It brought back memories of that dreadful day in London. 'She's stolen!' the voice continued. 'I saw you ride away from Deerhurst on her!'

I shivered at the idea he had watched me ride away that day. 'You followed me here?'

'No, I guessed you'd come here. I knew all about Henry Bridges. I told you, you couldn't escape me! Hand over the papers!'

'You won't get the papers unless I get Belle back safe,' I assured him, backing carefully towards the water. 'I'll throw them in the sea!'

To prove my point, I pulled them from my shirt and held them out over the waves that now swirled around my feet.

A large shadow emerged from the darkness before me and loomed closer. The partially-shuttered lantern that he'd put down on the sand cast an eerie light. What I saw made me cry out in fright. Belle was held tightly on a leading rope attached to her halter. Her eyes showed their whites in fear and her ears were flat against her head. Standing beside her, holding a gleaming knife to her jugular, was my father's murderer. I could not mistake those pale, cold eyes, gleaming in the lantern-light.

'No!' I cried. 'Please put the knife down! I'll give you the papers, I swear!'

He backed away from the water a little, Belle fighting for her head. I was terrified she would make an unexpected move and receive a fatal cut.

'Walk towards me slowly with the papers held out before you, where I can see them! No sudden moves! Don't try anything stupid!'

Helplessly, I did as he said.

'Keep walking!' the man ordered as I came towards him.

Still holding Belle tightly, though the knife was no longer held against her, the man reached out and snatched the papers from my hand. 'Now stand with your hands on your head!' he demanded. I did so.

Retreating a short distance from me, he bent down to the lantern and examined the letters by its light. He must have been satisfied with what he saw, because he tucked them away in his own shirt.

I thought of my brother as I saw them disappear. I thought of his future and mine, stolen away by a man who had no right to anything and I felt angry at the injustice for the first time. 'Who are you?' I demanded. 'Who paid you to do such dirty work? Was it Lawrence?'

'Is it likely I'd tell you?' the man sneered. He blew out the lantern with a quick puff and kicked it away. Tucking his knife into his belt and pulling Belle roughly to him, he vaulted onto her back. 'No!' I cried. Guessing he was about to gallop off on her, I sprinted towards them. But when I reached them, the murderer grasped me by the hair and pulled me back against Belle's flank. This had been his intention all along; he'd known I would run towards him and now I was at his mercy. I saw the moonlight glint on steel as he pulled his knife from his belt. He intended to finish me the same way he had my father. 'Did you really think I was going to let you live?' the man hissed in my ear. 'You know too much!'

His hold on my hair was agonizingly strong. Trapped, I leaned back and screamed, slapping at Belle to make her rear up. With an indignant neigh, she rose up on her hind legs, pawing the air. The man was forced to release me, swearing most foully as he clung on to her mane, trying to stay on her back. The moment Belle's front hooves touched back down on the sand, he lashed out at me with the blade. I threw up my arms to protect myself, and Belle leapt forward at the same moment. As a result, the blade missed my neck, but I felt it open up a long tear in my sleeve. A hot flame of pain seared my arm.

There were sudden hoof beats nearby and I heard Henry's voice shout out my name.

'Henry, help!' I screamed.

The murderer put his heels to Belle's sides. With a snort, she leapt forward and galloped away with him, back up the beach.

In the faint light, I saw Henry wheel Cloud around to give chase. My arm was stinging as though I'd scalded it. When I put my hand to it, my whole sleeve was slick with blood. 'Henry!' I yelled with what strength I could muster. 'Henry, I'm hurt!'

He checked Cloud and looked back. 'He's getting away!' he called. I dropped to my knees, my vision blurring. 'Help me!' I said weakly. I was afraid of being left alone and bleeding in the darkness, afraid of Henry being hurt, and terrified for poor Belle.

I must have lost consciousness briefly, for the next thing I knew, Henry was kneeling beside me on the damp sand, tearing his shirt into strips to staunch the bleeding from the wound on my arm. 'Are you with me, Charlie?' he cried as I stirred. He drew another bandage tightly around my arm and I whimpered a little. 'Courage!' he said. 'You're a soldier's daughter, remember? I've seen worse, girl. The arteries are not touched as far as I can see. You'll live.'

'Belle,' I said and was shocked at how faint my voice was.

'I'm sorry, Charlie. The damned scoundrel got away on her. But you were right to call me back. You were losing blood fast.'

When the long wound was bound up tightly, Henry caught Cloud and helped me onto his back. The moon was obscured by clouds once more and fat drops of rain had begun to fall.

266

'How did you know I was here?' I asked Henry as he led Cloud briskly along the beach. 'Did you find the note?'

'I did that. I came back early. I have a letter from your brother.'

'What does he say?'

'I haven't read it yet. Tell me what happened!'

I briefly explained. Henry groaned. 'He took the papers from you?'

'Henry, I truly don't care about them any more! They brought death on my father. I wasn't sacrificing Belle to them as well!'

'You can see it that way, Charlie,' Henry replied, opening the gate at the head of the beach and leading Cloud through it. 'Or you can look at it another way; your father died to keep those papers safe for you and your brother. You owe it to him to realize the inheritance he wanted you to have.'

A sick feeling in the pit of my stomach told me he was right. I hadn't even succeeded in keeping Belle safe, either. The thought of my beautiful horse in that man's power wrung my heart.

We were out on the cliff path now, the rain lashing us. My hair was plastered to my head and my clothes were soaked. We had to shout to each other to be heard. Henry halted Cloud and swung himself up behind me, urging Cloud onwards along the cliff path in the pouring rain.

Over the wind, the rain, and the crashing of the surf below us, I could just hear a faint neigh. Cloud stopped abruptly and neighed back. 'Oh!' I cried, sudden hope surging through me. 'It's Belle!'

'It can't be,' said Henry, but he allowed Cloud to turn on the narrow path. The gelding stood, ears pricked forward, snorting eagerly. There was another neigh, followed by the pounding of hooves as Belle appeared, galloping towards us, nostrils flared and dark flanks heaving. At the sight of us, she slowed, raised her head, and let out another neigh. I slid clumsily down from Cloud, gasping with pain as I jarred my arm, and stumbled towards her. I leaned against her, crying with joy and relief. Belle nosed me and snorted a greeting as I patted her soaking wet neck, stroking her with my uninjured arm.

'You clever, beautiful horse,' I praised her. 'Did you throw the evil man off? I hope you trampled him to death!'

The short night was fading as we reached the cottage. I refused to let Belle out of my sight, so Henry tethered both horses in the front garden, gave them an armful of hay and a bucket with some oats and helped me to the window seat in the kitchen where I could watch over them.

Henry stirred the fire, put the kettle over it, and lit a couple of candles.

'Look!' he said as he took my brother's letter from his coat and handed it to me. 'This is postmarked Portsmouth. It looks as though he has arrived in the country.'

We broke the seal and spread the letter out on the table in the pool of candlelight. 'He's arrived, safe and well!' Henry said as we read. 'He's on his way to see me just as soon as he can arrange things. By God, that's good news!'

'Dear Robert,' I said, sitting back with a small sigh. 'Though I should prefer him to be safe in the Americas right now, I shall be so happy to see him.'

Henry reached the end of the letter, caught his breath and looked up at me. 'Oh,' he said in quite a different voice.

'What is it? What's the matter?' I sat up, anxiously, wincing as my arm throbbed.

'He's changed his plans,' Henry looked up at me. 'There's a postscript. Look! Robert says he has heard you are at Deerhurst Park and is going directly there to see you!'

'But that will take him straight into danger!' I cried. 'And he doesn't even know it!'

'Pack your bag, Miss Charlotte,' said Henry grimly. 'And if you have any girl's clothes, bring them. We're going to Deerhurst.'

We stopped only to clean my wound and bind it up afresh and to take some breakfast, then we were on horseback once more, heading north-west.

'How many days ago is Robert's letter dated?' I asked Henry as we cantered side by side across the downs, jumping low stone walls as we came to them. From behind one wall, sheep suddenly scattered, baaing loudly, and Belle shied, jarring my arm. I gasped.

'Are you all right, Charlie? You've gone white as a sheet!' exclaimed Henry.

'I'm well enough. At least, I won't be until I see my brother safe, but I'll do.'

'The letter was dated four days ago, but there's no knowing when he added the postscript or when he left Portsmouth, nor how he's travelling. We'll ride as swiftly as we can without injuring your arm or the horses,' Henry told me.

We covered the distance far more quickly than I had done on the way down. We used the roads and Henry was more familiar with the direction than I had been.

'How did he know to go there, Henry?' I asked. 'Has he been led into a trap?'

'Don't worry yourself, Miss Charlotte,' said Henry in a tight voice that betrayed his own anxiety. 'There may be a good reason. He may not be in any danger.'

'But . . .'

'No, Charlie, we aren't going to talk about it.'

'Do you at least know if father would have said anything to him about Deerhurst?'

'I'm certain he did not before we left America. Whether he wrote to him since we parted, I can't say.'

'Won't you get into trouble for leaving your post?' I asked Henry as we rode across the border into Somersetshire.

'There's little enough smuggling done at this time of year,' said Henry. 'They're busy getting the harvest in. Anyway, if I lose the position I shan't repine. It's a miserable way to earn a living.' He gave me a strained grin. 'If this ends well, perhaps you or Master Robert will give me a place.'

'How would we not?' I said at once. But a favourable outcome seemed unimaginable to me.

A long meadow stretched out ahead of us, and Henry urged Cloud into a canter. I pushed Belle faster. She responded valiantly, but she was weary after several days of hard riding. I patted her and praised her and she lengthened her stride.

We fell silent as we left Bath and started up the long hill towards Deerhurst. We rode steadily, sparing our tired horses, both our minds busy with memories and fears. I wondered where my brother was. Had he been lured into a trap? If so, by whom?

'Henry, I can't take Belle to Deerhurst!' I cried as we reached the top of Lansdown Road. 'I *stole* her! And Lord Rutherford wants to shoot her!'

'You've no choice, Miss Charlotte!' Henry replied briefly. 'Your brother might be there already! There's neither time nor money to conceal her anywhere other than in the park itself.'

'My grandparents might help us,' I said dubiously. 'Though Mr Saunders . . . I don't think he believed me. And now I no longer have any papers to prove it all to him.'

When we finally arrived at the closed lodge gates, the sun was already low in the west. Mr Saunders came out to attend us at Henry's call.

'Charlie!' he gasped when he saw me on Belle.

'Saunders,' said Henry, stretching down a hand to him. 'Do you recognize me? It's been many years.'

Saunders stared at him hard with a look of puzzlement on his face. 'It seems to me I do . . . Bless me! You're Bridges' brother!' he exclaimed. 'Henry Bridges!'

Mr Saunders flung open the gate and Henry slid down from Cloud and shook him by the hand.

'Charlie tells me you doubted her,' Henry said, wasting no time. 'But you didn't need to. I've watched her grow up. She's your Emily's daughter all right!'

Mr Saunders eyes found mine. 'It's true then?' he said. 'Emily did not die when she left us? And you . . . you really are our granddaughter?'

I nodded and the old man embraced me, then abruptly released me and turned to the lodge house. 'Mary!' he cried. 'Mary, Charlie's come back to us!'

Mrs Saunders rushed from the house and cried out as she saw me. 'Oh, Charlie, I thought we'd lost you too! But why . . . ? Why did you steal that horse? Don't you know you're wanted by the law?'

'Can we speak indoors?' Henry asked.

As soon as the horses were hitched and we were in my grandparents' tiny parlour, he poured out the whole story. Mrs Saunders began to weep softly again as he talked of my parents' love for one another and how determined they had been to spend their lives together, no matter what sacrifices they had to make.

Mrs Saunders got up and embraced me tearfully. 'So she *did* marry young Andrew all those years ago! I've grieved and prayed for my daughter for so many years, and now God has seen fit to send me a granddaughter in her place,' she said.

From the corner of my eye, I saw Henry take Mr Saunders aside and talk to him in an urgent under-voice, after which Mr Saunders disappeared.

Mrs Saunders began a tearful explanation of why she had opposed the unequal marriage and how bitterly she regretted it. 'For if we'd supported her,' she cried, 'perhaps she would have written to me during all those years and let me know she was well and happy and had a fine child!'

Henry broke into her flow of words: 'She had two, Mrs Saunders, and it is the other child I'm most concerned about at present. Charlotte, as you can see, is very well. But your husband tells me he opened the gate to Robert first thing this morning.'

'He did?' I cried.

Henry glanced at me anxiously. 'It sounds like him. Mr Saunders doesn't know him, naturally. He only saw a young soldier in uniform who gave his name as Robert Smith. I've sent Saunders down to speak to my brother and enlist his help. We need to find out where Robert is now.'

Henry looked at me gravely. 'Apparently it was a letter from Mr John Lawrence that brought Robert here, Charlie.'

I felt suddenly sick and sank into one of the chairs by the empty fireplace, putting my head in my hands. 'Oh, Henry,' I said faintly, once I was able to speak at all. 'Is it true? Is it Lawrence indeed who . . . ? Then I am very much afraid I betrayed Robert to him. I spoke about my brother, with no idea that he . . . that I . . .' I stopped, too choked up to continue. My fears for my brother overrode all else. But beneath the fear there was also horror that the man I'd loved might be guilty of such infamy; that all along he was scheming to inherit the estate and title, even to the point of deceit and murder. The shadow of guilt was darkening around him. Mrs Saunders put a comforting arm around me. 'I don't understand,' she said. 'What does young John Lawrence have to do with this? He's a good man through and through, you can be sure of that.'

'I fear he has deceived you, Mrs Saunders,' I said in a shaking voice. 'Just as he deceived me.'

'I hope that isn't true,' said Mrs Saunders. 'For he knows who you are, Charlie. He came here and questioned us. I saw no reason not to trust him when he guessed so much already.'

CHAPTER THIRTY-THREE

The sound of clattering hooves on the driveway made us all look up hopefully, but Saunders entered the room alone.

'Bridges has gone into Bath on an errand,' he told us.

'That's unlucky!' exclaimed Henry.

'He must have gone through the village,' continued Saunders. 'For I didn't see him here. I asked in the stables and a young soldier did indeed come to the house. Not this morning, but this afternoon. In company with a man who's been here several times before; the family's lawyer, I believe. Johnson, he's called.'

'The magistrate!' I interrupted faintly. 'Henry, he's the one who was in league with the man who murdered my father. It is certainly him!'

I turned back to Mr Saunders: 'He was with my brother, you say?'

I got unsteadily to my feet and looked back at Henry. 'I don't understand,' I said to him. 'Why would the magistrate or lawyer or whatever he is help Robert? Why did Lawrence write to Robert? I'm so confused I can no longer think straight. But I'm terribly afraid. Robert's in that house alone with people who mean him no good. We *must* go to him! Now!'

'Hold on, young Charlie,' said Saunders barring the way. 'You can't just go charging in there! And you've no reason to think anyone will be in danger in Lord Rutherford's house!'

'Haven't I?' I asked solemnly. I shed my jacket and pulled up my shirt sleeve to reveal my bandaged arm. A little blood had soaked through the bandage on the journey. 'If you'd seen my father's murdered body, you wouldn't tell me my brother has nothing to fear,' I added.

I looked around at their horrified faces. 'You must all do as you think best,' I told them, pushing past Saunders. 'I'm going down there now.'

'Charlie, wait!' said Henry. 'If you are wanted for stealing Belle, you cannot go down there as Charlie the stable boy! That's a complication we don't need right now. Put on your girl's clothes!'

'That will take time!' I cried impatiently.

'It's time well spent. Quite apart from the theft of Belle, you need to win Lord Rutherford over with your story *despite* the fact that you've no papers to show him. Appearing dressed as his stable boy would be a disaster.'

It took far too long to get changed. Fretting impatiently, I fought with the buttons and hooks on my old gown dug up from the bottom of my satchel where I'd packed it all those months ago in London. All the time, I feared for Robert's well-being. He might have been in that house for several hours. What was happening there? I needed to know. A red-eyed Mrs Saunders came to my aid, buttoning my dress for me, brushing my short hair, and threading a ribbon hurriedly into it so it looked more feminine.

'Thank you,' I said kissing her cheek.

The two men were waiting downstairs, ready to accompany me. 'I'm coming too,' my grandmother told me. 'There are plenty of things *I* have to say to his lordship! Off you go!'

She gave me an encouraging push, and we all spilled out of the tiny house. I took Belle out of sight of the carriageway and tethered her behind the lodge house. She was in the shade there with grass within reach. Saunders brought her water and I patted her farewell lovingly, promising to return soon.

Henry swung himself up on Cloud and then reached down a hand to me. 'It'll be quicker if we ride down,' he said. 'Your grandparents will follow on foot.'

I put one foot on his and allowed him to pull me up in front of him. Henry held me securely about the waist as he wheeled Cloud around and headed along the carriageway at a canter. It was horribly uncomfortable to sit sideways across the pommel, but in my petticoats I could scarcely sit astride. The house came in sight as we reached the brow of the hill. It was bathed in sunshine, sitting at the bottom of the hill, a jewel in isolated splendour in the midst of rolling parkland. The scene couldn't have been more peaceful. Deerhurst hid its dark secrets well. Behind me, Henry gasped. 'But the house!' he exclaimed. 'It's newly built,' I explained.

Henry checked Cloud and reined him in to a walk down the hill then trotted him through the gates.

'To the front,' I cried, as Henry turned Cloud towards the stable yard. 'The front door, Henry!'

I dared not waste a moment getting to Lord Rutherford. I slid from Henry's arm and down from the saddle the moment we reached the front of the house. I ran up to the front door and grasped the bell, sending a peal through the front hall. I stepped back and waited impatiently, rocking on my toes while Henry dismounted more slowly behind me.

Every moment seemed like an age. I was so close to Robert now and yet this vast oak door and thick stone walls still divided us.

At last I could hear bolts being drawn back on the other side of the door and it swung inwards. A very superior-looking butler stood in the doorway, immaculate in his livery and fine, powdered wig. I didn't remember ever having seen him before, but that was not surprising as I'd so rarely been to the house.

'I wish to . . . to see Lord Rutherford!' I blurted out.

'Lord Rutherford is engaged,' said the butler. He looked me up and down in a way that made me acutely aware of my short hair, my shabby gown and my patched, dirty boots.

'It's important!' I said. 'It's Robert Smith I've come to see. Is he here?'

'I think the tradesman's door will be more suitable for you,' said the butler disdainfully. 'Make enquiries with the housekeeper there. If you must.'

He shut the door firmly in my face.

'Wait!' I cried out, but it was too late. I turned and looked helplessly at Henry. 'Now what?' I asked.

'We must do as he says,' said Henry stoically, turning to walk around the house, Cloud's reins in his hand.

It took time to gain admittance through the tradesman's entrance. Eventually, a footman admitted us to a vestibule just inside the back door. It was simply furnished with a couple of hard-backed chairs and a small table that had seen better days.

'His lordship does not deal personally with . . . er . . . callers,' the footman informed us as disdainfully as the butler. 'You can give your message to me and I will convey it to the appropriate person.'

'Who will that be?' I asked.

'That, miss, will depend upon the nature of your communication,' said the footman, speaking to me as though I were something unpleasant that had stuck to his shoe.

'Does his lordship have visitors with him?' I asked frantically. 'Has a young man called Robert come to see him?'

'That, miss, I couldn't take it upon myself to say,' replied the footman.

'If I write a message, will you take it to Lord Rutherford?' I asked.

'I will take it to Mr Lawrence, his man of business,' replied the footman coldly. 'He is occupied today, but either he or his assistant, Mr Brown, will deal with it in due course.'

Henry and I exchanged looks. The expression on Henry's face told me not to write anything at all that Lawrence might see. But I had no choice. Dressed as I was, no one would ever believe my true identity. How should they, when I scarcely believed it myself?

'I'll write him a letter,' I said at last, ignoring Henry's gesture to stop me.

'I will fetch you pen and paper,' announced the

footman. He turned and left the room through a door to the main house. Henry and I looked at one another.

'Both this man and the butler are new since I left the place,' said Henry as the door clicked shut. 'If only my brother were here! He is known and trusted. He would help us!'

'If only *my* brother were *not* here!' I sighed.

I crept to the door the footman had left through, hoping I might get into the house to search for Robert, but the footman had locked it behind him. We were free to leave through the door we had come in by, but not to gain access to the mansion.

After a few minutes, the lock clicked and the door opened. We both turned, expecting to see the footman again, but it wasn't him. Instead, Miss Judith stood in the doorway, her golden hair catching the rays of the late afternoon sunshine that reached into the room. I stared to see her.

'Who are you?' she asked curiously. 'What are you doing here?'

Instinctively, I recoiled, retreating into the shadows. I didn't want Miss Judith to look at me too closely. After Lawrence, she was the person in the house most likely to recognize me. I didn't believe Lord Rutherford had ever actually looked at me.

'We are here to see a young man called Robert who we believe has called on his lordship,' Henry replied cautiously.

Miss Judith looked from Henry to me. Her eyes rested on me, taking in my short hair and shabby gown. A small crease appeared in her brow, but she gave no sign of recognition. 'If you wish to see Robert, you should come and do so,' she said unexpectedly. 'He arrived with my father's lawyer some hours ago.'

She swept out of the room on the words; we followed eagerly.

'The excitement is positively non-stop today,' she said brightly, leading us along a long corridor and through another door. 'First a long-lost cousin appears and then two more strangers come looking for him and are turned away at the door. I'm dying of curiosity. Who are you, exactly?'

'I'm Robert's sister,' I replied. 'My name is Charlotte.'

'This grows stranger still,' Miss Judith said with a malicious smile. 'I think I'm going to enjoy this, I really do!'

I didn't trust her for a moment, but she was taking me to Robert and I cared for nothing else at this moment. We turned a corner and came face to face with the footman. With a pen and ink in one hand and paper in the other, he stopped short, jaw dropping to see us walking through the house.

'I'm escorting the guests to my grandfather myself,' Miss Judith told him, waving his incoherent protest aside. 'You are not needed.'

'But Miss Lawrence . . . !' he expostulated. Miss Judith swept onwards and we followed.

'I heard you knocking,' she told us as we mounted a staircase. 'I was in the room above the front door. Your mistake, of course. You should have gone directly to the back.' She cast a disparaging glance at my attire as she spoke. We'd reached the main house now; the carpets were thick, hushing our footsteps. The walls were freshly papered and hung with portraits. Somewhere nearby a clock ticked loudly. It paused, made a grinding noise, and then began laboriously to chime the hour. Six o'clock. It was evening now.

On the first floor, Miss Judith flung open a painted door and walked into a huge salon hung with costly drapes and filled with expensive, polished furniture. I paused on the threshold, blinking at the grandeur before me before I could take in the people in the room.

'Grandpapa,' announced Miss Judith. 'We are overwhelmed with new relatives today. Behold another long-lost cousin! She claims to be Mr Robert Lawrence's sister!'

I stepped into the room, my eyes desperately seeking Robert. Though I spotted a soldier in regimentals at once, I did not find Robert's beloved features. I swept the room again. At first I only registered disappointment that he was not present. Then I recognized other faces. Mr Lawrence had risen at my entrance and was staring at me. Lord Rutherford sat in a large chair, his cane resting next to him. He appeared strained and pale. Opposite him sat another man instantly recognizable as the magistrate from London. I'd expected to see him, so he was not as great a shock to me as the man next to him. When I looked at the young soldier again, I recognized him, though he was not my brother. There, sitting in an easy chair, uniformed and groomed and looking very much at home, was my father's murderer himself, whom I'd last seen on the beach at Studland. He had the same wavy brown hair, the same pale blue eyes and the same mole beneath one of them. There could be no doubt.

I gasped and shrunk back. 'You . . . here?' I gasped, clutching my throat as though I felt his knife there once more.

'Where I belong,' said the murderer complacently. His arm rested in a sling, looking for all the world as though he'd been injured in a battle recently.

I looked around me fearfully. 'Are you all in this?' I asked.

Miss Judith rustled forward, her silken petticoats hushing and swaying. 'Do you not know your own brother? You were eager enough to meet him.'

'Who is this person?' demanded Rutherford icily. 'Why did you bring her in, Judith? I told the servants to deny me!'

'She said she was Robert Lawrence's sister!' said Miss Judith innocently. 'I thought the two of them should be reunited without loss of time.'

'She is not my sister, grandfather,' said the man to Rutherford before I could speak. 'As I told you earlier, both my mother and sister perished of a fever in America. This wench was a servant in my family. She is the thief I told you about, who tried to steal the family's papers from me. She must have had some idea of pretending to be Charlotte and worming her way into your family.' The false Robert then got to his feet and pointed dramatically at me. 'Worst of all, my lord: this despicable wench was the murderer of your son and my father, Andrew Lawrence!'

Lord Rutherford gasped and shrunk back in his chair. Lawrence looked startled and Miss Judith's eyes sparkled with excitement.

'*No!*' I cried, appalled, looking around at them all. 'It's a lie! He was *my* father; *you* killed him! You tried to kill

283

me too! You did this!' I bared the bandaged cut on my arm. Lawrence took a hasty step towards me, but then stopped.

'Father left the papers to me! We were everything to each other until you destroyed our lives. I don't know who you are, but you are *not* Robert!'

'I am Robert, but I'm certainly not *your* brother! You are a thief and an impostor.'

The murderer turned to Lord Rutherford. 'Grandfather,' he said again. 'She is a low person who has a mind to better herself by unspeakable crimes. She is utterly ruthless! She has even been working for you here as some kind of servant to learn more about you, hasn't she?'

'Not to my knowledge!' spluttered Lord Rutherford. 'We don't employ her sort here!'

'She's been masquerading as a boy, my lord.'

'What?' cried his lordship, outraged. He looked from one to the other of us, but I could see he was inclined to believe the suave soldier in the smart uniform, rather than the shabby intruder in a worn gown.

I began to see how clever the murderer's story was. He had enough truth about him to make me look a liar. For all I knew, either Lawrence or Rutherford or both had plotted this with him. What was I to do?

I looked at Lawrence, realizing he must know me. As his eyes met mine, I saw he did. But he stood quite still, impassive, and even more impossible to read than usual.

'Egad!' Miss Judith exclaimed suddenly. 'I do believe . . . yes, it is that stable boy who was working here! What was his name? Charlie! That was it. You are

Charlie! What have you done with my horse, boy?'

'That boy?' cried Rutherford explosively. 'Then you stand proven a thief, boy! The varmint stole a valuable horse from our stables! We must call for a constable!' He rang the bell vigorously for the servants.

'Wait!' I cried. 'Do what you like with me. I don't care!' I turned to the murderer and the magistrate. 'Tell me! Where is Robert?' I cried wildly. 'What have you done with him?'

The murderer turned to Lord Rutherford. 'It seems the poor creature is mad as well as dishonest,' he said pityingly. He turned back to me and said slowly and clearly, as though to a witless idiot: 'I am Robert Lawrence. You were our servant, Abigail.'

'That's a damned lie!' said Henry, finding his voice at last, stepping forward to stand beside me. 'I was a friend of Andrew Lawrence, Lord Rutherford's eldest son, and I followed him to America! I watched his children Robert and Charlotte grow up. This is certainly Miss Charlotte,' he put his hand on my shoulder, 'and I don't know where Robert is, or who you might be, but you are nothing like him, except a similarity of height and colouring.'

The man pretending to be Robert looked taken aback for a moment, but quickly recovered himself. 'So you've paid some other menial to lie for you,' he sneered at me. 'That proves nothing.'

'What the devil is going on here?' interrupted Lord Rutherford irascibly. 'Johnson, you said you had found my grandson as I commissioned you to do. Have you or haven't you?'

'Of course I have,' said the man who I had believed to be a magistrate in London. 'It is all just as I told you,' he said. 'This is Robert Lawrence. You've seen the evidence! All his papers! And painful though it will be for you to hear it, my lord, I found this girl with the blood of your son upon her hands! With my own eyes, I saw her guilt! But she escaped me. I have been hunting tirelessly for her ever since, in the hope of bringing her to justice.'

'So you say,' said Lawrence calmly, stepping forward. 'And yet the posters you distributed from here to London refer to a Charlotte Smith. Not Abigail.'

As he spoke, he pulled the dreadful poster from his coat and held it up for all to see. 'Smith was the alias her father used. How do you explain that?'

'I used the name she was calling herself!' said the magistrate, thrown on the defensive. 'The girl has been pursuing us, determined to lay her hands on money. Do not, I beg your lordship, be taken in by her or to be persuaded to buy her off. She should hang for theft!'

'Was she following you before or after she took employment here?' asked Lawrence, apparently bewildered. 'For I would swear we worked her far too hard here to allow her any such freedom.'

'Before!' cried the magistrate. 'Naturally it was before! I was hunting for your son, Lord Rutherford, but sadly, I reached him just too late!'

The truth crashed upon me at Lawrence's words. Neither Lord Rutherford nor Lawrence had been scheming against us. It was this man. He'd been paid to trace the heir, but instead of bringing him to Deerhurst, he'd had him killed for his own ends. I looked at the murderer and the magistrate and realized that between them they planned to usurp my father's and my brother's place. I could see it all so clearly, but how was I to convince Lord Rutherford?

While I stood frozen, working it all out, Lord Rutherford signed to the butler and the footmen who had entered at the ringing of the bell. 'Take these two intruders away,' he ordered. 'Lock them up and bring me the key! The constable shall have them! I don't know what you were thinking of, bringing them in here, Judith!'

Miss Judith smiled. 'Why, it's been most entertaining, hasn't it, Grandpapa?' she asked. 'And I still want to know where my horse is!'

The servants both came forward to grab me and take me away, but as they seized my arms, I cried out: 'Don't you see? He's cheating you! That man murdered my father, not me!'

'How dare you,' spluttered Lord Rutherford. 'Get out!'

'I don't care about the inheritance!' I yelled as I was dragged away. 'Have it, for all I care. Keep your stupid money! I just want my brother! What have you done with Robert?'

'My lord, do you not remember me?' asked Henry frantically as he too was dragged away. 'I am Bridges' brother, Henry! I served you faithfully in the stables for years here! When I left, I served your son! I followed him to America . . . Can you not summon Bridges to ask him the truth of this?'

I fought my captors, desperate to hear what Lord Rutherford would say to this. But though his expression was arrested for a moment, he waved the servants to take

Henry away. He looked, I thought, grey, shrunken and defeated. Judith, standing beside him, looked gleeful and amused.

My last glance as I was forced from the room was for Lawrence. He was watching me, his face carefully blank. I couldn't tell what he was thinking, but he had spoken for me. I had a tiny shred of hope left that he might believe me.

Both Henry and I were shut in a small, airless box room that was mainly used as a storage room for brooms and the like. Neither of us resisted once we'd been dragged from the room, merely accompanying the servants quietly. When the lock clicked shut behind us, I looked at Henry miserably.

'I'm so sorry, Henry,' I said. 'They got the better of us and it's my fault. I thought Robert was here!'

'You and me both, Miss Charlotte,' agreed Henry sadly. 'I fear we're in a peck of trouble now.'

'I'm more worried for Robert. Did he come here? Or was it that . . . that impostor who came through the gates this morning all along? And if he isn't here, where can he be?'

Henry bit his lip, his face pale. 'Charlie, I think we must prepare ourselves for the fact that they might already have done away with Robert.'

'I won't think that,' I said firmly, though my voice shook. 'Until we find him, there's still hope.'

Time passed. I heard the stable clock striking seven in the distance. A short time after that, we heard footsteps and a key turned in the lock.

Both Henry and I braced ourselves, expecting the

constable already. But it was Mr Lawrence who stepped into the room.

My heart beat faster at the sight of him. I was both glad to see him and terribly afraid. I couldn't see what he had to gain by setting up an impostor, but I hadn't forgotten that it was apparently his letter that had lured my brother here. We stood looking at each other uncertainly.

'Charlie,' Lawrence began after an awkward silence. 'I've been working at this mystery from the other end. You're telling the truth aren't you? Will you explain it to me?'

'Of course I am!' I said. 'And I will! I'm the daughter of Emily Saunders and Andrew Lawrence. You already knew that though, didn't you? You spoke to my grand-parents.'

'Yes. Though they did not know who your father was. Why did you never tell me? All this time?'

'I did not know! And if I had known, I still would not have known whether I could trust you. You had that poster in your bag! I thought you would turn me in!'

'Oh, Charlotte! You saw that? When I took that down, I had no idea it was you! I was suspicious of Johnson, Lord Rutherford's lawyer. I had some fears that he was untrustworthy so I did some checking. It appears my fears were well-founded.'

'Oh. But is it true you wrote a letter to my brother? Why?'

'Because I was concerned about you,' Lawrence replied. 'You must believe me. I knew nothing then of your connection to the family. But even before I knew you were a girl, I thought your family should know your whereabouts. It was clear from everything you'd said that you were very young, well educated, and dangerously adrift in the world. You had mentioned your brother's first name and where he was posted. You'd entrusted the surname Smith to the Saunders. Once I knew all that, he wasn't difficult to trace.'

'That was it?' I asked. 'Truly? Why didn't you tell me?'

'I kept silence because I feared you would think I was interfering.'

'You did not try to lure him into a trap, so you could have him killed?'

'What?' exclaimed Lawrence. 'No! How could you think such a thing of me? What motive could I possibly have?'

'The fact that with her father gone, Robert is the only person between you and the succession,' said Henry. 'That could be motive enough!'

Lawrence shook his head. 'I've never expected or coveted the inheritance,' he assured Henry. He turned to me. 'Do you believe I would be capable of such a thing, Charlie?'

'No, not now,' I said. I felt quite weak with relief. 'You would have nothing to gain from a false heir. I believe you. But you are imposed upon. That man upstairs is not my brother! You do not believe I murdered my father, do you?'

'No, Charlie, of course not. Your story makes sense to me; it confirms what I had already suspected.'

'Her parents never told her who they were,' said Henry. 'When she came to me in Dorset, I told her! I held her father's papers.'

'The papers those men have now shown to Lord Rutherford?' asked Lawrence, his eyes widening. 'How did they come by them?'

'They threatened to kill Belle,' I said tearfully, remembering my terror that night. 'I gave them up.'

Lawrence caught his breath. 'My God!' he exclaimed. 'What is this infamy?'

'That man upstairs is a liar and a murderer!' I cried.

'They took a risk coming straight here with Charlie still alive to tell the tale,' Henry broke in. 'Perhaps they had found out the real Robert was on his way and made haste to get here before him, trusting to the tale of Charlie being a thief and a servant to prevent her thwarting their plans.'

'It's a good story,' I admitted. 'And I lent it truth by stealing Belle. But they were going to *shoot* her!'

'I know, Charlie, I know,' said Lawrence. He fell silent, deep in thought. Henry and I exchanged glances again.

'Mr Lawrence,' I said timidly. 'My brother must be out there somewhere,' I indicated the park with a sweep of my hand. 'We need to search for him!' Quickly, we explained our theory of what must have happened.

'You're right,' agreed Lawrence at once. 'And we should see if Bridges has returned. Come with me, both of you.'

He led us back to the room where we had waited before. There Mr and Mrs Saunders and Bridges were waiting.

'Henry!' exclaimed Bridges, as we entered the room. 'By God, it's good to see you! Even if you've turned into an old man!'

'What about you, James?' asked Henry, his voice thick with emotion. 'What a crop of grey hair you've sprouted!' The two men embraced and then Henry turned to Mr Saunders for a more detailed description of the man who had ridden through the lodge gates this morning. 'Did he have pale blue eyes or dark? Was he injured?' he asked.

'Dark. What do you mean injured?'

'Did he have his arm in a sling?'

'No,' said Saunders definitely. 'He did not. The man I opened the gates to this morning was unharmed.'

'It was the real Robert this morning, then!' Henry said definitely, turning to me.

'Perhaps the impostor was hurt overpowering Master Robert,' suggested Mr Saunders.

'Perhaps they have concealed him nearby, hoping to move him under cover of darkness,' said Henry. 'We must pray they've kept him alive.'

'I hope they think he can be useful to them,' I said with a voice that shook. 'There must be a great deal they still don't know about the family.' I could see that none of the others were so optimistic. They expected to find a body. I swallowed hard and clenched my fists to keep my courage high.

'Where do we even start to search?' asked Mr Saunders helplessly.

'We must think like those nasty, murdering rogues,' replied his wife. 'Where would they hide someone quickly nearby, someone who they attacked on the ride down to the house?'

'The summer-house?' I suggested.

'I'll check there, but it's in view of the house,' said Bridges doubtfully.

'The crypt?' Mrs Saunders suggested. 'I'll walk up there.'

'The barn at the Home Farm?' I said. 'I'll go there to look.'

'I'll go with you,' said Lawrence.

'I'll go with Charlie,' said Henry protectively.

'You won't find him in any of those places,' said a girl's voice behind me. I turned to see Miss Judith in the doorway. She looked coolly amused.

'Good God, Judith, have you left his lordship alone with those scoundrels?' demanded Lawrence, hurrying from the room.

'What could *I* do?' asked Miss Judith with a shrug.

'Keep him company; be a witness!' he snapped over his shoulder. I could hear him outside giving orders to the servants who hurried upstairs. No doubt the servants would guard the old lord, though I did not imagine even those rogues dared harm him here in his own home where their guilt would be plain to all.

As Lawrence came back into the room, I turned to Miss Judith.

'You know something?' I demanded eagerly. 'Please tell us!'

'What possible reason could I have for helping you, stable boy?' she asked disdainfully. 'No, really, I think I might almost prefer to have the young man upstairs as grandpapa's heir than a couple of bumpkin cousins from America. And anyone, absolutely anyone, would be better than dull John as heir.'

'I understand you still resent me for foiling your

elopement recently, Judith,' said Lawrence. 'But I was concerned for your safety and acting on your grandfather's orders. If I did wrong, please don't revenge yourself on others.'

'So dull, and so very worthy,' said Miss Judith with a sigh.

'Miss Lawrence, you are better than this,' cried Mrs Saunders. 'Don't play these games! What have you seen today?'

Miss Judith looked at her. For a moment it looked as though she would defy her too, but then she shrugged and gave in. 'Try looking in the icehouse,' she said.

We didn't stop to ask how she knew. We all turned and ran out of the house and down through the formal garden behind. I'd never been to the icehouse, but I'd seen the kitchen servants going back and forth. Lawrence and I swiftly drew ahead of our older companions. My heart was hammering with dread and hope. As we approached the trees where the icehouse lay half concealed, I felt sick with fear. Would I find another corpse instead of my living, breathing brother?

Lawrence caught my hand in his and pulled me faster. 'Courage, Charlie,' he said. When we reached the icehouse, he pushed open the heavy door, ducked, and entered the building ahead of me. The vast stack of ice that was stored here was mostly gone so late in the summer, so the building lay almost empty, though still cold, half dug into the earth as it was. The light was dim, and I stared about me blindly. I thought I heard a slight noise behind the remaining ice stack, so I followed it. There was nothing there but a pile of sacks.

A sickening sense of disappointment flooded me. He was not here! I was about to declare that Miss Judith had been lying or mistaken, when I thought I saw the sacks move.

I ran forward, throwing myself on my knees in the dirt beside them and flung back the sacks. A body in torn underclothes and bound with ropes lay there: face down, pale, and motionless. I whimpered with fright. It was my brother's soft brown hair, so similar to mine. For a moment, I was too afraid to turn the body, terrified that his throat would have been cut with that evil knife.

Kneeling on the other side of the body, Lawrence bent and lifted it in his arms to turn it. The face was my dear brother's. A gag was bound cruelly tight across his mouth, but the deep blue eyes that met mine were very much alive.

CHAPTER THIRTY-FOUR

Lawrence freed the gag and I fought to untie the ropes on my brother's wrists. 'Robert! Robert, you're safe!' I kept repeating, giddy with relief.

Robert coughed and spluttered as he was freed from the dreadful gag. I flung my arms around him and hugged him tight while Lawrence freed his ankles.

'I say, Charlie old girl,' my brother managed to gasp at last. 'Let a fellow breathe!'

I released him, stroking his grubby face, unable to believe that he was really here, alive and well. Between us, Lawrence and I helped him to his feet and supported him out of the building. Mr and Mrs Saunders, Henry, and Bridges had all reached the icehouse now and greeted us with relief.

Lawrence and Mr Saunders supported Robert back to the house. He was in pain as the blood began to circulate in his hands and feet again after so many hours. He was also dazed from a blow to the head and from lying so long in the dark.

We reached the house just as the constable arrived. Lawrence sent a servant scurrying for some clothes of his for Robert to wear and led us all into a library lined with countless bookcases and furnished with sofas and armchairs with a view out over the gardens. There, Lawrence took the constable aside and spoke earnestly to him. I could see Henry's suspicious eyes on Lawrence, but for myself, I no longer harboured thoughts that he was guilty of any crime.

I persuaded my brother, who was still horribly pale, to sit down upon a sofa, then I sank wearily down beside him. I had to break the dreadful news to Robert that our father was dead. After his ordeal today, he was no longer surprised, though deeply distressed. He wept, his arms around me, grieving for the father he had loved.

'What's happened to you, Charlie?' he asked when he could speak again. 'Have you been ill? Is that why your hair is cut short?'

I shook my head. 'No, I've been in danger but quite well.'

'You've been up to your tricks again, haven't you?' asked Robert, striving for a more cheerful tone after his tears. He tugged at my shorn hair. 'Dressing as a boy? What a ragamuffin you are, Charlie.'

'You sound like Mr Lawrence,' I said, half laughing and half crying. 'That's what he calls me. I had no choice! I needed to hide from those same men who attacked you and father. They were looking for a girl.'

'Oh, Charlie!' exclaimed my brother, hugging me tight. 'What a time you must have had of it! I realized something was terribly wrong when I heard from John Lawrence about my *brother*! Why did you not write to me?'

'I was so afraid those men were watching the post or had spies to take letters,' I explained.

'Then you were wiser than me,' said Lawrence walking over to us, the constable at his heels. 'I did precisely what you were careful not to do, and brought your brother here. In my defence, I'd written to him before we went to London. I had no idea you were already in trouble or that I was putting Robert in danger. And I had not the slightest suspicion of who either of you really were.' He turned to Robert. 'I was concerned for your sister, who I thought then was your younger brother. She was so clearly well-born and so young to be making her own way as a stable boy.'

'Is this what you've been up to Charlie?' exclaimed my brother, shocked. 'A stable boy? I'm relieved you *did* write to me, Lawrence!' he said, stretching out a hand.

Lawrence shook it with a smile. 'Please, call me John! I think we must be related, you know.'

'What?' exclaimed Robert, brows knit. 'How can that be?'

'It's a long story, Robert,' I said. 'But it seems our name isn't Smith at all. These are our mother's parents.' I drew Mr and Mrs Saunders forward. They had been waiting patiently all this time at the side of the room to be introduced to their other grandchild.

Robert was astonished, but delighted, to meet them. While they introduced themselves, Lawrence drew me quietly into an adjoining room. 'Charlie, I've told the constable all I can,' he said. 'But you are going to have to explain your story to him yourself, to convince him to arrest those two scoundrels above stairs. Can you do that?'

'Of course,' I said.

'You look weary,' he said. 'I wish I could spare you this.'

'No, it's important. I'm ready now.'

'He's in the room next to this, ready to listen to you. Would you like someone with you? Your brother, your grandmother or your friend Henry, perhaps?'

I hesitated. 'Would you stay with me?' I asked. 'I'd feel safe . . . with you there.'

Lawrence sighed. He stepped forward, taking one of my hands in his and pressing it. 'I was afraid you no longer trusted me,' he said. 'I tortured myself, when you fled with no word to me, thinking you'd run from me. I was afraid you thought . . . that my intentions towards you weren't honourable.'

I shook my head; returning the pressure of his hand. 'That wasn't it . . . it was seeing you with that man! And I'd seen the poster too . . . it's true: I *didn't* trust you.'

'But you don't suspect me of plotting for the inheritance now?'

I looked up into his kind, warm hazel eyes. My heart flipped over. 'I couldn't think such a thing of you.'

'But you did.'

'Most unwillingly, I assure you.'

'I can't tell you how relieved I am to hear it. This is scarcely the moment, I know, to speak of love, but, oh, Charlie, it is so good to see you!'

I smiled shyly up at him. With a quick glance at the door to check we were still unobserved, Lawrence drew me into his arms and kissed me. 'I would have married you, no matter what Lord Rutherford said,' he whispered to me. 'When you were a penniless stable girl.'

I put up a hand to touch his cheek and he caught hold of it, pressing my fingertips to his lips. My heart fluttered.

'I hope you will still wish to do so if it turns out that I am somebody altogether more distinguished?' I asked.

'That would depend on whether you would stoop to marry a mere steward, Miss Lawrence,' he replied seriously. 'Our positions are quite reversed, you see.'

'I care nothing for that,' I assured him. 'How could I? And please, continue to call me Charlie!'

'Only if you will call me John.'

'Very well, John,' I drew reluctantly back from his embrace. 'But I don't think I should keep the constable waiting any longer, should I?'

I thought, as Lawrence accompanied me, that he still looked troubled. Dimly I perceived that there was perhaps a greater gulf between us now than there had been before and it sat uneasily with him; he would prefer to be the one who generously overlooked the difference.

The constable questioned me at length. He then spoke to the others: my brother, the Saunders, Henry, and his brother. It must have made a most bewildering tale for the poor, baffled man. At length he felt he had our story clear, and Lawrence was ready to escort us back to Lord Rutherford.

'Have you said anything to them?' I whispered as we all followed him upstairs. 'To his lordship or to the impostors?'

'Not a word,' he replied. 'I couldn't speak to Lord Rutherford without alerting the other men and I didn't wish to set them on their guard just yet. They are at dinner, partaking freely of the wine, and I hope we will take them by surprise.'

Lord Rutherford, Miss Judith, and their two companions were startled when so many of us trooped into the room. My brother, hurriedly dressed in a slightly-too-small shirt and breeches of Lawrence's, was still badly bruised and dirty after his ordeal. There was not a presentable guest among us for such a grand dining room, save only Lawrence who was as neat and immaculate as ever.

'What is the meaning of this?' demanded Lord Rutherford from the head of the table. 'I ordered those two locked up for the constable!' he cried, pointing at Henry and me. 'I don't wish to be troubled further with them! What are you thinking of, John? And what the devil are my lodge keepers and groom doing in my dining parlour?'

'The constable is here with us, my lord,' said Lawrence quietly. 'He would like a word.' He walked over to the sideboard where some bottles and crystal glasses were laid out, poured a glass of cognac and brought it to my brother, who was looking very pale. 'Drink this,' he said in a low voice, pulling up a chair at the table. My brother sank gratefully into the chair and sipped at the cognac.

While he did so, Mrs Saunders boldly addressed Lord Rutherford: 'I'm here to tell you, your lordship, that if we hadn't done our best between us to separate Andrew and Emily all those years ago, we'd all have been spared a great deal of loss and unhappiness. I'm not putting all the blame on you. We thought Emily would be happier marrying in her own class too. But you can't deny your part in that sorry tale. Well, we both lost our children as a result.'

'What has that to say to anything?' blustered Rutherford, staring around at his bewildering array of ill-assorted and unexpected extra dinner guests. He put down his cutlery and groped for his napkin.

'They ran off together and hid themselves is what,' said Mrs Saunders. She was unleashing anger and sorrow that had been pent up for many years. 'All these years we thought Emily had put an end to her life, but she didn't! She ran all the way to America with your son and they raised these two lovely children you see before you!'

'Impossible!' cried Rutherford. 'That girl is a servant and a thief.'

'I've been both,' I agreed. I found it difficult to speak up before so many people, two of them my mortal enemies. I braced myself and stepped forward. 'I worked as your servant and I stole your horse to save her life. But I seem to be your granddaughter for all that. I'm not saying I'm pleased about it, but it's true.'

'I can vouch for her, as I said last time I was in this room,' said Henry. 'And my brother will speak for me, won't you, James? I assume you will believe a man who has served you faithfully all his life, your lordship?'

Bridges cleared his throat. 'It's true that he's my brother, my lord,' he said gruffly. 'And it's true that he ran off with Master Andrew twenty-four years ago.'

'And this girl, your granddaughter and ours, is the spitting image of my Emily,' added Mrs Saunders. 'I could see that as soon as she came here. Even dressed as a boy as she was!'

Lord Rutherford looked at me with undisguised horror. I would have found it amusing, if it were not so serious.

'And this is your grandson, Robert, who these two men attacked this morning, tied up, and hid in the icehouse!' Mrs Saunders added, pointing at my father's murderer and his accomplice.

Lord Rutherford glowered at Robert in his ill-fitting clothes. Robert looked back, still pale and bewildered. Even I could see the similarity between them, and wondered that it had not struck me before. Robert had a great look of the old lord, though his features were still softened by youth and by the sense of fun he had inherited from our mother.

I looked at my two enemies: the lawyer and the impostor. Both had blenched at the sight of Robert walking into the room. They must have known their tale was told, but it seemed they were still determined to bluster it out. The murderer, still pretending to be Robert, took a large gulp of wine, pushed back his chair, and got to his feet, looking towards Lord Rutherford.

'I can see these two have bribed your servants to speak for them and concocted some tale,' he said insinuatingly. 'But I assure you, my lord, I am your grandson. I have brought you ample proof. I hold all the papers to prove myself.' He indicated the sheaf of papers on a side table as he spoke.

'I'll take a look at those, sir, if that's all right with you,' said the constable stepping forward and taking the papers into his possession. The impostor looked uneasy. 'What can *they* show you?' he demanded, pointing at us.

Lord Rutherford's eyes swivelled back to Robert and me. He looked confused and unsure of himself; I'd never seen him at a loss before. He passed a tired hand over his face. 'It's a fair point,' he said. 'What proof do you have?'

'I had all the papers that man holds, until he stole them by holding Belle at knifepoint,' I cried angrily.

Robert shrugged. 'I have no proof at all,' he admitted. 'For this is all news to me. He turned to me. 'Related to a lord?' he asked. 'I have to admit, it don't seem in the least likely, Charlie, old girl. Where'd you get this notion?'

'There is a great deal to explain,' I told him. 'I only began to suspect it recently myself, though the puzzle had been falling into place for a while.'

'Tell you what though,' said Robert shaking his head. 'I don't understand why these two men should attack me, hide me away, and steal my uniform if they did not wish to do some mischief! It's not honest, egad!'

'We did no such thing!' cried the lawyer. 'It's all a lie!'

'You did,' said Miss Judith, speaking for the first time. 'For I saw you. I was out for a ride and I watched it all from the copse. That's how I knew where to direct the rescue party.' She smiled triumphantly as everyone gasped.

'It was you who came in to look at me?' asked Robert, astonished. 'Why did you not untie me?'

'I thought it would be more amusing and instructive to let things play out,' said Miss Judith. 'And I was right, wasn't I?'

'You still have no proof of your identity!' insisted the murderer, his eyes flicking from one of us to another in growing panic.

'Wait!' I cried, suddenly remembering that I did have

proof. I pulled the lace that hung about my neck and drew the ring from inside my bodice. Pulling it over my head, I walked to the head of the table and held it out to Lord Rutherford.

'My father's ring, my lord,' I said as he took it and examined it. 'It never left his finger until he returned to England. These despicable ruffians never knew I had it, so they could not steal it from me. It bears the Rutherford crest, so I assume you will recognize it?'

'Indeed,' breathed Rutherford, turning the ring to read the letters engraved inside. 'Andrew Stephen Lawrence. It was my gift to him on his twenty-first birthday. Just before he left Deerhurst.' His voice shook. I knew we had reached a turning point.

He looked up at me with new interest in his eyes. 'Charlotte, you said your name was? That was my dear wife's name. Andrew's mother.' Then his gaze moved to my brother. 'You do resemble Andrew most strongly,' he admitted.

At those words, the man pretending to be Robert made a dash for the door. The lawyer was slower to move, seemingly frozen in horror at the unravelling of their plan. But as my father's murderer ran from the room, he fell straight into the arms of the butler and three footmen, who swiftly overpowered him.

'Take care, he's sure to have a knife!' I cried. A quick search revealed the knife that had done so much harm concealed in his boot and it was taken from him. Servants then seized the lawyer too.

'I trusted you,' snapped Lord Rutherford, staring at him in growing disgust and horror as he struggled in his captors' arms. 'I paid you handsomely to track down my son and heir, and you had him murdered! My own *son*!'

He was pale and shaken. Lawrence hastened to pour him a glass of wine. 'We both trusted him,' said Lawrence quietly as he took the glass to Lord Rutherford. 'This has been a disgraceful betrayal, my lord.'

'You're mistaken!' cried the lawyer, terrified. 'I've served you faithfully for many years, my lord! It was nothing to do with me! I believed this man's tale! I believed he was Robert Lawrence, your grandson! I brought him to you in good faith!'

'Don't put it off on me!' snarled the murderer. 'It was all your damned idea for me to impersonate the heir so we could profit one day!'

'Take them away,' shuddered Rutherford, dropping his head in his hands. 'My own son!' he repeated, distraught. His shoulders shook for a moment and I wondered if he were crying. After a moment, he straightened himself with an effort and cleared his throat fiercely. 'There will be a deuce of a scandal over this,' he said in what was a good imitation of his usual sharp tone. 'I shall never be able to hold up my head again.'

'I don't think you will have any difficulty with that, my lord,' said Lawrence with a slight smile. He looked over at me and his smile grew warm, lighting up his eyes.

Lord Rutherford was looking at me too, but with a much less enamoured expression in his eyes. 'I think it will be devilishly difficult to live down. A couple of American savages as my heir and granddaughter? A girl who has been working in my own *stables*? Dressed as a

306

boy?' His voice gave way in sheer horror at the thought. 'There is nothing else for it; you will have to be married as soon as possible before it becomes known. I shall find you a suitable husband!'

'With respect, my lord, I should prefer to make my own choice.'

'What? Nonsense! Good God, what would you know about how to choose a husband? We've had one shocking *mésalliance* in the family, it seems; we hardly need another!' Lord Rutherford glanced at my shabby dress and short hair and could not repress a shudder. 'No doubt your upbringing was shocking. But . . . '

'You are speaking of my parents!' I interrupted with a touch of anger. 'I would consider myself privileged to be as happy as they were!'

I was inclined to announce my attachment then and there, but meeting Lawrence's eyes across the room, I saw him shake his head slightly at me. Understanding he wished me to leave the matter to him, I bit back the words I had been prepared to utter.

In any case, Lord Rutherford was in full flow once more: 'You understand nothing, my girl, believe me!' he said. 'Take my word for it, marriage in our class is not about love, as I've explained to Judith many, many times!'

'But you are wrong, grandpapa,' interpolated Miss Judith from her place at his right hand. 'It's what I've been telling you forever. But you cling to the past. People these days marry for love. You've forbidden me to do so and made me very unhappy.'

Support from Miss Judith was so unexpected that I could only blink at her. But her face was set and I could suddenly see the unhappiness in her eyes where before I had only seen malice.

Lord Rutherford seemed startled at her unexpected defection. He looked around at us all in sudden bewilderment, as though he had forgotten we were all standing in his dining room. 'Well, there is time to discuss this,' he admitted. 'Lawyers will look over all the papers tomorrow. If I can find some I can trust! Please forgive me if I retire now. I am tired!'

Lawrence stepped forward and assisted him in rising from his chair. 'You had all better take a seat and have a glass of wine,' Rutherford said once he was on his feet. 'Benson, are those felons safely under lock and key?' he demanded of his butler.

'They are, my lord. The constable has sent for men to escort them to gaol and is questioning them now.'

'Good. Can you please have bedchambers made up for our visitors?' He waved at Robert and myself.

'I have already done so, my lord,' replied the butler, with a respectful bow.

'Benson, is there enough food for all our guests? Send a message to the kitchen, will you?'

Miss Judith rose and took her grandfather's arm. 'I'll accompany Grandpapa,' she said to Lawrence.

On his way out of the room, Lord Rutherford paused by my brother Robert and looked him over once more. 'Very like your father,' he murmured. He shook my brother cordially by the hand. 'You are still single, I hope?' he added.

'Why yes, my lord!' My brother had some colour in his face and a small twinkle back in his eyes.

'No one unsuitable in mind?'

'No one in mind at all, my lord. Please feel free to match-make for me. Happy to consider all candidates!'

'I'm very pleased to hear it,' said Rutherford before leaving.

Robert winked at me and I smiled. But I had one more thing to ask his lordship. 'One last question, my lord,' I said. 'Do I have your promise that if I bring Belle to the stables, she will not be harmed?'

'Belle?' asked Rutherford, all at sea.

'My . . . your horse that was Miss Judith's,' I said. 'You were going to have her shot.' I looked at Miss Judith as I spoke.

'Oh.' Rutherford rubbed a hand wearily over his face. 'Yes, very well. What is a horse among such revelations as we've had today? You have my word, as long as she doesn't savage anyone.'

'She won't.' I turned to Miss Judith, raising my brows in a mute question.

'Oh, very well,' snapped Miss Judith. 'I don't want the stupid nag. I have Autumn Gold now.'

'I'll bid you good night,' Rutherford said to Robert and me. 'We'll meet again at the breakfast table, I daresay.'

I dropped him a small curtsey. 'Of course,' I said.

'Good night, my lord,' said Robert.

Lord Rutherford left the room leaning on Miss Judith's arm and everyone fell quiet for a moment. Then Mrs Saunders came to embrace us both. 'Welcome to Deerhurst, Robert,' she said to my brother, kissing his cheek. Henry clapped us both on the back. 'We did it, Miss Charlotte!' he said, his eyes suspiciously moist. 'Your father would be happy to know it.' He turned to Robert. 'He loved this estate. He wanted you to know it and to inherit it one day. It meant a lot to him.'

Robert shook him by the hand, looking distressed as he thought of our father. Henry clasped his hand tightly.

'Come,' said Lawrence with his usual calm good sense. 'Sit down, everyone; eat something!' He signed to the butler to fill everyone's glasses. 'It's been quite a day. I imagine you are all in need of sustenance.'

After dinner, we said farewell to all our friends, both old and new, and Lawrence took Robert and me down to the stable yard so that I could see Belle.

'I sent Ben up to fetch her during dinner,' he told me, as I stroked her soft brown nose and leaned my cheek against hers. 'I knew you wouldn't be able to relax until you'd seen her comfortably bestowed.'

'That's true,' I admitted. Belle looked very happy to be back in familiar surroundings, and blew contentedly in my hair.

'I hope you will be able to accustom yourself to sleeping in a bed, rather than in her stable?' added Lawrence with a smile.

My brother shook his head in horror and uttered a strangled yelp of disapproval.

'What?' I demanded. 'There are worse places to sleep!'

'I imagine you'd appreciate a bath before retiring?' Lawrence asked Robert.

'That would be welcome,' admitted my brother running a hand ruefully through his dishevelled hair.

'You can borrow anything you need from me,' said Lawrence.

'Thank you! You're very good,' said Robert. 'So . . . you two know each other well then?' He was looking from me to Lawrence with his eyebrows raised.

'I should tell you your sister has agreed to marry me,' John told my brother. 'I hope you are not unhappy with that?'

'Lord! I'm very happy. Congratulations!' Robert wrung John's hand and kissed my cheek. 'It's the old man you're going to have trouble with.'

'I know,' I sighed. Lawrence looked serious.

'Oh, never fear! He'll come round,' said Robert optimistically. 'I'll keep him busy looking out for a bride for me! I'll willingly make up to every rich, high-born, squinty-eyed heiress, to keep him happy. That'll take his mind off you two. What more could a brother do for his sister?'

'Nothing more!' I said, kissing his cheek with a grin. 'You're a wonderful brother! I suspect you'll enjoy yourself very much and in the end will marry exactly whom you please!'

'I will! But as you say, it will be fun. And what is life without a few larks?'

Marie-Louise Jensen was born in Henley-on-Thames of an English father and a Danish mother. Her early years were plagued by teachers telling her to stop reading and stop writing stories and do long division instead. Marie-Louise studied Scandinavian and German with Literature at the UEA and has lived in both Denmark and Germany. After teaching English at a German university for four years, Marie-Louise returned to England to care for her children full-time. She completed an MA in Writing for Young People at Bath Spa University in 2005.

Her books have been shortlisted for many awards including the Waterstones Children's Book Prize and the Branford Boase Award.

Marie-Louise lives in Bath.

www.marie-louisejensen.co.uk

MARIE-LOUISE JENSEN

Smuggler's Kiss

It's not a crime to steal a heart

It's not a crime to steal a heart

In the autumn of 1720, Isabelle runs away,
changing her life forever.

But though Isabelle has fled, she is still trapped.
If the secret of her previous life is revealed then the
smugglers who have found her will not let her stay on
board The Invisible—and she has nowhere else to go.

To survive, Isabelle must help her captors—even though
she detests what they do. But soon her principles are
thrown into confusion and she finds herself becoming
fiercely loyal to the crew—and to one mysterious
smuggler in particular . . .